Writing *in the* Sand

"Last night someone left a baby on our doorstep. A baby boy. Premature. He's in hospital. Well, obviously."

My heart beats in my throat. "Hospital?"

"First thing Dad did was ring for an ambulance and the police."

"The baby wasn't ill, was he?"

"Just small, Mum said. Born too early. She was right – he's in the Prem Unit."

Somehow I keep my voice steady. "So no one saw anything odd going on?"

"Not a sausage. And they're worried about the mother. With the baby born so early, they say it's likely the mother's in need of medical attention."

My heart thuds.

Writing in the Sand

Helen Brandom

USBORNE

For Corinne

First published in the UK in 2014 by Usborne Publishing Ltd., Usborne House, 83-85 Saffron Hill, London EC1N 8RT, England. www.usborne.com

Copyright © 2014 by Helen Brandom

The right of Helen Brandom to be identified as the author of this work has been asserted by her in accordance with the Copyright, Designs and Patents Act, 1988.

Cover photography: Sami Sarkis/Photographer's Choice RF/Getty Images.

The name Usborne and the devices ♈ ⬡ are Trade Marks of Usborne Publishing Ltd.

A CIP catalogue record for this book is available from the British Library.

ISBN 9781409563914   03009/1   J MAMJJASOND/14

Printed in Chatham, Kent, UK.

Chapter One

It would be easier if I didn't have to pretend all the time. I can only imagine what it must be like, not worrying about saying the wrong thing. Not having to tell half-truths.

I don't need to pretend to be *happy*. I *am* happy most of the time. I've got my mum, Kirsty's a brilliant friend, we live by the sea, GCSEs will soon be over, and it's nearly summertime. What's not to be happy about?

What I'd love most, though, would be to feel normal more often. Like now.

Revising GCSE Geography might sound boring. But to me, sitting in Kirsty's bedroom sharing her laptop, it's a good feeling. It's what I think of as normal – and I take a moment to let it wash over me.

Kirsty's fingers move over the keys and the screen fills with diagrams, then explanations on cyclones. But I've stopped concentrating. Screwing my eyes up, the flat yellow and blue in the diagram on screen turns into warm sand and blue sea, and though I ought not to – and only for a moment – I let myself run along a beach in Australia with Liam.

Kirsty says, "Here, this could be important—" She breaks off. "You're not even listening, are you?"

"Sorry." Then I say, "It's Liam's birthday."

She pushes the laptop away. "Today? I didn't realize."

I sigh. "No reason why you should."

"Does it still hurt?"

"Not like it did."

Kirsty's fingers hover over the keys, and though I can't honestly think why he'd email on his birthday, I say, "D'you mind?"

"Mind what?"

"Seeing if there's anything for me."

"Sure." The diagrams disappear and she brings up my email login, keying in my password as if it's her own. We stare at the empty inbox, and she says gently, "Shall we call it a day?"

I push back my chair and stretch. "Okay."

I'm following her downstairs when she says, "You didn't send him a card, did you?"

I shrug. "I thought about it. But we made a clean break, so…" I jump down the last two stairs. "You know what it's like."

She gives a short laugh. "I do." She gives me a quick hug. "It'll get better, Amy. Honestly."

The house is unusually quiet, with no sign of Kirsty's

parents. I glance towards the kitchen. "I thought your mum and dad would be back by now."

"They're duvet-hunting."

I laugh, and she says, "Plus other stuff – in the sales. New kids arriving tomorrow."

I often wonder how it is for Kirsty, with her mum's foster kids needing such a lot of attention. Sometimes it's like the house is bursting at the seams. A complete contrast to my situation. Just me and Mum.

"How many kids?"

She looks mock-guilty. "I forgot to ask."

I make for the front door. "Oh well, you'll soon find out."

She puts her head on one side. "Can't you stop for coffee?"

"Better not, I left a pile of washing-up. Mum'll wonder where I am."

"She *knows* where you are."

"Yeah, but still…I'd better go." I pull open the door. "Thanks again. Don't know what I'd do without you."

She grins. "Any time."

Chapter Two

"Amy?" At Mum's voice – sleepy, from her chair – I'm back in the real world. The frying pan slips from my hand into the water – scummy and going cold.

Washing-up (whether it's lunch dishes or messy bits and pieces left over from last night's tea) is a good time for sorting my head out. Or trying to. This afternoon I'm not doing too well. My mind wanders – again – thinking about Liam and the party he's probably having on a beach somewhere. He'll have made friends in Australia. Girls from school, evenly tanned all over. I never met his mum, but obviously she'd be there. For a few moments I'm there too; I'm slim and wearing a green strappy dress (like the one in a shop window he'd said would look good on me). It's early evening. The sun's still beautifully warm and the surf is rolling in. I run down to the sea and pretend I'm surprised when he catches me up and puts his arms round me.

Mum says, "Did you hear something?" and the dream fades.

I listen. Yes, I can hear it. A whooshing sound coming through the gap at the bottom of the back door, the gap where we stuff newspapers in winter to keep out the draught.

I look across at Mum. Her hair, dark like mine but straight, is tied back with a black ribbon. She has brown eyes and skin people envy – they say it's like porcelain. The time I told her this, she said she didn't fancy being compared to a teapot. Teapot, cup or saucer, she has to accept the fact: she's beautiful.

Beautiful but frail. More than anything, I wish for her to get better.

She's been dozing, waiting for the painkillers to work their magic. We hear the whooshing noise again. I wring out the dishcloth and stand still, listening hard. Now though, the only sound is rain splashing off the gutter.

Then there it is again, a definite snuffling. We both look towards the back door. Mum's face lights up. "If you ask me, that's a dog."

"Shall I have a look?"

She eases her position in the chair. "Go on then."

I open the back door, and it flies in – a tornado on legs. Quite long legs. It's shaggy and wet.

It shakes its head. Droplets hit Mum in the face and she laughs – something I wish she did more often.

Perhaps it's lost. Mum and I, we must be wondering the same thing because, with difficulty, she leans forward. "Has it got a collar?"

When I say, "Come here," it looks at me like we've known each other all our lives. It sits down for a second, head cocked to one side, then stands up again and pads over to where I'm waiting. I feel its neck. No collar.

"I wonder if it's a stray," says Mum. "It's not much to look at."

She's right. It's fairly ordinary. Shaggy mid-brown fur. A bare patch on its rough tail. Long claws that go *click-click* on the lino.

But its eyes… They're a deep luminous gold.

When Mum puts out a hand, it rubs the side of its face against her fingers. She scratches behind its ear and you can see how happy it is.

I stroke the dome of its head. "What d'you think it is? Boy or girl?"

Mum says, "Have a look."

As soon as I kneel down, it rolls over. I take a quick peek. "It's a boy." My mind rushes ahead. I've already decided he's a dog nobody wants, and wonder if we can keep him. Not that it would be exactly practical. With Mum the way she is.

She's frowning. "I wonder who he belongs to."

"Whoever it is, they've managed to lose him."

"We ought to notify the police," says Mum.

When I need to, I can think at the speed of light. Now is one of those times. "I've got a better idea. Why don't we put a card in the post office window?"

"Saying what exactly?"

"Something simple, like: *Found. Brown dog. Please enquire inside.*"

My reasoning is that if we stick up a card, there won't be too many folk finding out about him. But if the police are notified, he could go on a database.

Mum makes sure she fondles both his ears equally. "That's not a bad idea." She leans back, and the dog leans forward. He's making sure Mum can still get at those ears. She frowns. "He's not what you'd call small. He must cost a bit to feed."

I say, "We'd find a way."

"Amy – he seems really sweet, but don't get too keen; we're not in a position to—" She breaks off as the phone rings. Irrationally, I panic that someone's already noticed their dog's gone missing and has maybe spotted it's turned up at our house. I pick up the phone. "Hello?"

Mum watches me. I listen to the caller. I'm nodding. Mum looks worried. Although of course the call isn't about the dog, I make a face at her. Then I say into the phone, "No, it's half-term – I go back Monday." The caller asks if she can visit. I can't tell her no, so I say, "Yes, okay," and she tells me what time she'll be here tomorrow. She has a jolly voice: "I'll expect to see the kettle on!" We say goodbye, and I put the phone down.

Mum strokes the dog's head. "The Social?"

"The new person. Mrs Wickham – eleven tomorrow."

Mum sighs. "Sorry, love, it's going to mean a tidy-up."

Don't I know it. It means starting upstairs and working down. It means I'll have to make it look like caring for Mum is a walk in the park. It means she'll have to try her hardest to look less disabled than she is. It means we'll have to convince this Mrs Wickham that we manage perfectly well. No way can we let her think it looks like Mum ought to be in residential care. No way can it look like I can't cope.

I think of everything I'll have to do, and wish I had more energy. I wish I didn't keep getting the sudden stomach cramps I've had yesterday and today. Which I wouldn't dream of worrying Mum about.

My spirits lift at a sudden thought. A dog in the house... This could be a definite advantage. Maybe it would make us look less like "those poor things on Dune Terrace" and more like a family. Which wouldn't be a problem if my sister still lived at home. Lisa, she's called. She lives in town with her boyfriend. Or he lives with her. I don't know which way round, because I'm not sure who pays the rent. Occasionally she turns up, making out she wants to see how Mum's getting on, though usually it's actually because she wants something. A bit of a waste of time, because there's never much to want round here.

I can't say I'm bothered whether she comes or not, except for Mum's sake. But I wish it wasn't like this. She's the only sister I've got.

12

I touch the bare patch on the dog's tail. He doesn't mind.

If you're in a family, you need a name. Looking at him, I try the question out in my head. Then I say aloud, "What shall we call him?"

Mum says, "You choose."

I stroke his brownish fur. "Toffee?"

"That's good," says Mum. "I really like that." She looks into his eyes. "Toffee?" she says, and he wags his tail like mad – his way of smiling. If he *could* smile, he'd be grinning all over his face.

Chapter Three

I started cleaning last night. I dusted and wiped and vacuumed until I was ready to drop. I didn't get it all done, and in the end I *did* drop – into bed. But not before I looked in on Mum. Visits from the Social get her worked up, and I crossed my fingers she'd sleep through. Asleep – her dark hair spread out like a fan – she's so lovely.

Toffee was asleep too, lying beside her bed. I'd tried organizing a makeshift basket for him in the kitchen, but he knew where he wanted to be. With Mum. I'll swear she got upstairs more easily with him behind her.

Early evening I'd taken him out. I'd made a collar and lead from one of the belts I used to wear before what Mum calls my puppy-fat stage (which, annoyingly, I seem to be a bit slow in shaking off). Toffee, on the other hand, doesn't have any spare fat, puppy or otherwise. Once he'd got over rolling around in the soft sand of the dunes, he was quite a good boy, which made me wonder how old he is. But I suppose it doesn't matter. All I know is he loved every minute.

*

I'm up at the crack of dawn this morning, and Toffee's eyeing the back door. He already knows my belt's hanging on the hook with our other outdoor things. I take him down to the beach. It's not cold out, just fresh – and he races along like he'll never stop. I wonder where he's from, where he was born – and if our Northumberland stretches of sand are what he's used to. Or has he never been here before?

We can't spend too long because of the imminent visit by the Social. When I yell, "Toffee!" I think at first my voice has been lost in the wind. But he hears me and it makes me laugh, seeing him whirl round and hurtle back towards me.

Dog food. It's been at the back of my mind since yesterday, that we're going to have to budget for it. Why does money have to be such a worry?

Back home, I feed him a bowl of cornflakes, moistened with a splash of milk. Not as much as he might like, but I've got to watch that last half-pint – what with Mrs Wickham wanting the kettle on.

I fill a white enamel pie dish with water, and walk round the kitchen – which isn't much of a hike – looking for a natural place for it. Toffee turns in tight circles, waiting for me to put it down. Then he parks himself firmly beside the washing machine – he's obviously decided where he'd like it. This is a bit of luck because it covers a missing lino tile – going a little way further to making it look like we're managing nicely, thank you.

I pop upstairs. Mum's in her room, doing her hair. I make sure I sound happy and relaxed. But when I say, "Need any help?" her eyes fill up.

"Mum, don't *worry*. Mrs Wickham sounds okay. Very nice. Quite upbeat, really friendly."

"It's not that."

"What is it then?"

Worry lines spoil her face. "I don't know… It's just… Sometimes it all comes over me."

"What does?"

"Everything – you doing so much for me, when you ought to be concentrating on school."

"Mum, me helping at home is what keeps us together."

"Amy love, you do so much more than that. Look at you – you *run* our home. It makes me feel so damned inadequate."

"Well it shouldn't, it's not—"

I was going to say it's not her fault, but she butts in. "You're the one with your life ahead of you. You're the one who matters. Look at me, I'm bloody useless – just a washed-up, middle-aged—"

"Stop it, Mum. I hate you talking like this."

"You'd be better off without me."

I go cold. "Don't you go saying stuff like this in front of

Mrs Wickham." I take a breath. "Mum, listen. We manage fine. I'm happy. You're happy – most of the time. I don't have problems at school."

"I know. It's just…" She trails off.

"Just what?"

"Your last report was so good – I can't bear the thought of holding you back."

"Don't be daft." I put on my bossy voice: "Now shut up, and let me tie your ribbon."

Afterwards I go downstairs, her words running round in my head. I wish she didn't feel this unnecessary guilt. I hope she's not getting mad ideas about what's best for *me*. Tough love and all that rubbish. If only she could accept that I need her as much as she needs me.

For a second I wish Lisa would walk through the door. So I could shake her. Till she rattled. Shake some sense into her, make her see she should be here, backing me up. Trouble is, she acts so thick I'd probably be wasting my energy. I don't think Lisa's got a clue what it must be like for Mum, always hoping she will come home. Or maybe Mum thinks Lisa had a right to walk out and lead her own life. What if she believes I should do the same thing?

I get the niggling doubt I've had before. What if I've got it wrong? What if Mum *would* be better off without me? Would she get better medical treatment in a care home?

I get a cloth from under the sink and polish the draining board until my wrist aches.

Hearing Mum start to come downstairs a while later, I hurry into our tiny hallway to make sure she's managing. She is, but all the same I wait at the bottom to see she makes it into the kitchen okay.

When there's finally a knock at the front door, Mum – dressed in jeans and a green shirt, is sat at the kitchen table. In front of her there are three mugs on a tray cloth embroidered by her gran. The blusher on her cheeks stands out like two boiled sweets, but she looks better than she did half an hour ago. On my way to the front door, I grab her sticks and shove them in the cubbyhole under the stairs. There's no need to advertise her walking difficulties.

I open the door to a dumpy woman with grey hair so short it's almost stubble. Perhaps she knows it's a mistake, and bought the dangly earrings to make up for it. "Hello there," she says, "I'm Mrs Wickham. You must be Amy." She seems nice, and I swallow my silly impulse to say, *Sorry, Amy emigrated to Australia.* Instead I ask her to come through. This takes about three steps before doing a little dance to decide who's going into the kitchen first. In the end, she edges in front of me.

I say, "We could have gone in the front room, but the—"

"Oh no," she says, "I much prefer the kitchen, it's the heart of the home."

Mum makes a little movement like she's going to stand

18

up, but I give her The Big Stare that says, *Don't you dare move, you might fall.* I ask Mrs Wickham if she'd like a cup of tea.

"Actually," she says, "I could murder a coffee."

My mind goes into Grand Prix mode. Coffee. Have we got any? I open a cupboard, at the same time standing well in front of it. I don't want Mrs Wickham clocking what we have or haven't got. I spot a jar of something instant. And old. I get it out. There's about a teaspoonful of coffee sticking to the bottom. I wave the jar. "Coming up!" I tell her. Then, "Tea for you, Mum?"

Mum gets the message. "Great – thanks, love."

Switching on the kettle, I murmur, "Me too, I'll have tea."

Up until this moment Toffee hasn't moved from his place beside the washing machine. Then suddenly, like he's sat around long enough, he makes for Mrs Wickham's left foot in its sensible beige sandal. Too late for me to stop him, he makes a grab at her puffy ankle and does that thing you really wish dogs wouldn't do.

She tries pushing him off, but he's hanging onto her like a dead weight. "Get *off!*" she says.

Mum says, "Do something, Amy."

"Yes, do something, Amy," says Mrs Wickham.

"*Bad dog!*" I say and, putting my arms round his middle, I pull as hard as I can. For a horrible moment I think I'm going to end up dragging Mrs Wickham off her chair.

But Toffee sees sense, turns round in a flash and licks my nose.

Mrs Wickham checks to see her foot's still attached to her leg. "I'm more of a cat person," she says.

Mum says, "So sorry about that. Not much of an introduction."

"I'm thankful I'm not the postman," says Mrs Wickham.

I take Toffee out the back, and leave him cocking his leg against the drainpipe.

Mrs Wickham opens her briefcase and gets out a file. About us. Turning over a page, she smiles. "Alison Mitchell says lots of nice things about you." She takes a sip of coffee. "By the way, she's had the baby – a little girl." She laughs. "Now she'll find out what it's all about!"

Mum had liked Mrs Mitchell. "Give her my congratulations," she says. "What's the baby called?"

Mrs Wickham wrinkles her forehead. "Gosh, somebody did tell me... No – it's slipped my mind."

"Ah well," says Mum, "so long as they're both doing well."

"I'm sure they are," she says, but I can tell she's a lot more interested in Mum than in Mrs Mitchell. "Now then," she says, tilting her head so one long earring nearly touches her shoulder, "how are we getting along?"

"Good," I say. "Brilliant."

Mrs Wickham looks at Mum. "And *you*, Mrs Preston, you're—"

I interrupt because I'm still worried Mum's not going to

play it the way we usually do: the way we put someone off when they try to find out what life is really like for us. I treat Mrs Wickham to my carefree smile. "Mum's doing great," I say, "really great. Don't you think she's looking well?"

When Mum says, "I certainly *feel* well," I have to hide my relief. "All my pills," she says, "are doing a good job—"

Mrs Wickham interrupts. "There are that many?"

"Well, not really," says Mum. "I suppose I'm mainly referring to the celecoxib."

Mrs Wickham makes a note. "That's for your arthritis?"

Mum says that's right, and loses her deformed fingers in her lap.

"Have you noticed an improvement?" asks Mrs Wickham.

"Oh, definitely." At this rate Mum should be getting an Oscar. Even I begin to believe her, until I remember the look in her eyes when she needs her painkillers. And the relief when they kick in.

When Mrs Wickham asks how she copes while I'm at school, Mum is amazing. I'm almost reeling at the way she gives a convincing rundown of how she keeps on top of things.

I say, "I come home at lunchtime."

Mrs Wickham says, "Would you like to stay for school lunch?"

"Why would I want to do that? I'm only five minutes away."

She says, "I was only thinking, you must be quite stretched with your GCSEs."

So she's worked that out.

Mum includes me in her smile. "There's not long to go now."

Mrs Wickham makes another note, and I wonder if it's because I sounded less than polite. I can't think what the big deal is about me and school meals. You'd think I was about ten.

We – Mum and I – have wondered about asking for help. But we're not risking it. No way. With both of us happy enough, there's no point in stirring things up – perhaps even giving the Social the wrong idea. All right, we could get some very nice woman popping in to help, but there's no guarantee they wouldn't send a nosy parker. I'm not saying intentionally – but if someone caught Mum on a bad day, it might be a job convincing them that things are okay. Most of the time our arrangements work out fine.

But there were times – times I was going out with Liam – when I was torn in two, thinking I ought to be at home with Mum.

Mrs Wickham turns over another page of printed notes. "Let me see…" she says. "How is your other daughter?"

No one has any idea Lisa has moved out. Not even Kirsty. Which I hate. The thing is though, I'd have to ask her not to say anything. It wouldn't be fair, and she might worry about me. If she doesn't know, there's no risk she'll let something slip.

Mum responds to Mrs Wickham's enquiring look. "Lisa's fine," she says, "working hard."

"Good," says Mrs Wickham. "And what's her job?"

Mum hesitates.

Quickly I say, "She's in retail." Which is true: two weeks in Asda, six in Tesco, ten in Aldi. The last was a record. "She's learning as she goes."

Mrs Wickham closes her file and stands up. "Wise girl. There's no substitute for experience."

Mum gives a little smile. "That's what I hoped to do."

"Oh yes?" says Mrs Wickham.

"I did work for a while," says Mum. "Bottom rung of the ladder at M&S. Then I got married and had our Lisa." She pauses. "Next thing we knew, Amy came along. After a bit I wasn't so well…and this thing started."

I catch Mrs Wickham's quick glance at Mum's hands, at the "thing" that twists them out of shape. Does Mrs Wickham know what happened to Dad? I suppose it's in the notes somewhere, how he left when we were little. When Mum began to get ill.

When I show her out, she pats me on the shoulder. "Try to keep that dog under control."

Chapter Four

Mum's worn out after Mrs Wickham – says she feels like a piece of chewed string. She stays in her chair while I make us a snack: cheese on toast. Which is not at all what I'd really like. What I'd like at this minute is a packet of chocolate digestives. I don't mean I'd eat the whole packet in one go. But two or three would be good – after I'd eaten the cheese on toast.

When we've finished, I take her plate and wipe crumbs off the worktop.

She smiles at me. "Thanks, love, that filled a little corner."

I count out the pills she takes after meals, and hand her a glass of water. She's hardly given me back the glass before she's ready for sleep. I can reckon on her having a good nap for at least an hour. Her eyes close, and I look at her. Peaceful and pretty – letting go of those ideas about me doing too much for her. I stop and think for a moment. How would I feel if I was a sick mum relying on my kid for support? I might feel the same. A bit guilty.

Toffee seems to sense we need to be quiet, but it doesn't stop him pawing at the back door. The house is so clean and tidy I think it's best not to stay in and mess it up. I collect my belt from the hook and open the door. He makes sure I'm following him, then rushes into the yard.

I squat down, buckle him up with my version of a collar and lead, and we go round to the front lane.

There's no view of the sea from downstairs in our house. The dunes, pillow-shaped, get in the way. Toffee tugs on his "lead", and I risk letting him run on his own. Leaping through the tufts of marram grass, he throws up puffs of fine soft sand. I hurry to keep up with him and now, reaching a ridge of sand, we see the sea. The tide's out, though it's on the turn.

Toffee runs and runs. Trying to keep up with him, I think how this must be great for burning calories. They're on about it all the time on the news – obese teens not getting enough exercise. (Not that I'm obese.) Plus, we apparently live on a diet of Mars bars… Well, not in our house, we don't; there's no spare cash for treats. So looking on the bright side, my limited access to chocolate must give me a head start. All I need to do is take exercise more seriously.

Toffee could be the answer. Taking him for a run two or three times a day could help me lose weight. With a bit of luck, I'll soon be as skinny as I was at thirteen. Though don't get me wrong, I wouldn't ever want to be that flat-chested again.

I'm looking into the distance. There's a figure jogging towards us, and I squint as the sun comes out from behind a cloud. She – it's Kirsty – comes closer. Toffee shows interest and I hold him by the scruff. I wave, and after a few seconds she waves back; she's short-sighted but doesn't like to admit it. Besides, she's not expecting I'd be here with a dog. I'm pleased to see her. Nearly an hour with Mrs Wickham has made me feel I've lost sight of reality.

And it's not just today – I've felt a bit jittery these last couple of days. Mum's noticed, even though I didn't mean to make anything of it. She says it's my hormones – which seems to be her answer to everything. Still, it would be a relief if it meant I was finally settling down. Kirsty and I are the same age, but she came on three years ago and is as regular as clockwork. Not like me; I'm all over the place. I started the summer before last, but it's utterly unpredictable – in fact, a complete pain. A while back, because I never know when it's coming – and just in case there was something wrong – I saw a woman doctor at the practice. She said it isn't unusual for periods to be irregular for the first three to four years.

Kirsty pounds up to us. "Hi!" She leans forward, bending over in an n-shape to get her breath back. Toffee wags his tail. Surprised to see him, she says, "Who's this?"

"Toffee."

She looks puzzled. "He's not yours, is he?"

"For now he is."

"How d'you mean?"

"It's not definite." I curl my fingers in his scruff. "But it's possible he'll stay."

"When did you get him?"

"Yesterday." I make it sound like you get a dog every day.

"After you were round at ours?" She gives me a look. "I didn't know you were thinking of getting a dog. You didn't say anything."

I pat Toffee. "He's a rescue dog. You don't always know when they're going to turn up." I'm not sure why I don't just tell her exactly what happened.

"Great," says Kirsty, "think of all the exercise you'll get!"

It was the way she said it. I could virtually read her mind. Here she is, jogging along, delicately pretty, ponytail as blonde as the beach, legs to die for, sun-kissed midriff taut as a drum. And here's me stood beside her, taller but a bit of a podge. I stand up straight and tug my plaid shirt so it covers my bum. "I won't need to go to the gym – not with Toffee keeping me toned."

"*You* were going to the gym?"

I laugh. "As if!"

She strokes Toffee from his shoulders to his tail. "He's a real sweetie."

"Glad you like him."

"He's beautiful."

I look at him. I love him already, but I can't honestly say he's beautiful. "Don't you think he's more cute than beautiful?"

She looks him up and down, like she's judging at a dog show. "No – he's too big for cute." She nudges me. "Come on, race you to the rock!"

We start running towards Croppers Rock. Toffee alongside Kirsty. Me miles behind.

I get a stitch and stop for a few seconds. Toffee must sense I'm not running. He skids to a halt in the wet sand and looks round. Which makes Kirsty turn.

"You okay?"

"Just a stitch!" The sharp pain eases off, but I realize I'm not feeling too clever; plus I really do need a new bra. Running in this old thing's making me sore – and I'm puffing like I'm eighty. Toffee rushes back towards me.

I think I must be worn out from getting the house ready for Mrs Wickham. Kirsty looks at me like she's surprised at my pathetic performance, but she doesn't comment on it. Instead she says, "Everything all right at home today?" She pauses. "Mum said to make sure I ask." She strokes Toffee. "Which I am doing."

"We're fine. We had a Mrs Wickham round this morning. She's new – from the Social. She seemed pleased with Mum. You know – the way she's managing."

She pulls a face. "Don't you mean, the way *you're*

managing? With or without Lisa's help." Kirsty knows my sister well enough to realize she won't be pulling her weight, even if she's not aware that Lisa's actually left home altogether.

Kirsty says she'd better be heading back. "It's hell on wheels at ours."

"They've arrived then?"

"Yeah – teenage lad from a children's home. And twins of eighteen months – boy and girl."

Mum wonders if Mrs Kelly fosters kids because she can't have more of her own; though we don't know that for certain. She's the sort who'll take a kid in, any hour of the day or night, if their family can't cope.

Kirsty jogs off like she hasn't a care in the world, and I'm glad for her. It was a different story in January when she split up with Harrison – just when I was so blissfully happy with Liam.

Even though Kirsty was the one who ended it, it still upset her. Looking back, I probably wasn't much help, being so wrapped up in Liam. She'd been totally into Harrison – crazy about him, in fact – though I don't know if he really cared that much about *her*. If you *really* love someone, you don't keep trying to force them to do things they're not ready for. Which was what he was doing. I'm just glad she didn't give in.

Unlike our Lisa, who's more than happy to throw herself at anyone who turns up. Currently Darren Baines. Though you can never quite tell what's happening with those two – one minute he's a waste of space, the next she's bending over backwards for him. I only wish she'd spare me the graphic details.

When she's gone a little way, Kirsty turns round to blow Toffee a kiss. I love that. Now, watching her get smaller, I picture her mucking in to help her mum with the new intake of kids. It'll be all go. Busy and noisy.

Liam arrived at the Kellys' last summer. I remember thinking it must be humiliating, finding yourself in care at fifteen. He was in a bad place when we first got together. He didn't want to talk about it, but from what I gathered, his mum was in hospital with depression after his dad began a fifteen-year sentence in a high-security prison. I was shocked, but Liam tried to play it down, saying his dad had been a rotten husband and his mum was better off without him. It was pretty obvious he hadn't been much of a dad either.

I don't like myself for thinking this…but if his life hadn't all been so awful, Liam and I would never have met. I know it's not a good thought, but it doesn't change how I felt about him.

I think I was about eleven when I asked Mum how I'd know when I was in love. "You'll just know," she said. And she was right.

Those early days were wonderful. Mum – glad that I'd found "such a nice lad" – encouraged me to get out and enjoy myself. If I ever looked doubtful, she'd say, "I'll be all right, love. Go on, make hay while the sun shines!" I knew it wasn't easy for her, and cracks of guilt opened up when I worried I might be betraying her trust. One minute I'd be lying in Liam's arms, thinking, *If this is making hay, it's all I've ever wanted* – the next I'd ask myself whether I was still giving Mum the care she needed. Most of the time I made doubly sure I was doing just that, then suddenly I'd realize we were out later than I'd promised and my stomach would seize up with worry. I don't think Liam always understood why I was in such a rush to get home. If I got anxious, he'd say, "It's not like we're out that often."

The months we were together, I lived in a world I hadn't known existed. Sometimes I literally caught my breath at the thought that this was happening to me, that I'd met someone I wanted to be with for the rest of my life. Being so much in love felt like a dream I could never have imagined, like it had fallen out of the sky. Quite how it was for Liam, I couldn't be sure. If I ever tried asking him how he felt, he'd clam up and I wished I hadn't said anything.

Mum says one of the ways I'm so different from Lisa is having my head screwed on. Not always, though. Looking back, it was stupid to imagine a future with Liam, free as a bird – travelling the world. Weekends in Paris. I got carried away. Mad really.

I was happy for Liam when his mum came through the breakdown. But at the same time – loving each other the way we did – it felt like fate had played a mean trick. When

Australia thing came up, I had to come to a decision. Putting thousands of miles between us had never been part of the deal.

Kirsty hardly believed I could be so cool. In my heart though, I just never believed that once Liam got to Oz we'd be able to stay together. All the same, I cried buckets. It was hard, very hard. I guess Liam took it pretty well – which I was thankful for, but it hurt too. Kirsty had already been through it – splitting up with Harrison – and when I found myself going through the same thing, I felt guilty for not totally understanding how bad it must have been for her. Although I did think it was a bit different for me and Liam. Kirsty and I, we're as close as you can get, but I don't think I ever really told her just how special Liam was. He wasn't like Harrison, and I'd been sure he wanted me for myself. It had felt so right. All of it.

At the beginning, when Liam and his mum flew to Oz for a short visit – wanting to make sure living with her sister would work out – it was kind of exciting. Liam called twice, putting on an Aussie accent. It didn't feel real, not like they'd make up their minds to live there permanently. As it turned out, they fell in love with Australia, and decided to make the move. (I reckon leaving his dad locked up on this side of the world had a lot to do with it.) When they flew back to London for a week, I talked to Liam on the phone but we didn't see each other. Then they were gone for good.

Though I'm glad for him – really glad – that his life has turned round, it doesn't stop me missing him. Ever since I saw a programme on TV, one fact has been at the back of my mind: that one in three British families looking for a new life in Australia comes back.

Toffee's pleased with himself. He's found a stick. He lollops towards me and drops it at my feet. Bending to pick it up, I breathe in the salty smell of wet seaweed. Then I move to where, very soon, the sea will slide in and wash away the oversized capitals I'm scratching in the sand.

LIAM.

Chapter Five

Saturday, and we've got to think of getting in some proper dog food.

Mum's had tea and cereal. She's still in bed and I'm down here, listening to Radio 1. Funny how something in the background helps you concentrate.

I've seen the dried stuff Toffee needs. Beef and vegetables. In two sizes. More economical to buy the big one. In itself it's not too expensive. The problem is it'll be every week. *A dog's not just for Christmas*, etc.

I stare into space, waiting for the DJ to play something different.

With a high-pitched twang, the intro to a new song starts. The solution hits me.

Lisa...

...Who can't hold down a job for five minutes. Who you can bet right now is scrounging some sort of benefit. What does she ever contribute? Nothing. She'd argue she doesn't live here any more, so she doesn't owe anything. Wrong.

She owes Mum – who gave her everything. When Dad walked out, though I don't remember what that hard time was actually like, Mum held the family together. Although she was already getting sick, she made sure we had balanced meals and clean clothes. She kept the house looking nice even though we never had anything new. She came to parent-teacher evenings and carol services. She did all those things.

And then – with Mum worse, despite what she lets the Social think – Lisa falls for that pig-headed Darren and announces she's leaving. No apologies for not pulling her weight. Just the opposite: she said she was doing us a favour – one less mouth to feed and more space. Perhaps she meant it.

The day she left, a while ago now, Mum was too shocked and weak even to walk to the door and see her off.

I'd caught up with her at the end of the terrace. "Lisa? When will you come back and see us?" She wanted to shake me off, but I stood my ground. "Mum will want to know."

She looked past me, like I was holding her up. "Soon."

"How soon?"

"Look, I don't know, okay?"

"*Lisa*, can't you think of Mum for two seconds?"

"One – two – three – *four*." She paused. "How's that?"

"Why are you being like this?"

"Like what?"

I tried to keep calm. "Acting like you don't care."

She gave me a stare. "Give me a break, Amy." She paused. "I'm just not cut out for all this heavy stuff."

"I'm not talking heavy stuff, I'm talking *our mum.*"

"What if you are?" She stuck out her chin. "You don't know what you're talking about. If you did, you'd realize."

I wondered what *she* was talking about, what it was I'd realize.

She looked at the ground. "Whatever you might think, I do care."

"*Saying* you care isn't enough. You have to show it. You know, do things for her. Stick around."

"For God's sake, Amy. Get a life."

I stayed calm. "I'd get more of a life," I said, "if you helped more." I looked at her silly bleached hair. "Even someone with half a brain cell can wash up and make their own bed."

"I've had enough of it," she said. "If you must know, I can't stand her being ill all the time." She nearly smiled when she said, "I thought you'd be glad to have the room to yourself."

"It won't make up for me having to do everything on my own."

She took a step towards me. "Look, I'll come back. Now and again."

I said, "What's your new address?"

She huffed. "Got a pen?"

"No."

Eventually, scrabbling about in the bottom of her pink fluffy handbag, she dug out a pencil and wrote on the back of one of our old shopping lists. "There you go."

I read her childish writing: *24a Ladder Lane.*

She said, "You can get a bus. The 213." Then she added quickly, "This doesn't mean you can keep coming round. I've got my own life to lead."

She spun around and began to walk away. I raised my voice: "Have you ever thought about my life?"

"You're the one does the thinking, Amy."

It was obvious I was wasting my time. Folding the piece of paper, I watched her totter away on her scuffed heels.

This morning, sitting beside Mum on her bed, helping her get dressed, I tell her I'm getting the bus to Lisa's. It'll be my first visit to her new place and Mum doesn't quite hide her hope that this might be a new beginning for Lisa and me. She leaves it a few moments before she asks if there's a particular reason why I'm going today.

"Bits and bobs. Let her know the Social's been. That we're okay for a bit." I pause. "Anyway, it seems ages since we were in touch."

She says, "Oh, right…" and leaves the sort of pause that signals there's more to come. "Amy, love, our Lisa's not a bad girl."

"Course not."

"She's just a bit thoughtless. A bit headstrong." She puts out a hand to me. "To tell you the truth, I think deep down she feels she can't cope."

"Yeah? Well… Did you want your striped top?"

"No – the blue one'll do another day." I reach for the blouse and she says, "It's probably my fault she's like she is."

I don't like the sound of this. "Don't be daft, Mum."

"I'm serious. I'm not sure I dealt with her the right way. You know, when she was little. Even as a toddler she was a rebellious kid. I suppose I wasn't expecting it to be like that. I'd imagined this dear little girl who'd go along with what me and your dad wanted—"

I pause. She never mentions Dad.

She says quickly, "She *was* a dear little girl, of course, it's just she had a mind of her own."

I fasten some buttons she can't manage. "You'd have been worried if she didn't think for herself." I fiddle with the top button. "And Dad?"

"Well, you know, some men aren't that fussed about kids…unless they stop them getting their eight hours."

With Dad more or less a no-go area, I'm wary about quizzing her. "So what did he do, that his sleep was so vital?"

"Most of the time he worked nights. A noisy kid didn't go down well." She plucks at her jeans. "Lisa was a nightmare – screamed the place down if she didn't get what she wanted. I think…" She falters. "…that's where I'm to blame. To be honest, I didn't know what to do. Your dad said she needed a good smack, but I could never do that." She looks up at me. "You were different. You were so easy." She manages a little laugh. "You were almost too good to be true."

When I reach for her socks – one's just under the bed – she puts a hand on my shoulder. "D'you think you and Lisa might do something together today? Go out and have a bit of fun?"

Fun – me and Lisa? I put my hand inside a sock, ease it onto her foot. "Like what?"

"There must be something."

It's hopeless, but I say brightly, "I could tell her about Toffee. See if she'd like to come for walks."

Mum's face lights up. She never stops believing some miracle might happen, like Lisa turning into an unselfish, caring human being.

She says, "You'll give her my love, won't you?"

"Of course I will."

Ladder Lane isn't on the bus route, and the driver doesn't have a clue about the nearest stop. A girl with a runny-nosed baby tells me when she thinks we're near. I ring the bell and get off. But I take a wrong turning, and it's not until I notice The Ladder Discount Store (with a window full of cheap batteries and black bin liners) that I spot Ladder Lane. I trail down the dreary-looking street of terraced houses, which might have been quite nice once, with patterned tiles on their garden paths.

I check which side of the street is even-numbered, but I'm confused until I realize a 6 is actually a 9 swung upside down because of a missing screw. I cross the road and start looking for 24. I stand outside what I think must be Lisa's. The house is next door to 26, so I reckon I'm looking at the right one. Though the bell for 24a works, it's a little while before I hear footsteps clip-clopping unevenly down the stairs. Lisa opens the door.

It takes a lot to shock me, but even I think she looks wrecked. Her peroxide hair's spiked up stiffer than ever. Her face is swollen from crying. There's mascara under her eyes – like a spider's stood in black ink before sliding down her cheeks. She stares at me. "Oh, it's you."

It doesn't hide much, the matted pink dressing gown with a grubby bunny on the pocket. I take a quick look over my shoulder. Wouldn't she rather passers-by didn't see her like this? I say, "Aren't you going to ask me in?"

She stands back and I step into the hallway. When she shuts the door it's almost pitch-black – until a door opens on the right-hand side of the narrow passage. A deeply wrinkled old woman comes out, pulling a wheeled basket. She eyes Lisa.

"What was that all about last night?" she says. "I need my beauty sleep, you know."

I open the front door for her, and she winks at me.

After the woman has bumped her basket over the front step, I close the door behind her.

Lisa's already climbing the stairs. "You'd best come up."

I follow her. Someone's painted 24a, badly, on the door to the flat, which is really only a bedsit with an unmade bed taking up most of the room. The greasy-looking green velvet headboard is disgusting, rubbed bald in two patches – I suppose by the different pairs of heads over the years. Behind the bed, just on that one wall, there's peeling wallpaper picturing exotic birds perched on twisted branches. In a corner of the room, half-hidden by a sagging orange and brown curtain, there's a teetering pile of old pizza boxes, ready to slide off the mini draining board. Do they call that the kitchen?

I need the loo, though I only went just before I left home. "Where's your toilet?"

She says, "You passed it on the half-landing."

"Won't be a minute."

The door has BATHROOM written on it. Inside, the bolt doesn't work properly. If you sat on the loo, next to the bath, you'd be too far away to stick your foot out and stop someone coming in. I'll be hovering, not sitting. There's a notice over the bath: CLEAN THE BATH AFTER USE. How many people use this bath? However many there are, there's no sign of anyone cleaning it. I pull the old-fashioned lavatory chain, holding it high above the handle everyone else probably uses. After a quick glance at the wash basin, I reckon there's less risk of catching anything if I don't wash my hands.

Back in the room, I tell Lisa she's practically out of bog roll. Then I ask, "What did the old woman mean?"

"What?"

"About last night," I say. "What were you up to?"

She slumps onto the bed. "Just a fight. No big deal."

"You and Darren?"

Her lips narrow to a thin line. "That low life is yesterday's news. I don't ever want to hear his name again."

When she gets up and starts rummaging in her make-up bag on the window sill, I spot four pound coins on a bedside table. She finds a cleansing pad and sits on the bed again. Pulling at the skin round her eyes, she attacks the leftover mascara. I tell her she'll dig an eye out if she's not careful.

She looks at me like she's a little girl, and I'm the big sister. "I'm thinking of coming home," she says, and screws up her left eye. "Mum won't mind, will she?"

I don't let on this'll make Mum deliriously happy. I don't let on this'll make *me* happy. "You'll have to pay your way. Mum's not too good, there's extras she needs."

"Like what?"

I look at the coins. "Food and stuff."

She falls back onto the rumpled sheets, snorting a false laugh. "Yeah, well, we've all got to eat." This is so typical – her never taking anything seriously – that I want to retaliate: tell her the real extra that Mum would benefit from would be seeing *Lisa* do her fair share of chores round the house. Without moaning all the time. But I hold back because my eye is on those coins.

So all I say is, "Food's expensive, you know."

"Whatever," she says, and I can see she's so pleased at the thought of getting out of the bedsit, she doesn't care what her money would be used for.

"Well," I say, "as long as you understand you'll have to contribute."

"No worries," she says, "I'll get a little notebook and we'll—" At this point it rings – the mobile I didn't know she had.

She flicks it open, glances at the screen, slaps it against her ear. She turns her back on me, but I can hear the low crackle of a man's voice. She butts in: "Change the bloody record, Darren." She pauses for a second. "Anyway, Amy's here and I'm going home. Mum needs me." Whatever it is he says now makes her stiffen: "That is *not* what you said last night." She moves nearer the window, gives the skirting board a kick. "It didn't sound like that to me." While he rabbits on, I watch her shoulders relax. "Yeah, yeah," she says, and gives her hips a little wiggle. "Okay, but look – if you *ever*—" She breaks off, listening to him intently. She licks her finger, runs it along an eyebrow. "All right, but this is the last time." She swings round, a silly grin on her face. A moment later she turns away again, the phone still stuck to her ear, and hurries to look out of the smeary window – like Darren could already be outside. I scoop up the coins and put them in my pocket.

Clearly, he's not here yet but when she says, "Okay, sweetheart – as soon as?" I gather he'll turn up any minute. I look round the manky room. Once out of here, why would anyone want to come back? She signals to me, sliding her eyes towards the door.

But I'm not leaving, not until I get her mobile number.

After a big slurping goodbye kiss into the phone, she raises her eyebrows at me. "What're you hanging around for? You'll have guessed what that was about."

"I'm very happy for you," I say. "Just one thing, Lisa – can I have your mobile number?"

When I realize she's thinking up an excuse for not telling me, I say, "If I can call you, I won't have to keep coming round."

Sighing hard, she finds a scrap of paper and writes it down. I make sure I can read it, then put it in my purse.

When I get back in – stagger, more like – with a large bag of dog food, Mum's watching a talent show. "Listen to this lad," she says, "he's got a gorgeous voice."

44

Though my arms are aching under the economy-size Adult Beef & Vegetables, I stand watching the TV. Slowly the bag slides from my arms, then thuds to the floor. It startles Mum. "What sort of hole did that make in the housekeeping?" I tell her it was on offer, and that we'll have to guess Toffee's weight so we can judge how much he'll need each day. We study silhouettes of dogs on the bag, and decide he's bigger than a fox terrier-type, but a bit smaller than a German shepherd.

I fetch the scissors and cut the bag open. Toffee goes crazy at the smell. I take the kitchen scales from the cupboard under the sink, and weigh out the approximate number of grams. Then I pour the helping into a soup bowl that'll be his from now on, and put it on the floor. He clearly loves this crunchy stuff – much nicer than the scraps we've been feeding him. It seems to be the right amount, because once he's finished he sits quietly beside Mum.

She's been working up to the question: "You saw our Lisa all right?"

"Yep."

"And?"

"She sends her love."

"Is Darren still hanging around?"

"Seems like it." All the way to the supermarket I'd been telling myself the four pounds was his, not Lisa's.

For apparently no reason she says – and it's not quite a question – "I suppose you've not heard from Liam lately."

Chapter Six

Sunday. Mum's voice, amused, breaks into my thoughts. "Are you going to sit reading all morning?"

She can't have noticed that I've barely turned a page. I've been dreaming the dreams I usually save for when I'm staring out to sea – where only the sand reads my thoughts about Liam. Millions of billions of trillions of grains of sand, all washed away in one powerful frothy suck. I know one day there'll be someone else. There has to be. This can't be it. I'm sixteen.

I stand up and lean against the sink. Through the window I watch a family carry picnic things towards the dunes. The mum looks fed up, and I want to call out and tell her how lucky she is. Mum hears their voices. "Why don't you get some fresh air?" she says. "Take Toffee out."

I turn away from the window. "Okay."

"You could go and see those twins at Kirsty's."

Yes, I think. I'll do that.

*

Weekends at the Kellys' are the same as any other day. Like Mrs Kelly says, "No peace for the wicked!" The house is a complete contrast to ours. I think of Mum: quiet, longing for a nap that will take her somewhere pain-free. Today at Kirsty's, with these twins, it's non-stop jabbering. Mind you, I've heard it noisier than this. While Liam was here, there was a kid who could only talk at full volume; shouted every word. Turned out his mum was going deaf and he'd forgotten how to speak normally. He wasn't here for long. His dad got back off the oil rig, and his mum came out of hospital.

Good as gold, Toffee sits beside me while I help Kirsty give the twins their dinner. I'm feeding the little boy while Kirsty feeds the girl. My toddler, Aidan, is easy to deal with – apart from grabbing the spoon and wanting to feed himself.

Mrs Kelly checks a tin of roast potatoes in the oven, then folds flour into the buns she's making. "Amy, love, let Aidan try on his own." I do what she suggests, but the spoonful of pasta in tomato sauce flies over his shoulder. Toffee catches it in mid-air, and we all double up laughing. The other twin, Eleanor – food smeared over half her face – beams at me. While she's still grinning, Kirsty manages to slip a spoonful of pasta into her mouth, instead of onto her eyebrows. Kirsty and I plough on, until Mrs Kelly says she thinks we've done our bit with their first course. Pudding is easier. Little pots of fruity yogurt quickly vanish.

Sunlight from the door into the hallway is suddenly blotted out. I look up. This must be the teenager. Wow, he's big... Not actually fat, just man-sized. Shoulders like he's built for American football. Kirsty waves a little plastic spoon at him. "Hi, Shaun – this is Amy." He pulls out a chair and sits at the table. "What've you been doing?" she says.

He shrugs, and biceps like a weightlifter's bulge out of his short-sleeved grey T-shirt. "Nothing."

I want to tell him he must have done *something*, even if it's only breathing, but that would be cruel because he doesn't look happy.

Kirsty and I exchange glances. We carry on making a fuss of the twins, and she says, "Shaun's coming to our school."

He looks at Mrs Kelly and says, "Am I?"

How weird – him not knowing which school he's going to.

Mrs Kelly stops stirring the bun mixture. "Yes, you are...I thought I told you."

I look at Shaun's big round face. Something that, to me, would be so important, doesn't seem to mean much to him.

Kirsty tries getting his attention. "I don't envy you, Shaun, having to sit in our revision classes. Still," she says, "it'll give you a head start for when you come back in September." I take a quick look at her. Surely he's older than us?

He glances at the twins for a second. Then his eyes, kind of grey, slide away. He makes a point of not looking at me. Like I'm not here. But he notices Toffee and rubs the fur under his chin.

Our eyes meet again, Kirsty's and mine. The little downturn of her mouth tells me she reckons Shaun's a lost cause.

Mrs Kelly puts a mug of coffee and a slice of cake in front of me. "You look a bit tired, Amy. Everything all right?"

Toffee wants to nose my cake. I push him away. "I'm fine, thanks, just wishing it wasn't Monday tomorrow." This isn't strictly true. The only thing I don't like about Mondays is leaving Mum alone after the weekend. And it's not like we've even got an exam tomorrow, just revision for English Literature, my favourite subject.

I stop my mind from drifting. Lick my finger and press it into the cake crumbs on my plate. I could easily have eaten another slice. "Lovely cake, Mrs Kelly."

She smiles, pleased. "I got the recipe off the telly." I'm surprised she ever has time to watch.

When she gives Shaun a slice, Toffee sniffs at it. For the first time Shaun looks at me. "Can he have a bit?"

"Better not," I say, "I don't want him getting into bad habits."

Shaun nods, and finishes his cake in two mouthfuls.

There's the sound of Mr Kelly knocking mud from his

boots on the back step. He comes in. Spots Toffee. "Hey, who've we got here?" He pulls off his socks. "And hello to you too, Amy."

"His name's Toffee," says Kirsty. "He's a rescue dog."

I'm surprised when Shaun says, "A rescue dog?" like he wants to know more.

Mrs Kelly says, "A dog without a home."

Shaun pushes back his chair. "Like me," he says, and leaves the room.

While Mrs Kelly pretends to shoot herself, Kirsty's dad says, "You can't watch every word, Susie."

I take a few sips of coffee but, unusually for me, I don't want the rest. Mrs Kelly goes to the cake tin. "D'you think your mum would like a piece?"

"Oh, she'd love one. Thank you." Kirsty's mum never misses a chance to pop something in a bag for Mum.

Before I leave, Mr Kelly gives me two freshly-picked lettuces to take home. "A bit of a glut out there," he says. "Hope you can make use of them."

"Oh great, thanks." I try to sound matter-of-fact. I don't want him to know I think he might look on Mum and me as a charity case.

The tide's half in when I make my way back from Kirsty's across the sand. Toffee is so obedient I don't need to bother with my old belt. But I know I must get a real dog collar soon, and – positive thinking – put his name and our phone number on it.

It's a beautiful day and the sea is mirror-calm. Just a few sailing boats bob about, waiting for the wind to whip up. There are couples strolling; other people on their own, some with dogs. Toffee eyes the nearest – a posh-looking white poodle – then decides staying with me is a better bet. Gazing out to sea, I pick up on a daydream – me, Liam and Toffee racing about on a beach in Australia.

"Ow!" I'm brought down to earth by the real Toffee crashing into the backs of my knees. "That wasn't *funny!*" I tell him. He drops a stick at my feet, like this makes up for nearly sending me flying.

The sand is perfect, just damp enough for drawing. But I keep getting a low-down stabbing pain, and feel it again when I bend over for the stick. It starts to subside, so I decide to forget it and draw an oval in the sand. I give it eyes and a nose, then the mouth. Now some hair and ears, flat to the head. Toffee puffs around. I keep pushing him away from my work of art. I look at it. It's the best I can do for now. To be honest, I'm a rubbish artist. I brush sand off the stick. Slowly, carefully, I write *LIAM*. For a second I stare at it, then promise myself it's the last time I'll do this.

"What does that say?"

My heart lurches. It's Shaun. I hadn't heard him creep up on me. "Hey, you made me jump!"

He says, "Why's that?"

"I didn't know you were on the beach."

Toffee, wagging his tail in wild circles, tries to get at the plastic bag Shaun's holding. Shaun raises his arm, keeping the bag out of Toffee's reach. He jerks his head towards the cliffs. "I came down from the top," he says. Which amazes me because it's practically a sheer drop that must have landed him between a stretch of rock pools and Croppers Rock.

"What? You *slid* down that?"

Shaun doesn't seem to think this is anything much. Telling him he's lucky not to have two broken legs, I shove my toe into the sand and scrub out LIAM.

When he says, "What did that say?" most of his attention is still on Toffee and he sounds only half interested.

"Nothing, really."

"It must've said something."

So he is interested. "Didn't you see?"

He says, "No."

My laugh is too loud. "Len – it said *Len*."

"Who's Len?"

"My grandad." (My grandads, both dead before I was born, were Ted and Maurice.)

He says, "Have you got a gran?"

"I did have. Nana Kathleen, Mum's mum. But she died four years ago." The familiar pang hits me as I realize for the thousandth time how much Mum and I miss her. She was everything to us. I think how different things would be if she was still alive. How she'd be dealing with Lisa.

She loved both us girls to bits, but she was firm with Lisa in a way Mum never is. It's always felt like Mum's scared of Lisa, scared she'll take offence. When she was just a kid, Lisa would threaten to run away. She'd yell, "Then you'll all be *sorry!*" and go to the door – to make sure it wasn't raining. Nana Kathleen didn't stand for any of her nonsense. "What're you going to do for money?" she'd say, and watch Lisa stomp up to our room.

I bring myself back to the present, point to the dunes – a signal to Toffee that we're going home. I smile at Shaun. "See you later."

Deadpan, he says, "When? How much later?"

"I don't mean anything definite. I mean I'll see you sometime. Like I'll see you at school tomorrow."

Suddenly I want to be at home with Mum. I've hurried a little way off when Shaun calls out, "Amy!"

I turn round. He's following me, dangling the plastic bag. Mr Kelly's lettuces! I think of the cake for Mum at the bottom, turning to crumbs. "Thanks, Shaun."

He says, "See you later then."

Was that a smile? If it was, it must have been meant for Toffee.

Chapter Seven

Monday morning, and Mum gives me the *Found – Brown dog* note she's written for the post office window. "You can ask Mrs Goodge to copy it onto a card for you," she says. This makes me feel really down. I'd been thinking she feels like me – that Toffee is here to stay, that it's not entering our heads he might belong to someone else. It's not like we enticed him, even *found* him. He found us, and any fool can see he wants to stay.

There won't be time to take the card to the post office before school. I'll go on my way home at lunchtime.

I settle Mum in the kitchen, with stuff she might need. Give her cushions for support, and put hot water in a flask for her mid-morning drink. I leave her sticks handy, so she can make it to the back door to let Toffee out into the yard. And I remind her, like I always do, to be very, very careful if she wants to go upstairs to the loo. Which she might want to. I know she'll try to hang on until I get back, but if she gets desperate she'll make her way upstairs, crawling.

I think she's probably entitled to a kind of portable toilet that could be kept downstairs behind a screen, but making enquiries might open a can of worms we don't need.

If we could truthfully say Lisa lives here permanently, maybe we'd relax a little. Age-wise, though sadly not in any other way, she almost classes as a responsible adult. Me, I've only got a couple of years to go – though sometimes I feel about thirty-five.

It's the first day back after half-term, and the racket outside school is even more ear-splitting than usual. Maybe I've got used to the calm while on study leave. Like me, Kirsty usually walks to school, but this morning – I suppose because Shaun is starting today – her dad drops them off at the gates. She gets out of the car, followed by her dad and Shaun, who gets some odd looks. Although he's not smiling, he's pleased to see me. When he says loudly, "Hi, Amy," I notice his voice doesn't have much of a range. It's like it's all on one note. Pupils swarm about, in and out of small groups. Three giggly Year Ten girls nudge each other and give me a look.

I say, "Hi, Shaun," and glance sideways at the girls. One, a redhead with way too much make-up, raises her eyebrows at me.

Kirsty joins me while her dad makes for the main door with Shaun. With a warm smile, Mr Smith, our form tutor, comes out of the building and holds the door open for them. I can't hear what he says but it's clear he's directing them towards the Head's office. I wonder what Shaun will make of Mr Wilson – who's not what you might think of as a typical head teacher. Liam described him as *dead casual, like he's on another planet.* That's the impression he gives, but Mum and the Kellys think he's brilliant. Mr Kelly says he gets what he wants out of his staff. Well, most of them.

Mr Smith crosses the playground and pushes between knots of students to get to his car. Kirsty watches as the Year Ten redhead sidles up to ask him something. He answers while moving round to the boot. She follows, then looks disappointed when he taps his watch. She joins her friends, who are giggling, and they make their way into school.

Kirsty's remark comes out of the blue: "Have you ever seen his wife?"

I follow her glance. "Mr Smith's?"

She nods, and I say, "No. Have you?"

"Yeah, last week. She picked Mum up for a council meeting they both wanted to go to."

"What's she like?"

"A bit stuck-up. She's a bank manager." She pauses. "Mum thinks she's lovely."

"You mean to look at?"

She says, "I suppose so. Though I can't see it."

"Isn't that a bit mean?"

"I'm only stating a fact." She changes the subject. "By the way, you've got a secret admirer."

"What d'you mean?"

"Shaun," she says, "he fancies you."

"Don't be daft!"

"He does," she says.

As he closes his boot, Mr Smith spots us and calls out, "Morning, girls!"

Kirsty hurries towards the car, and I follow. She says, "Can I carry something for you, sir?"

He reaches for a pile of exercise books. "Thanks, Kirsty." Taking them from him, she gives me the tiniest look of triumph. He says, "You can put them on my desk," and there she goes, trotting off, her ponytail shimmering in the morning sun.

I get the feeling I'm going to sneeze. I shove my hand in my pocket for a tissue, but there isn't one. Instead, as I pull my hand back out, Mum's note for the post office falls to the ground. I start to bend over for it, but get that low-down twinge again. It must show, because Mr Smith says, "All right, Amy?" and picks it up himself. I tell him I'm okay.

He hands me the note and I say, "It's about a dog we found. He just turned up at our back door." Mr Smith looks genuinely interested and I show him the note.

He takes it and smiles. "A brown dog, eh? As it happens, I'm very partial to dogs."

My heart lifts at the thought of someone liking Toffee without even seeing him. "We've called him Toffee because of his colour."

He grins. "Caramel or treacle?"

"Definitely caramel," I tell him, and we both laugh.

"And you hope no one's going to claim him."

I nod.

"Fingers crossed, then." He hands me the note, and I put it back in my pocket.

Shaun's come to sit in the revision session with us. Mr Smith has put him at the back, probably because he's head and shoulders taller than anyone else.

We're revising English Lit and Mr Smith suggests Kirsty reads aloud from *Lord of the Flies*. Which she does, describing how Ralph courageously searches the island for "the beast". She reads clearly and dramatically, with real feeling.

Mr Smith says, "Thank you, Kirsty. That was great – very expressive." He catches Neil Betts yawning; books bore him, even *Lord of the Flies*. To be honest, I'm surprised he bothered to turn up this morning. In a minute, Mr Smith's going to get his own back – he'll ask Neil to read. But Neil's let off the hook because the Head opens the door and beckons Mr Smith. "Can you spare a minute?"

As the two of them leave, to stand just outside the door,

a couple of chairs scrape back. A feeling of relaxation runs round the room. Mr Wilson's "minute" could turn into anything up to a quarter of an hour. When Kirsty realizes I'll carry on revising, she draws an imaginary halo over my head. My grin indicates she can think what she likes.

One afternoon last term Mr Smith asked me to stay behind to discuss my homework. Until that moment I'd been thinking I'd done quite well, but now I was starting to think I must have written total nonsense.

I suddenly felt deflated.

The chair he pulled forward for me squeaked in the quiet classroom. "This is a good piece of work, Amy."

I thought I hadn't heard properly. "Sorry?"

"It's great," he said. "Sit down for a moment."

"Thank you."

He smoothed open my exercise book. "You've given me what I asked for. And no more. No waffle."

He leaned back, hands behind his head. He smiled at me. "Well done."

I thought that was all he wanted to say; that I should thank him again and leave. But he didn't seem in any hurry. "You're a clever girl, Amy. Forgetting GCSE results for the moment, what are your post-A Level plans? Have you thought about college?"

Warning bells clanged in my head. College, university.

Leaving home. No one to look after Mum. Careful – don't give too much away.

A question mark hung in his voice: "Perhaps you've not thought about it yet."

Was he waiting for me to say something? "I'm not sure I'd want to move far away."

He chuckled. "So it won't be Oxford or Cambridge. Do I sense you're a home bird?"

As well as silly dreams about Australia, there *are* times I wonder what it would be like to take off. Go anywhere. Right now I can't, of course. But maybe – if Mum's health improves – one day I might.

I changed the subject. "University costs such a lot."

"You're right. An arm and a leg these days – though it's possible you'd be eligible for financial support. And loans aren't generally repayable until you're in a good job." He looked away for a second, like he didn't want to pry into my private life. "But there are other options," he said. "Higher education colleges and apprenticeships. University needn't be the be-all and end-all." He paused. "You're still young…but have you thought of what career you'd like to follow?" He raised an eyebrow. "Any burning ambition?"

"Not really. Though definitely not anything to do with figures."

"There's nothing wrong with your maths."

"I know, but I'd hate to be stuck in accountancy or something like that." I chased around in my brain for something positive to say. I wanted to tell him I'd like to be a writer and that I sometimes write short poems, but I thought it might sound too ambitious. Then I thought I'd go for it anyway. "I'd like to write."

He pushed his hair back from his forehead. "Well then – how about journalism?"

I thought for a few moments, imagining standing outside a court, taking notes in shorthand; or pushing a microphone in the face of a grieving relative. I shook my head. "I don't think I could intrude into people's lives."

He seemed to be thinking for a moment, then he said, "I know what you mean. I don't think I could do that either."

We both laughed, and I decided I'd better stand up. Look like I was ready to go home.

He stood up as well. "There's still time to think." He smiled. "If you ever want to discuss anything, my door's always open."

I'd walked home that afternoon, happier than I'd felt for ages. Me at college? But I didn't want to say too much to Mum. The trouble is, with my worries over leaving her, I never look much further than the next set of exams.

I pull myself back to the present just as Mr Smith returns.

He hasn't forgotten who was about to read. "Neil," he says, "if you'd carry on, please – where Kirsty left off."

I glance sideways at Neil's sulky profile. I bet his mind was a million miles away from *Lord of the Flies*. Mr Smith waits a few moments. "Bottom of the page, Neil. Come on."

Neil says, "Oh, yeah," and reads painfully slowly until Mr Smith says, "All right, Neil, thank you very much," and Neil slumps back in his seat.

When I give Mum's note to Mrs Goodge in the post office, she says, "You'd like me to copy this onto a proper postcard, pet?" I think for a moment, because Mrs Goodge – so small that Kirsty and I call her "The Borrower" – has awkward, very loopy handwriting and shocking grammar. She's got a thing about labels – they're everywhere: *Sweets for Those with Nut Allergy's*; *Photo-copying, Just Ask*; *Post Office closes 12 Saturday's*; *Childrens SAFE felt-tip pen's*.

But it's kind of her to offer, and I say, "Thank you. Can you copy the words exactly, please."

She takes two felt pens from behind the till. "Which colour, pet?" She holds out red and brown. I choose brown because it won't hit folk in the eye like red.

As I leave the shop, I look hungrily at snacks in the chill cabinet and think how good it must be to have no money worries; if you could just choose your favourite sandwiches – tuna mayonnaise, cheese and pickle, free-range egg and cress. I'd have a mound of poached salmon in seeded bread with wild rocket. (Mrs Goodge doesn't sell that but I saw the idea in a magazine.)

Back home, Toffee's all over me. First I make a fuss of him, then sort out a pot of tea and peanut butter on toast.

I help Mum upstairs to the loo. While she's in there, she says, "Did you take my ad to the post office?"

I lean on the door, waiting for her to finish. "Yeah – hope nobody reads it!"

Chapter Eight

Last night I felt like I was coming down with something. Mum says it's times like this she wishes, more than ever, that she wasn't sick. "If only I had my health," she says.

I wonder if I should call Lisa – warn her we might need her.

Lisa? Have I gone mad? At the worst, I've only got a bug. We'll muddle through. Anyway, if I'm not better quickly all I need do is call Kirsty and ask her to get another bag of dog food. I've got cash put by. I'm sure to be okay by Friday and we've got enough food for ourselves to last till then, at least. It's Fridays I go to the supermarket and get stocked up. It takes me ages because I look for all the *Whoops!* labels – pointing out reduced items. It's time-consuming but you can save money.

I've got definite cramps this morning – and some bleeding. So finally my period's decided to put in an appearance.

It's a relief in a way; proof that my pains before were nothing to worry about.

Though I tell Mum about my period, I don't make too much of the cramps. They can't be as bad as her arthritis and she doesn't need anything else to worry about.

I don't tell Kirsty, but she spots me wincing. "I hope you've not got that stomach bug going round."

I tell her I'm sure I haven't and leave it at that.

It's just a period, no big deal – I don't need to spell it out.

End of the afternoon, and we're halfway through a Geography revision session, discussing farming in rural areas. So far Shaun hasn't said a word. Miss Havers picks on him. "Shaun, isn't it? Can you tell us the difference between sedentary and nomadic farming?"

Shaun says, "Yes," and Miss Havers waits for him to go on. But he doesn't.

She gives a big sigh and looks across at me. "Amy?"

I'm aware of the question but my cramps suddenly get so bad I ask Miss Havers if I can leave the room. I sense Kirsty looking at me. "Shall I go with her?" she asks Miss Havers.

Miss Havers says, "Thank you, Kirsty, but I think we can be fairly certain Amy can manage on her own."

I'm halfway to the door when Kirsty says, "But what if she's got this bug?"

I don't hear Miss Havers's reply because I'm out of the door and heading down the corridor. I'm feeling so awful, all I want is to double up on the loo.

It's quiet, thank goodness. No giggling Year Sevens, skiving in a cubicle. I sit down. Put my head on my knees – or as near as I can. I'm feeling bloated. But that's okay; I know some girls get like this every month. Until how old? Fifty?

I've sat here for about ten minutes. Miraculously, the pain's going away. I don't need the spare pad I've got rolled up in a hankie in my pocket. In fact, there's not much more blood than there was earlier on.

I wash my hands and look in the mirror. Normally I've got a pinkish sort of complexion – rosy – but today I look pinched and pale. My hair looks a darker brown. It's curlier than usual because it wants washing. I meant to do it first thing this morning, but with the way I was feeling, it was the last thing on my mind.

When I get back, it's noisy in the classroom. Miss Havers has left, and everyone's packing up their stuff, ready to head home.

With my belly settling down, I feel quite euphoric at the absence of cramps. They seem to have gone completely.

*

By bedtime it's pouring with rain. I give Mum her sleeping pill, put a glass of water on her bedside table and tuck her in. Toffee curls up on an old quilt at the end of her bed. All of a sudden, thinking of someone reading the card and claiming him, I find it hard not to cry.

Mum mistakes the look on my face. "Still having those cramps?"

"Kind of."

"They'll have worn off by tomorrow." She reaches out for my hand. I sit on the bed and stroke her hair. Her breathing deepens. She's asleep.

Chapter Nine

I go downstairs to make sure the back door's bolted. I check the front too. Then I draw back the curtain over the sink – I hate coming down to a dark kitchen in the morning. The rain has stopped and there's a full moon. Clouds are scudding across the sky. Every now and then the moon disappears.

I head back upstairs. It's weird; I haven't drunk more than usual this evening – just a mug of tea, then a couple of glasses of water – but I can't stop going to the loo.

Now I'm not sharing with Lisa, I love my bedroom. When she was here it was a complete tip. For Mum's sake I'd be prepared to share again, but I'd rather not. I get into bed and read for a bit, though the trashy romance Kirsty lent me isn't really my bag. I'll find something else when I go to the library for Mum. She needs topping up with a fresh pile of thrillers. Gory murders with too many bodies and too much information. Strange how Mum gets such a kick out of stuff like that.

*

It's the pain that wakes me. I rub my belly, trying to soothe it. *Wow*, where's this come from? The cramps are worse, much worse. The pain's excruciating! What if I've got a superbug as well as a period? I want to cry out, but no way can I wake Mum. On a scale of ten, the pain is fifteen. Should I try to get out of bed? I try rolling onto my side… it's fractionally more comfortable. But here it comes again! I pull the pillow over my head. If only I could scream, but I mustn't, I mustn't. Instead I bite the pillow. Bite it and bite it. Rub my face from side to side.

If it carries on like this, I could be forced to go into Mum…

…Now though, thank goodness, it's not quite so bad. In fact, it's kind of fading away. And it's gone…

…Even so, I hold my breath: it was so awful I'm half expecting it to come back. I start to relax. Is that it? I take a breath so shallow you could hardly call it a breath… Good. Everything's calmed down. I roll onto my side, but still I'm not risking anything; I'm dead careful how I breathe… Ah, that's better… I so need to get some sleep.

It's like my insides are pulled in tight and I'm awake again. I know I must have slept because I dreamed Toffee could talk. It was so sweet…

Oh, please *no* – there's another niggle. *More than.* God! Nearly too late. I desperately need the loo, and I don't mean for a wee. Can I get there? I have to – I can't make a mess in the bed. I lower my feet to the rug. I'm better standing up. I go to the door, lean on it. The harder I lean, the more the pain eases…

No! It's on me again – this massive urge. I open the bedroom door. With my hands between my legs, I scurry along the landing. I sit on the lavatory seat. Nothing happens and the pain lessens. Perhaps if I sit here long enough it'll go away altogether. I want to moan, partly with relief. But I can't because I'm nearer to Mum now than in my own room.

Without warning I need to throw up. I slide off the seat, swivel round and hang my head over the pan. I retch and vomit. Tears stream down my face.

I creep back to my room, crawl into bed and lie as stiff as a board, listening for every creak in the house. I pray Mum didn't hear me in the loo. The exertion of the pain has wiped me out. So much – it's left me gasping for breath. I'm practically panting. In fact, if I carry on breathing this way, it feels possible the pain might ease off. Careful of every move I make, I dare to stretch out. I don't trust my own body. I feel floaty. And so hot I throw off the duvet.

It's back – the pain. Back with a vengeance, and I don't care what mess I make in the bed. All I want is to get rid of whatever's causing this bloody agony. It's like I don't recognize this is me. Me and my body pushing hard, again and again, down into the bed. My lungs struggle for the deepest breath I ever took. Which I hang onto...until something slithers – out of me – onto the sheet.

A baby.

I'm paralyzed with shock, and for a moment stop breathing altogether. At first I daren't touch anything: not the duvet, not my nightie, not my own flesh. My arms lie rigid. I stare at the ceiling, half blind, while a mad drummer beats inside my chest and a slippery warmth squirms between my legs.

My arms loosen, and I move my hands up and down over the baby. It's a boy. Somehow I grasp his wetness and pull him onto my stomach. He cries a tiny cry. My voice shakes in a whisper: "Oh my God, what are you doing here?"

Chapter Ten

Stunned, I feel something else finding its way out. I don't have to wonder what this is: it's the placenta. From Biology I know what it looks like. Liver. With me not even knowing a baby was inside me, this is what's kept him alive, and it's still attached to his belly button by the umbilical cord.

In the half-light I reach into my bedside drawer and fumble for my nail scissors. I've seen births on TV and know what the cord is like. Ugly. Grey and twisted. I'm glad I can't see it clearly. But I have to see it better than this, so I turn my bedside light on. The idea of cutting through the cord near his tummy is scary, so I start separating it close to the placenta instead.

Though I'm sure it can't be hurting him, I keep saying I'm sorry: "I'm sorry, *I'm so, so sorry*." It takes for ever, and when I've finished, I lay the cord across his middle and push the placenta aside. I hope I haven't done the wrong thing.

*

We haven't moved. We're lying on the bed, while I think what to do. God – *what am I going to do?* The baby turns his head, nuzzling. He's so small. Not even a normal doll size. His lips move, but his eyes are mostly shut. I turn off the light because I think if it's dark he's less likely to cry and wake Mum.

It's like my brain aches, trying to work something out. This baby, he can't stay here. Tears roll down my cheeks. Gradually, it comes to me. There's only one place I can go.

I prise open the tiny fingers that grip the little finger of my left hand, move him to the safety of the middle of the bed, and tell myself I'm strong enough to stand up.

Careful not to make even the slightest sound, I draw the curtain back. It hits me then – how just a few hours ago, when I closed this old blue curtain, I was still me, with just my GCSEs to worry about and the same old day-to-day stuff. Now I'm another me. Numb, scared witless. With a newborn baby.

I won't talk to him any more. It's best if I don't.

I won't talk to him. But I know what to do.

In my wardrobe, on the floor at the back in a plastic bag, there's a cardigan I got at the hospice shop in town. I bought it for Mum's next birthday. Looks like it's never been worn. Perhaps someone died, or it didn't fit or they didn't suit red. I pull out the soft cardigan and spread it on the duvet. I fish under the bed for the shoebox I keep socks in, tip them out and put the box on the bed. I unfold the cardigan and lay the baby on it. I have to hold his arms and legs down so I can wind the soft red woolly stuff round and round him and the cord. Once I've wrapped him up he doesn't move. For one short moment, when moonlight touches the bed, I think he looks at me. I place him, swaddled up, into the shoebox. My knees feel weak and it's like I'm looking down on myself, looking at the Amy who's so keen on packing things neatly. Who parcels things up for Mum when her crooked fingers won't fold paper.

You read about mothers putting a note in with the baby. Perhaps the baby's name and a message: *Tell him his mum will always love him.* Something like that. But I don't know what I'd call him. I haven't had long enough to think about it. Or anything else. I don't even know if I love him. It's better if I don't. There's no point. I tell myself again – don't talk to him, try not to even look at him.

It's hard work, getting dressed, and I'm bleeding. I put on some knickers, take a pad from my drawer, pull off the sticky strip. Wobbling, I place the pad between my legs. My jeans feel stiff and it's painful getting them on. I pull on two sweaters. I feel hot, too hot, but reckon on taking one off if the baby looks like he needs more covering.

The beauty of the red cardigan is that no one has ever seen it. Anyway, not on Mum.

Though I think I've done everything, I nearly forget the placenta. I know it shouldn't, but it disgusts me. Scooping it into the plastic bag, I'm shaking like a leaf. I hold the bag like it's shopping, and slide my other hand under the shoebox on the bed.

On the landing, willing the baby not to cry, I stand stock-still outside Mum's bedroom. Not a sound. I creep to the top of the stairs. Then he snuffles. Not the baby – Toffee in Mum's room. He'll know something's up. I bend down, put the baby on the floor. Quieter than I would have thought possible, I open Mum's door a fraction. No sound from her, but Toffee's nose pushes through the crack. I open it enough to let him onto the landing. I grab one of his ears. He goes still. He understands. Even when he gets the scent of the baby, he controls himself, just sniffs it up and down. He's more interested in the contents of the plastic bag, and I push him off before grappling with the shoebox again.

Downstairs, when I put the baby on the kitchen table, he lets out a squawk and tries to turn his head. I need to get out of the house fast, but first I have to write a note. I grab a pencil from the jam jar beside the draining board.

Dear Mum, Toffee needs to go out, hope he didn't wake you. Won't be long.
Love A XXX

I'm so careful. Every step is a considered move. I have this baby in a box. I must not trip. We leave by the front door, and start off towards the dunes. Toffee goes ahead, looking back every now and then to make sure I'm keeping up.

If the clouds would clear I'd be able to see better. Thank goodness, though, that I know almost every centimetre of this path. Starting down the slope towards the beach, I dig my heels in, steady myself by leaning back. It's an incoming tide, and all I can hear are waves crashing against Croppers Rock.

We're on the flat, and here's where I'll throw the placenta into the sea. With the baby under my other arm, I give the plastic bag a feeble swing into the surf. In the murk, I watch it disappear. What's the betting it'll wash up somewhere further along the coast? Too late, I think how it would have been better if I'd taken it out of the bag.

Stopping for a second on the strip of beach, I push my face into the box. He's so still and quiet, I'm scared he's stopped breathing. I begin to wonder if the shock of being born has been too much for him. I grope under the red cardigan to see if I can feel his heart. I can't, but he gives a little splutter. He's alive.

The tide is coming in fast and at last the moon comes from behind the clouds, its broken reflection bouncing across the waves. Toffee runs ahead. Does he know where we're going? I resist the need to walk faster, partly because

I'm taking such care, but partly because my whole body is throbbing and tender. Toffee bounds on and on, only stopping when eventually he gets to the bottom of the steps cut into the sea wall.

A cat appears, stalking along the wall. Toffee, his bark almost lost in the smash of waves against the breakwater, rushes after it. When it's gone – into thin air – he sits waiting for me, as if there never was a cat.

These steps, usually no bother to me at all – even when I take them two at a time – tonight feel like Everest. Before I get to the top, I stop. Suppose someone's having a night-time walk? Worse still, taking their dog out. I peer up onto the paved seafront. It's deserted. Clutching the shoebox, I manage the top step. I turn left. Toffee knows where I'm going and runs on, like we're having the best game in the world. I almost wish he wasn't with me.

Kirsty's house is the first in a row of three. It's the largest, with an extension on the end nearest me. My legs feel shaky and I sink onto the pavement. Toffee tries to lick my face. I have to calm him down. "Good boy, good boy," I whisper, and he flattens himself.

The house is in darkness. I feel heavy, so heavy. I long, overwhelmingly, to go to sleep – hidden from the house by this low hedge.

I have to keep my eyes from closing. I try to stand up. I'm holding the shoebox in the crook of my left arm – using my right hand to press on the ground for support –

when the top of the hedge glows green. Toffee rears up. Forcing him down, I look up and see, on the side-end of the house, a small first-floor window ablaze with light. I stare at it. For how long? I don't know, but now there's blackness again. I've stopped breathing, and it's seconds before I dare take a proper breath.

It's too much to hope Toffee won't follow me, so when I walk – unsteadily – to the front door, I don't try stopping him. For a reason I don't understand, I encourage him to have a last quick peek at the baby. Which he does, sniffing – then looks up at me. Does he expect me to do the same? I think I should kiss my baby.

But I don't. I put him down on the step and ring the bell. For a few seconds my head spins and I have to lean against the door. Recovering – but with my heart bursting in my chest – I turn, grab Toffee, and run down the path. I can't say how I manage to run, but I do. I run, then collapse behind the hedge. In a rush it comes to me that when the front door opens, Toffee will expect to be invited in. Holding him down, I stretch myself across his back and stroke his head fiercely.

Staring up at the house, my neck cricks.

One after another, lights go on. The front door opens and a wide stream of light colours the garden. Mr Kelly looks down the path. Next he looks down at the step. He sees the box, and calls back into the house. "Susie!" He's bending down, picking it up. Mrs Kelly comes running and they both look towards the road. Mrs Kelly calls, "Hello? Is anyone there?" She's wearing a short nightie. What is it makes me notice this when I'm hunkering down again, grabbing Toffee and crawling along the pavement?

I don't see any more, but, after a moment, I hear someone shut the front door.

Chapter Eleven

The tide's right up now; there's hardly any beach left. I've pulled my trainers off, and the water swishing over my feet is like every cool thing in the world. Cool, cool, cool. I'm tempted to paddle in further, but I know there's something dark about this thought. Toffee loves the sea, but I fear for him. If he decides to have a swim and gets into difficulties, I'm in no state to go after him.

My right foot meets a massive hidden pebble. Almost a small boulder. Bruised, my toe starts to hurt, like the rest of me. I stumble, and now I'm sitting in the lapping saltwater. I know I should move, make an attempt to stand up. But the cold sea, seeping into my jeans – making wet balloons between the harsh denim and my sore skin – feels so good. Too good, because it makes me want to stay here with the water washing round my waist. Now up to my breasts. They're sore, and this soothes them. In front of me, at eye level, the reflection of the moon stretches away in a narrowing ribbon of light, until it meets the real thing high above the horizon. I don't feel the cold, and somehow I know this is wrong. I think of Mum alone at home. Beside me, Toffee shakes himself, and the spray on my face knocks sense into my stupid head.

I don't, after all, want to slip under the water and drown.

Wondering why I took my trainers off, I push them back on, and though my fingers don't want to work, I force them to tie knots in the laces.

I'm nearly home, and weeping. Which must be exhaustion. Also I'm worried Mum might have woken and noticed Toffee gone. I hate the thought of her going downstairs – even if she does read my note and assume everything's all right.

Each step up through the dunes seems hardly possible. Even Toffee has slowed down. Reaching the ridge top, I'm afraid to look at our house in case there's a light on.

But there isn't. The whole place is pitch-black, the roof and chimney silhouetted against the sky – lighter now because the clouds have moved away. But even as I sigh with relief, a light goes on. My heart hammers. I wait a few seconds, praying Mum will switch it off again.

She doesn't, and I know I have to reach the house and get indoors quickly. We cross the lane, Toffee and me, and somehow I make a rush for the front door.

I know Mum's at the top of the stairs, but – like I haven't spotted her – I softly call out, "Hi?"

Toffee, his tail circling madly, is up and beside her in three bounds. Mum grabs one of his ears. "Amy...?"

I struggle with the wet knots in my trainers, give up, wrench them off and start dragging my jeans down. I try not to let her see how heavy they are with seawater. "Sorry if we woke you, Mum. I heard Toffee scratching your door. He needed to go out."

"But you're drenched!" She strokes Toffee's head. "And this one's sopping wet."

Pulling the top sweater over my head muffles my voice. "There was a sudden downpour," I say, and hope she won't look out to see how wet it is.

"You could at least have put a parka on."

I try to laugh. "Mad, aren't I? But I didn't know it was going to rain." Bare-legged, I take a couple of steps to the bottom of the stairs. "Can I get you anything, Mum? Hot chocolate?"

She starts coming down. "You look as if you're the one who could do with a hot drink."

I start up the stairs. "Mum, go back to bed—" But my knees buckle, and the next minute I'm in a heap at her feet.

"Amy – sweetheart! What's wrong?"

"Mum, I'm so sorry, I—"

"There's nothing to be sorry about, love," she says, and I can tell how, for a few seconds, she's glad to be able to take on the role of a mum looking after her daughter. She puts a hand out. "Come along, let's get you into bed."

"Mum, I'm all right. Honestly. It's just I've got such a pain…" With my voice trailing off, I try to control the shudder going through me.

"You'll feel better tomorrow, love, the first day's always the worst."

I cling to the lifeline she's thrown me and look up. "Sorry, Mum – I know what you mean now." I rub my belly. "The last time I came on, the cramps weren't as bad as this." I take a deep breath, get to my feet. "I'll put my jeans in the washer."

"There's no need—"

"There is. I'll get them out of the way and give Toffee a quick rub down."

She starts to hobble back to her room. "Well, all right, but a good night's sleep is what you need, so get to bed soon."

I put my jeans in the washing machine, and weakly rub Toffee down with an old towel. I leave my trainers under the stairs, stuffed with newspaper.

Toffee follows me upstairs and I let him into Mum's room. I make sure she's tucked in. She smiles. "You daft kid," she says, and I kiss her goodnight.

In my room at last, I pull the sheet off my bed, roll it into a ball and push it into my cupboard. Then I pull off the under sheet too. It's lucky that it's a thick, fleecy one because underneath the mattress is still clean. Too tired to put on a fresh sheet – there's not a word to describe my tiredness – I pull on a T-shirt and lie under my duvet on the bare bed.

I'm almost too tired to think about Liam. But I do. Just for a minute before I fall asleep I think of what we did. And how I believed the first time didn't count.

Chapter Twelve

Mum's looking down at me. "Who's a sleepyhead, then?" For a second I can't imagine why, with Toffee beside her, she's in my room. Slowly, jumbled clumps of memory join up, and last night begins to fit together.

I struggle to sit up. Pull the duvet across my chest. I can't let her see anything's wrong. "Sorry, Mum – I'll make you a cup of tea."

"You won't," she says, "I'll make it. You stay where you are."

I mustn't let her. It'll be such an effort: running water into the kettle, struggling with a carton of milk. Also, I can't just lie here worrying how I'll hide what happened last night. And wondering if the baby's still alive. I keep telling myself he must be. He has to be. Then I remember how tiny he was.

I say I'll make the tea. "I'll bring us up a cup and we can go back to bed for a bit."

"Amy, love, you look washed out – and I'm not surprised.

You were a silly girl, you know. Why didn't you just let Toffee into the yard for a few minutes?"

"I don't know. He thought he was getting a walk, and I worried that he wouldn't settle if he didn't get one."

Trying to swing my legs out of bed, every bit of me feels like I've run a marathon. "I'm a bit shivery. Perhaps I've got this bug doing the rounds – as well as you know what."

Mum gives me a wry smile. "No revision sessions for you today. Stay at home. We'll watch a bit of telly together."

This had been such a treat when Lisa and I were little: being full of cold, or once having chickenpox at the same time, and watching TV nearly all day. I know I shouldn't skip revision – it's my Maths exam tomorrow. I can't face anything, though. Not today. Finally I ease myself off the bed. "It's okay, Mum, I'll bring us up tea and cereal."

"While you're down there," she says, "see Toffee into the yard."

"Yeah, course." I stroke his back. "He can do without his walks today." I'm aware of my voice sounding strained. I stand up straighter. "While I'm downstairs, I'll get the washer going. Anything you want me to put in?"

"Amy, I can do that."

"I know you can, but you're not going to."

"All right," she says, "then just my towels from the bathroom."

This suits me fine. When Mum's back in her room, I pull out the bloodstained sheets from my cupboard and bundle them up with the towels. In the kitchen I force everything into the machine with my still-soggy jeans. I measure out the washing powder and turn the dial to sixty. This is hotter than we ever have it, but I'm worried about getting things really clean – I need to get the stains out. If my jeans shrink, too bad.

After all this effort, I'm more aware how heavy and painful my breasts are. Hard instead of soft. I worry what they might look like, and whether Mum will notice if they're obviously different. I remember a stripy pashmina Kirsty gave me. It's wide and very long. I could try flattening my chest by winding it round. I wonder if an ice pack would help. Maybe frozen peas if we've got any – though they'd defrost, of course. I settle on the pashmina.

I put mugs ready on a tray, then go upstairs. I hope the pashmina is where I think it is. And it is – on a shelf at the top of my cupboard. I pull it out. Good, it's every bit as long as I remembered.

I start winding it round my breasts, but with each tightening pull it hurts more and I hope I'm not making things worse. I secure it by tucking in an end. I look in the mirror. It shows under my pyjamas. So I pull on a sweater and realize I'm going to absolutely boil.

I sit on Mum's creaky old bed for a while, trying not to look as hot as I feel. We have the tea and cereal together, and I help her get dressed. Knowing I'm not feeling too great, she does more for herself than usual. I normally do her hair, but today she won't let me. Even so, I feel exhausted.

Back in my room, I slowly heave myself onto my bed. And think.

Last night seems like a dream, but a vivid one where you remember every detail. It's not like the dreams where you grasp at strands in case you forget. And you do forget. With those dreams, you stop thinking for a moment, and what you most want to remember slips from your grasp.

Today, so far, I've managed to avoid picturing what must have gone on at the Kellys' after they shut their door last night. Kirsty's mum would know exactly what to do. She'll have unwound the baby from the red cardigan and found it's a boy. With his cord attached, and so tiny, she'll know he was newborn.

For the first time it hits me: they'll have called the police.

While I'm picturing a police car racing to the Kellys', Mum comes into the room. "How's your tummy?"

I put my hand somewhere round my middle. It's not flat like Kirsty's, but it's flatter than it was. "It's okay. Better than yesterday."

"Good." She pauses. "Aren't you hot in that sweater?"

"No – I'm kind of comfortable."

*

It's such a relief when we're sat downstairs with the telly on. We watch people buy houses at auction; then couples being given a choice of houses they might like to buy. A bit later there are people getting their houses ready to sell.

I pull a face. "None of this will ever happen to us."

"None of what?"

"Wondering what house to buy." I think of another programme. "We'll never even have enough bits and pieces for a car boot sale."

She says, "Never say never—" and the phone rings.

Does it show – that I'm starting to shake? What will they say – the police?

Amy Preston, can you explain why you abandoned your baby?

Mum says, "I'll answer it."

"No." I turn the TV down and, with my heavy breasts hurting under the pashmina, I pick up the phone. "Hello?"

"Hi. Are you okay?"

"Hi, Kirsty. Yeah, just feeling a bit off. Think I've got this bug after all."

"Poor you… But listen—"

"I'm worried about Maths tomorrow—"

"Amy?"

"What?"

"Wait till you hear this."

I look at Mum and wish she wasn't in the room. She's looking expectantly at me. She likes Kirsty a lot.

"Last night…"

I hold my breath.

She says, "Guess what?"

Last night a girl left a baby on your doorstep.

"Last night someone left a baby on our doorstep."

I say, "Oh my God," and can feel Mum's interest behind me.

"A baby boy. Premature. He's in hospital. Well, obviously."

My heart beats in my throat. "Hospital?"

"First thing Dad did was ring for an ambulance and the police."

"The baby wasn't ill, was he?"

"Just small, Mum said. Born too early. She was right – he's in the Prem Unit."

"Prem Unit?"

"The unit for premature babies. They're doing everything they can."

My tongue feels too large for my mouth. "But he'll be all right?"

"That's what everyone's hoping."

I have to ask her. "Did you see him?"

"Amy, he is *so* sweet. They've called him Robbie – after the first paramedic on the scene."

Robbie. I try giving that tiny little thing a name like Robbie. I suppose any name would be strange at first.

"How long will he be in hospital?"

"Quite a while, I should think. After that, Mum'll have

him back here until they try to trace the mother. You know, if she hasn't already come forward."

Somehow I keep my voice steady. "So no one saw anything odd going on?"

"Not a sausage. And they're worried about the mother. With the baby born so early, they say it's likely the mother's in need of medical attention."

My heart thuds. I can't get ill. I can't. How would Mum cope? Oh God, I'd have to get hold of Lisa.

Kirsty says, "Are you still there?"

"Sorry – I was wondering what sort of medical attention."

"I don't know, Amy. I'm not a doctor." She pauses. "Anyway, I'd better get back. Sorry to remind you, but it's Maths revision. I only came home in case there was anything new on the baby."

I put the phone down. Mum's ears are well and truly pricked up. "Come on – put me out of my misery."

I look at her. I don't even blink. "They found a baby on their doorstep."

"*No! When?*"

"In the night," I say, and give her the whole story. Well, not all of the story. Just everything Kirsty and her mum and dad know.

I need to say his name aloud. "They've called him Robbie, after one of the paramedics."

Mum thinks for a moment. "That's rather nice. Poor little mite, though."

I've been feeling pretty grim all day. I'm so tired I've gone back to bed. Now I feel even worse, thinking about little Robbie in hospital, with everyone hoping he'll be all right.

Just small, Kirsty said. Even me – with my lack of knowledge – thought he was very small. Premature? Well, of course he is. I'm groping around for dates, but I'm falling asleep…

Awake again, I can see things more clearly. It's perfectly obvious. I can work it out. It was the time – the *only* time – Liam and me lost control. I'd remembered someone saying you can't get pregnant your first time. Or if you do it standing up. It was the time I got so carried away I felt I could fly to the moon.

Liam and me, we were learning from each other. Though as it turns out, I've learned the most. I think of him in Australia. A father. I wonder about birth certificates for babies when no one knows who the parents are.

I hate leaving Mum to let Toffee out last thing and lock up. I can't ever remember feeling as weak as this – yet somehow I've got to get to school tomorrow for my Maths exam.

It's well before midnight and Mum tucks me in, or does her best. But I can't sleep. One minute I'm hot, the next I'm cold.

Four a.m. and I still ache all over. Like flu.

I get up at five and go to the loo – which hurts. Not surprising when you consider what my body's been through. Most mothers don't take their newborn baby for a walk, with the tide coming in fast and a dog rushing about. Mostly, they don't dump it on their best friend's doorstep and try not to think about drowning themselves on the way back. Most of all, though, they know they're pregnant, not like Number One Idiot, Amy Preston.

Chapter Thirteen

I'm having to miss Maths. Mum called school to explain, and now Dr Finch is here. I'm in bed, dripping in sweat. Mum says, "She's burning up." She clears her throat. "And she's got her period."

Dr Finch doesn't pay much attention to Mum's remark, and there's a nice cold feeling as he puts a thermometer in my ear. "Mmm…" he says, "thirty-nine. A bit on the high side." He touches my shoulder gently. "Now then, young lady. Have you any pain? Tummy? Or anywhere else?"

I close my eyes and think for a moment. "I've got a bit of tummy ache, but not too bad." I wish I could tell him about my painful breasts leaking watery stuff under the pashmina. "I've got awful earache."

Mum says, "You didn't say."

It's hard, looking into her worried eyes. "I've been aching all over, but that's where it's settled – where it's worst."

Dr Finch fishes in his bag. "Which ear, Amy?"

I choose the one he put the thermometer in. "This one."

"Let's have a little look," he says, and puts an instrument – also wonderfully cold – in my left ear. He's leaning over me, and I imagine him squinting, deep inside my ear.

"Nothing to see," he says, "but all the same I'll put you on a course of antibiotics. We need to hit this on the head." He pats my hand. "Not literally, I hasten to add."

I look up at him. "Mum won't be able to go to the chemist."

"No problem," he says. "We'll have them delivered." His hand rests on my pillow for a second. "Are you allergic to anything, Amy? Penicillin?" I tell him I don't think so – and Mum says she's sure I'm not. He writes out a prescription, ticks one of the boxes, and slips it into his bag. "It's very important," he says, "to complete the whole course of tablets."

Mum says she realizes this, and thanks him for coming out so quickly. He leads the way downstairs. I'm conscious of Mum's painful footsteps following his firm tread. He stays in the kitchen for a while, and I listen to the murmur of their conversation.

The front door closes, and Mum starts up the stairs. I struggle out of bed and onto the landing. "Don't come right up, Mum."

"I wondered if you wanted anything. A drink?" She hesitates. "D'you need that sweater on over your pyjamas?

I did wonder if that's why you're so hot. I mentioned it to Dr Finch."

"Oh, you didn't! Honestly, Mum, I'd rather be too warm than too cold. I was shivering earlier."

She looks awkward, and I assume Dr Finch didn't go along with her. "Well all right," she says, "but how about that drink?"

"I've got water up here. I'll try to sleep this off – whatever it is."

She's holding onto the banister. "You'll notice a difference once the penicillin hits the spot." She smiles up at me. A reassuring smile. "We'll make it through the rain."

I try not to sound too tired. "Yep – we always do."

I was in bed for two days, with Toffee dozing beside me a lot of the time. Now I'm starting to get up and determined to get back to normal. Unfortunately it's not as easy as I hoped. I thought once my temperature came down, I'd get my strength back. Wrong. I'm still quite weak, and sore. And feeling more than a bit low. I don't suppose my hormones will settle down in five minutes. Having said that, I'm not leaking like I was. I've unwound the pashmina, though I've kept a sweater on over my shirt.

I'm still bleeding. Mum's noticed all the empty pad wrappers and is worried in case I haven't got enough to last through my "period". She hasn't got that many herself and she obviously can't get out to the shops to buy any. I tell her not to worry, I've got enough for both of us. (Each time I'd hopefully bought them over the past year, I had no idea how thankful I'd be to see so many piled up in my drawer.)

I come downstairs. Mum's at the front door – she's let Toffee out and isn't sure which way he's coming back in. Now she's gazing down at the front doorstep. "Heavens!"

By this point I'm on my way to the back door where Toffee's pawing to come in. I call out, "Heavens *what*?"

"Flowers…" I can hear the discomfort in her voice as she stoops to pick them up. "There's a note."

I go through the hallway. "Can I see?"

She hands the flowers to me, and we go back into the kitchen. I look at the note, stuck in the middle of a not-very-big bunch of cornflowers and grasses.

To Amy, hop your feelin betta. Hop to see you sune. Yors trly, Shaun.

Mum reads it too. She tries to hide a smile. "Shaun?"

"You know, the big lad at Kirsty's."

"Big or not, he can't spell for toffee." At his name, Toffee thumps his tail.

I say, "He's dyslexic."

Mum says, "That's a word I bet he can't spell…a very kind thought, though."

Chapter Fourteen

Physically, I'm a lot better, and I think I look more or less my normal self. Mum's said, more than once, that whatever was wrong, I'm on the mend. But she can't see into my head. Emotionally, I'm one big wobble. (Not a brilliant word – more applicable to a jelly – but it's the best I can come up with.)

Kirsty phoned to find out how I am and to give me the latest on Robbie. It's like I'm tied to him with an invisible thread: each time I hear her voice my heart beats faster. Supposing it's bad news? At this rate I'll turn into a full-blown bag of nerves.

When I'm not worrying about Robbie, my mind chases around thinking about Liam. Which I don't want to do; I need our clean break to remain just that. My really massive worry is what would happen if Mum found out.

Nana Kathleen had a saying: *least said, soonest mended*. But this isn't like I've broken a favourite jug. I've destroyed more than that.

*

It's not easy back in revision sessions – struggling to get my act together so I can prepare for my last few exams. I'm hardly in the form room one morning before Nell Somers – bulging eyes and hair like she's had an electric shock – comes up to me. "Did you hear about that baby left at Kirsty's?"

I say yes I know all about it, but this doesn't stop her gabbling on with a list of ridiculous details I know aren't true.

Sophie Hardy chimes in, "The mother just shoved it under a bush, then someone else found it and left it on Kirsty's front step." She pauses for effect. "The *cord* was still *attached*."

Zara Mills says, "*And* it had hardly any clothes on. Hospital tests showed it was born outside in the rain. Totally irresponsible. It could have died, you know. If it was winter, it would've done."

This is typical Sophie and Zara talk. If they can get it wrong, or exaggerate, they do. It's sickening for me, having to listen to all this stuff. Sometimes it's like it didn't happen to me at all, then the next minute my heart's pounding and I have to stop myself from running home. Some of it's nearer the truth, mainly thanks to Shaun being on hand to put things straight. He stands there, ultra-serious, telling them the baby was left on the doorstep in a shoebox, wrapped up very warm. He knows this, he says, because he lives at the house.

When a group gathers round him, I feel quite ill; they've got it into their heads he knows more than he's letting on.

Zara says, "Did you see something? You did, didn't you, I can tell from your expression."

Sophie gives a cruel giggle. "Shaun doesn't do expression."

He says, "Nobody saw anything, we were all asleep." I remember the small lit window and think: somebody wasn't asleep. Probably Mr Kelly, him being the first to come down. Whoever it was can't have seen me. If they had, they'd have knocked at our door by now.

Sophie says, "Fancy dumping a *premature* baby."

Shaun says, "Perhaps the mother didn't know it was premature."

"Er, right. Like it's *this* tiny and she thinks that's normal?" says Zara, holding her hands out to indicate how small.

Sometimes, listening to stupid talk about Robbie, I can hardly breathe. But the rubbish has a plus side – like it not looking suspicious when I ask Kirsty questions. I reckon if I don't ask her about him at least once a day, it'll look odd. Though if I say too much, that might also look odd. Which is what happens on our way home today.

Apparently I've asked her the same thing twice: about the colour of Robbie's hair and eyes. She says, "What's wrong with you? You were the same yesterday. Like you've got this baby on the brain."

My heart thumps. Why can't I keep my mouth shut?

Tears well up and my voice falters. "I didn't realize I was getting on your nerves." She can't begin to imagine how I envy her for being the one who's free to ask about Robbie whenever she likes.

She puts her arm round my shoulder. "*Amy*, I didn't mean anything."

I blow my nose. "I know." I try to laugh. "I'll stop pestering you."

We link arms and she chatters away – making a point of telling me about her mum's visits to see Robbie. I decide it's best if I don't refer to him by name. Calling him "the baby" makes it sound less like I think he's special. She doesn't notice, and answers my questions like they're quite natural, even passing on the progress report following Mrs Kelly's latest visit to the hospital.

"He's putting on weight," she says, "and he's a real favourite with the nurses!"

Suddenly I'm down to earth with a bang, and thinking even harder about what I've done. Well, I know what I've done. I had a baby and abandoned it…how could I have done that? Then, remembering Mum, I ask myself what else I could have done.

What would it do to Mum now, though, if she found out I not only had sex, got myself pregnant, and had the baby in our house while she was asleep…but that I also took it to somebody else to look after?

Chapter Fifteen

Two more exams out of the way: Chemistry and Food Tech – *plus* I've heard Robbie's got on better than anyone thought he would, and now weighs enough to leave hospital and come home! Home to Mrs Kelly's.

The twins have moved back to their previous home. Apparently the Social made arrangements with a relative to help look after them. "Not before time," says Mrs Kelly. "Wouldn't you have thought their gran would have stepped in from the word go?"

I think: poor Mum, she wouldn't be able to step in; there are times she can hardly stand up. She'd feel awful, not being well enough to look after her grandchild. I tell myself it's best she doesn't know. She'd feel so useless. I feel useless too; more and more each day. My waking thought is Robbie and what he's doing, what he looks like.

By chance, I'd been at Kirsty's a few times after Mrs Kelly had visited Robbie in hospital. At the beginning, when he was still very small, his health had apparently caused some scary moments. At times like that Kirsty had been able to show her feelings, even having a cry when Robbie's breathing was a concern. Me, I had to make it look like I was very sorry, but not so much that I might break down. Mrs Kelly was always good with me. She didn't seem to think it odd if I asked questions about Robbie – even medical ones. In a way I found it easier to talk to her than to Kirsty.

Having thought so hard about my baby, and wondering what (or even who) he looks like now, I can hardly believe I'll be seeing him again.

But now it's a reality, the invite I've more than half dreaded. The one where Kirsty says I must come and see Robbie. Though I've *ached* for this, I'm worried sick over how I'll cope. Just thinking about it sends shudders through me. I tell myself there's no reason why anyone would look at us together and realize I'm the birth mother, and in my saner moments I know this won't happen. But it doesn't stop my imagination going into overdrive.

It'll be one day this week. Friday probably, after GCSE Geography. She'll let me know.

We bought drinks in the dining hall and now we're sitting in the sun. Kirsty says, "You won't *believe* how much Robbie's changed!"

I manage a laugh. "You forget I've never seen him, so I won't notice any difference."

"Sorry, course you won't," she says. "Even if you hadn't been poorly that next day, you'd have missed him. He was in hospital before you could turn round."

Now it's like she's suddenly remembered something. "Hey, did I tell you?"

"Tell me what?"

"It was on telly, on *Your North*. The doctors say he was probably in hospital within three hours of being born. Or even less."

"He was lucky then."

"Dead lucky. He could have been a dead baby if the mother had decided to leave him somewhere else."

"Good job she didn't then."

Kirsty says. "She must have known about Mum being a foster carer."

"That's obvious," I say. "I mean you're not exactly central. She must have made a special effort, going to yours."

"Unless she lived nearby." She goes quiet. "Don't think so, though. There's been all sorts of talk, but no one remembers a girl being pregnant."

I have to say something, because it feels unnatural not to. "Why does it have to be a girl? Why not a woman?"

"Older women don't dump their babies, do they?"

"I don't know."

"Well they just don't, do they?"

"How should I know?" It's like I'm snapping at her. "It's not exactly my specialist subject." Then I say, "Don't mind me – stuff to think about."

"Your mum okay?"

I say, "Not too great," which feels like I'm using her as an excuse. "Anyway," I say, spewing out a big fat lie, "our Lisa's being helpful for a change."

Kirsty looks surprised. "That must be a relief."

Shaun has spotted us. I'm still waiting for that first real smile, a smile that's not for Toffee. Even when I thanked him for the flowers I only got a flicker.

He says to Kirsty, "Have you told her?"

His frown worries me. "Told me what?"

Kirsty's lips tighten, and Shaun says, "She ought to know, it's *her* dog."

I'm quick. "What about my dog?"

He says, "Yesterday, Mrs Kelly saw a man looking at the card in the post office window."

I go cold; I knew we should have taken it down by now. "He could've been looking at any of the cards. Couldn't he?"

"No," says Shaun. "Mrs Goodge got the card out and he took it."

The way I start rushing towards the toilets gets me a few odd looks, but I want to be on my own. An arm goes out to slow me down. It's Mr Smith, coming out of the staffroom. "Amy? Are you all right?"

I wipe my hand across my face, feel the silly tears. I'm sixteen, for heaven's sake. "Sorry, sir."

"What's wrong?"

I swallow, but words won't come.

"Something you'd like to talk about?"

I nod.

"Come along," he says. "We'll find a quiet spot."

We're sat in the school secretary's office. After a barely noticeable signal from Mr Smith, Mrs Roper has left the room.

Mr Smith finds a box of tissues in the desk drawer and pushes them across to me. "Now then," he says, "what's the problem?"

I take a tissue and blow my nose. "It's Toffee—"

He nods. "The dog. I remember."

"Someone's interested in the card we put in the post office window. A man."

"You know this for a fact?"

"Shaun Baxter knew. Kirsty's mum told him."

"Told him what?"

"That this man took the card."

Mr Smith's blue eyes show concern. "It was always on the cards – sorry – I mean it was always possible Toffee's last owner would see the card and hope it's their dog."

I start crying again and feel so stupid. Mr Smith pushes the tissues nearer. "These things happen, Amy." He pauses. "How long is it since you found him?"

"He found us."

"How long ago?"

"I'm not sure…" Though I am sure because it must be about a week less than how many weeks Robbie is now. I say, "No, wait a minute – May the twenty-seventh. About then, anyway." If only I could pour everything out. If I could tell anyone, it would be Mr Smith.

My nose is running and I grab a tissue. I feel ashamed, and try to pull myself together. "I'm sorry."

He rests his chin on his hands; he's so patient. "Is there something else – other than Toffee?"

I nod, then wish I hadn't.

"Do you want to tell me?"

Words start to come together in my head, but they don't feel right. "It's nothing really." I hesitate. "I think I'm just feeling a bit fed up."

"Is everything all right at home?"

"Yes, fine."

"Well, I'm here if you want to talk some more. And don't forget you can always see Mrs Hart."

"Thank you." Mrs Hart is Pastoral Care, but I've never imagined opening up to her.

He stands up slowly.

"Look, I'm sorry not to have more time. I'm due in a meeting," he says.

I get up too. "*I'm* sorry – that I'm so pathetic."

"Amy, that's the last thing you are." He ushers me to the door, and for a moment I feel his hand on my shoulder. "It'll be hard for you if Toffee's owner comes along, but you will get over it. I promise you." He pauses. "Where should you be next?"

"Revision – Geography. The exam's this afternoon."

He smiles. "Good luck."

After break we're back in revision with Mrs Grant.

Kirsty passes me a note. *He's asked me out.*

I write back: *Who?* She writes: *Who do you think?* I write: *Dunno, I'm not a mind reader.* She writes: *HE is Jordan Mantle!*

Mrs Grant gets wind of what we're up to and comes marching over to us. Kirsty doesn't hide the note quickly enough. Mrs Grant reads it with deep scorn, screws it up and says, "May I remind you this is your final revision session. Make the most of it."

Everyone turns to look at us, while I concentrate on a giant bluebottle on the ceiling and Kirsty works at controlling what could be a fit of the giggles. I follow the fly with my eyes. When it zooms towards the window I think how Toffee would make a futile leap at it. Already the thought of life without him is like a knife in my heart. Tears spring to my eyes, and I can't stop them trickling out. What's the matter with me? I never used to be like this.

Back at her desk, Mrs Grant looks my way. "Amy – for heaven's *sake*."

It's not too bad, the Geography exam… Just as well, the way my mind keeps switching backwards and forwards between the questions and what might turn out to be Toffee's fate. I finish, put my pen down and look across the hall. Kirsty's already sitting back, her arms crossed. I won't get an A but I should be all right.

Chapter Sixteen

Grinning, Kirtsy comes up to me after the exam. "How did it go?"

"Okay."

"Only okay? I thought it was pretty good."

"Yeah, it was."

We walk to the school gates. "See you in a bit!" she says.

This is how I imagine stage fright. I've stood in the wings for days, waiting to make my entrance. I'm not great at acting, but I give her a cheery wave and start walking home.

I change out of my school things. Mum eyes me up and down. "You look very nice," she says. "Have a lovely time… Now listen, you're not to worry about me. I'll be fine."

I won't be able not to worry about her. She won't have a proper tea till I get back…though I admit she didn't manage too badly when I was feverish after Robbie.

I say the sort of thing she's expecting me to say: "I can't wait to see the baby. Kirsty swears you can almost *watch* him grow… And everyone says he's amazingly responsive."

Mum says, "Sounds like he had bright parents." She pauses. "Whoever they were."

I nod a couple of times. "Yeah… Well, I'd best be off."

Kirsty's waiting for me at her front gate. She leads the way up the path, and my heart beats faster. With Robbie away in hospital, I was never this nervous. Right now, I'm petrified.

Kirsty pushes the door open and I go into the hallway ahead of her. My heart thuds at the sound of a baby crying. Is it Robbie?

It must be him. The other little kids staying here, three of them, aren't babies. My mind skates from one thing to another – *anything* to help push back the rising panic I feel at the thought of coming face-to-face with my child.

Kirsty cocks an ear. She grins at me. "Sounds like they're in the living room."

There's a little choky sound, and after that the crying turns to hiccups. We follow the sound and find Mrs Kelly hoisting a very small baby onto her shoulder and patting its back. "Hello, Amy, love." She turns the baby round. His mouth puckers, then relaxes. She says, "Meet Robbie, our little star." She kisses the back of his head. "You are, aren't you?" she says. "A real little star!"

Kirsty laughs. "As you can see, Mum's besotted with him."

Her mum kisses Robbie's head again. "Who wouldn't be?"

I can't take my eyes off him. I'm trying to relate him to the red-wrapped scrap I carried along the beach in a shoebox. Though he's still very small, my baby is now a real little person. I smile. Which is an effort, because my skin's tightening like I'm turning into a waxwork. I will the smile to reach my eyes, and crinkle them up. "Oh, isn't he gorgeous!" At the sound of my voice, he fixes his attention on me. His eyes are the brightest blue.

I need to say something else. "Incredible eyes!"

"Like forget-me-nots," says Mrs Kelly. "They might stay blue, but you never can tell." She strokes his sparse covering of flaxen hair. "He could go darker, of course, but on the other hand he might always be fair." She shifts him into a half-cradling position and looks into his round pink face. "Trouble is, we've nothing to go on." She gives him a little tickle. "We don't know what his mummy and daddy look like." She tickles him again. "We don't, do we?"

Me – dark curly hair, greenish eyes. Liam – light brown hair and blue eyes.

I smile at Robbie. Though he's still a tiny little person, I've changed. I'm not the same Amy I was before he was born, and that evening with Liam feels like a lifetime away.

Kirsty sniffs the air. "Lush smell, Mum."

"Oh my giddy aunt – buns!" Mrs Kelly puts Robbie into

Kirsty's outstretched arms, then runs towards the kitchen.

Kirsty lowers herself onto the sofa, and I sit beside her. She wipes a bubble of dribble from Robbie's chin with her fingertip. She smiles. "Would you like to hold him?"

It was inevitable, this moment. It's the moment I knew was coming, yet I'm still unprepared for it. "Go on," she says, "have a cuddle. He won't bite – he's all gums."

I know I must. I edge closer to Kirsty and she lifts him sideways into my arms. I sit stiffly, trying to ease him into a position he'll be happy with. "Don't worry," she says, "he's tougher than you think. You can't break him – not unless you try really hard." I push back into the cushion behind me. His head rolls slightly, and I feel the weight of it through my sweatshirt. Kirsty says, "Being premature, he's small for his age – still a bit wobbly." She gives him a big smile. "Never mind, he'll soon make up for lost time." She looks serious for a moment. "Mum's incredibly fond of this little guy."

I say, "That's nice," and, looking at him in my arms, I'm so glad that Mrs Kelly is really fond of him.

"I think it's because he came here as a newborn. She was at the hospital every minute she could spare – usually evenings when Dad got back from work."

"That often?"

"Yeah – one set of parents in the Prem Unit thought she was Robbie's mum!"

For a few seconds we don't talk, then she looks at her

watch. "What d'you make the time?" But I can't see my watch, not without disturbing Robbie. She says, "I think mine might be slow." She's hugging her knees, but moves an elbow to nudge me. She says quietly, "I'm half expecting Jordan to come round."

I take my eyes off Robbie for a second. "You didn't say anything. I thought it was just me."

"I wasn't sure till I got his text."

I raise an eyebrow. "Really? And there's me thinking you were only *half* expecting him."

She says, "Sorry – you don't mind, do you?"

"Of course I don't."

Actually I'm glad. It might stop me imagining that Robbie and I are the centre of attention.

I try to look relaxed, but when I lean forward my hair flops onto Robbie's head.

Kirsty scoops it back. "You could do with a trim."

"I haven't had the time." I don't add, *or the money*.

She says, "Did you notice Mum's hair? Shaun cut it. You ought to let him cut yours. He adores doing hair."

Mrs Kelly's hair had been the last thing on my mind, but I pretend I'd noticed. I'm not sure about Kirsty's suggestion. What with Shaun seeming keen – and the flowers on the doorstep – letting him loose on my hair might be risky. He could start getting the wrong idea. I make sure I look interested, but not in Shaun. Not that way. "How does he know how to cut hair?"

She laughs. "He cut his own fringe when he was four. Apparently it gave him a taste for it, and he's been doing it ever since." She giggles. "I don't mean his own fringe." She pauses. "No – actually he taught himself. Looking at videos online."

There's activity and noisy chatter coming from the kitchen – kids and grown-ups. Mr Kelly is home, giving Kirsty's mum a hand with the tea.

I sit here on the sofa, holding my baby. In the odd state I'm in – where everything, including this child, is alien – the swirly-leaf pattern on the carpet feels like the only piece of reality.

Kirsty says that when the young ones have finished eating, they'll watch a bit of kids' telly while we have our tea. For the first time, I register the toys scattered around.

Robbie holds my little finger, the finger he held so tightly the night he was born. Today I leave it where it is.

Chapter Seventeen

The kids tumble in and plonk themselves in front of the telly. Kirsty takes Robbie from me and we go through to the kitchen. Mrs Kelly has made a fish pie. There are vegetables to go with it. Shaun's already here. He moves his chair. Is this because he wants to sit next to me? He gives me one of his strange stares. Mr Kelly sorts us out, deciding where we'll sit – me between him and Kirsty – while Mrs Kelly sits with Robbie in her arms, a bottle of formula on the table in front of her. The teat of the bottle barely touches Robbie's lips before his eager mouth fastens onto it. He sucks noisily, gazing into space. I wonder what he sees. Kirsty doles out the fish pie, and we help ourselves to vegetables.

Mr Kelly pops into the front room to check the younger ones are behaving.

Shaun takes two heaped tablespoons of carrots, then eyes me across a portion of peas large enough for three people. "Has that man been in touch about Toffee?" His words hit their target like bullets. I know he doesn't mean to sound the way he does. It's obviously not his fault he finds it hard to smile – and comes out with stuff that's the last thing you want to hear. I shake my head.

Robbie, full of milk, is falling asleep. Mrs Kelly eases him into a carry-seat beside her chair. "Ah, well," she says, "no news is good news." Straightening up, she leans over to touch my hand.

Back from the front room, and sitting down again, Mr Kelly says, "All quiet on the Western Front."

Kirsty turns to me. "He's a got a saying for everything, my dad."

Just as we're finishing our apple tart and custard, I get an itch behind my ear. I give it a discreet scratch, but a wayward strand of hair (*all* my hair is wayward) escapes and flicks across my spoonful of custard. I'm trying to separate a ringlet from the custard when Kirsty laughs.

"See, I told you you need a haircut. Shaun could do it after tea, couldn't you, Shaun?"

Mrs Kelly pretends she hasn't noticed the trouble I'm having. Head on one side, in a model pose, she pats her shiny bob. "Shaun cut mine. What d'you think of the new me?"

I nod enthusiastically. "It looks great. Really great."

Shaun says, "So I'll cut yours, Amy. Right?"

Mr Kelly seems surprisingly keen on the idea. "I'll set up the salon, shall I?" He takes his own chair into the utility room at the back of the kitchen, and calls, "Are those hairdressing scissors still in the drawer, Susie?"

"Right-hand side at the front! And take a clean tea towel from the bottom drawer." She looks at me. "Just to keep the worst of the hair off that nice top."

Shaun laughs. Explosively.

Kirsty says, "What's so funny?"

"The *worst* of the hair? Amy's not got any worst. It's simply the best!"

Mrs Kelly says, "You're absolutely right, Shaun. It's hair to die for... No pun intended."

Shaun frowns deeply, and Mrs Kelly says, "I wasn't meaning you'd want to *dye* it."

Serious, he says, "No self-respecting colourist would want to dye Amy's hair."

Shaun waits patiently for me in the utility room while Kirsty helps her mum clear the table. Robbie sleeps, oblivious to everything.

I make a face at Kirsty, pull my hair back. "What d'you think?"

"Live dangerously," she says.

Her mum nods vigorously. "He's really good – though you must tell him what you want."

"I don't know what I want."

Kirsty grins. "Just tell him you don't want it getting in the custard."

I have to admit I'm nervous, sitting here while Shaun drapes a Robin Hood's Bay tea towel round my shoulders. "How would you like it?" he says.

I try to play it safe. "Take off about five centimetres?"

"How about ten?" He reaches for a bottle that looks like it could be used for weedkiller. "I'll dampen it first," he says.

I say, "Okay," and he moves around my head, squirting the spray until my hair's quite wet.

There's no mirror in here, but I can feel him starting to twist and separate my hair into bunches. "It's great hair," he says, "in really good condition." For a long moment he steps back, then walks round, looking at me from all angles. Now he starts cutting, and I'm no longer scared of what he's decided to do.

We're silent – must be for about ten minutes – then, waving his scissors, he points out my curls piling up on the floor. Which, from where I'm sat, are starting to form the shape of a poodle fast asleep. He says, "Would you like to save some?"

"What would I do with it?"

"Stuff a cushion?" he says. And I don't think he's joking.

Kirsty looks in. "It's looking good, Amy. Ve-ry good." The doorbell rings. I haven't asked any more about Jordan and wonder if this might be him. I look at Kirsty, who's making out she couldn't care less who's at the door.

Her mum calls out, "I'll get it!"

There are voices in the hallway, then Mrs Kelly comes in. She gazes at me. "Wow! That's starting to look terrific." She turns to Kirsty. "There's someone to see you."

Kirsty blushes. "Me?"

Her mum says, "Now then…did he say Gordon?"

Kirsty takes a breath. "You mean Jordan?"

"Oh, that was it, was it?"

"Where is he?"

"In the living room."

Kirsty looks furious. "What! Not with those kids?"

"Yes, with the kids." She glances at me, like I'll share the fun of winding Kirsty up. "Last seen, he was playing with Lego."

Kirsty dashes off. She can't get there quickly enough. You can understand how she must be feeling: someone you're dead keen on arrives, and your mum gets him stuck into Lego with a bunch of three-year-olds.

Alone again, we're quiet. I don't dare have a feel of my hair, not while he's still snipping away. How much shorter will ten centimetres look? "Is our school okay for you, Shaun?"

He stops mid-snip. "S'all right, no worse than most."

"Mr Smith's great."

"Yeah, he's okay."

"We're lucky to have him. As our form tutor, I mean."

"Yeah."

"You know you can go to him, if you need to." Then I add, in case he might not like Mr Smith as much as I do, "Or Mrs Hart. She's Pastoral Care."

"I'm all right."

He puts the scissors on the draining board and starts running his fingers over my scalp. I tell myself this is what professional hairstylists do, to encourage a good shape. I can feel what his hands are up to and only wish there was a mirror so I could see his face. I move my head, and he takes his hands away. I look up at him. He looks perfectly normal. Normal for Shaun.

"Have you been to many schools, Shaun?"

"Quite a lot." Perhaps I shouldn't keep digging. But I do. I start cautiously. "Mrs Kelly's lovely."

"Yeah."

"And Mr Kelly."

"Yeah."

I ask where he was before he came here, and he reels off places I've never heard of. Some of them must be children's homes. Maybe I'm going a bit far, but I ask him about his family. Like, is he in touch? He picks up a pair of clippers I'd not noticed. When he clips near the back of my neck, I start worrying I might end up looking like a hedge. He says, "I haven't got a real family...not that I know of. No brothers or sisters. Not like you."

"Like me?" I look into my lap while he very gently smooths the clippers from side to side. "Oh, you must mean Lisa... She's not really around that much. I mean," I hesitate, "she's at work during the day." I change the subject quickly. "Did you know your mother?" This is what I most want to know, but said like that it sounded so blunt.

He's not offended. "I don't remember her..." He pauses. "She put me up for adoption." He brushes hair off my neck. "I've seen photographs."

"Do you take after her?"

"Photographs of *me*, not my mum. They wasted their film, though – no one wanted me."

I don't dare turn my head to look at him. "Why not?"

"I was that weird-looking. You couldn't blame anyone for not wanting a kid like me about the place. What would the neighbours think?"

I wonder if he's being funny, but decide he's not. He bounces my hair up with the palms of his hands. Now he's taken some of the weight out of it, I love the feel. He says, "Later it was foster homes. Lots. But I never fitted in." He touches my shoulder lightly. "Let it dry *au naturel*?"

"Yes, fine." Then I say, "But you like it here?"

He says, "Yeah...it's great." I can't tell if he's smiling.

Kirsty comes in. "Oh! That's fab, Shaun. Honest – she's going to look a million dollars."

I look at her delighted face. "Really?"

"It's a brilliant cut."

I put out a hand to Shaun, but don't quite touch him. "Thanks, Shaun, I'm really grateful."

"Not a problem. Any time." And we watch him walk out of the little room.

There's quite a bit of chat coming from the kitchen. I push my chair back; I want to find a mirror. "Kirsty, where's the nearest mir—"

She interrupts, almost in a whisper, "Amy – he's adorable round Robbie."

I pretend I don't know what she's on about. "Who?"

"*Jor-dan.*"

I still need to find a mirror, but she nudges me into the kitchen, then through into the living room. It's not exactly bedlam in here, but almost. Even with Mrs Kelly looking on, the little kids are jumping about, two of them bouncing on the sofa. And, by the window, Jordan makes goo-goo noises at Robbie, who he's holding in his arms.

An image swims in front of me: Liam cradling a baby. I scrub it out. My head doesn't want to make space for these kind of thoughts.

"Wow – *love* the hair," says Jordan, dropping the babytalk. But not for long; he's got Robbie's full attention and is making the most of it. "Aren't you a great little guy?" he says. "They don't find one like you on the doorstep every day of the week."

It makes Mrs Kelly laugh when he says, still in a "did-dums" voice, "Did they put out a note? *Thursday. Four pints semi-skimmed, two double cream – and a baby.*"

I say, "It was a Wednesday."

Mrs Kelly says, "Goodness, Amy, you've got a good memory."

Why did I open my big mouth? I lick my dry lips. "I remember because it was when I wasn't feeling well – and I remember Kirsty calling to tell me about Robbie. I didn't go into school for a few days… It was a virus or something – I even missed my Maths exam, so I could hardly forget."

Mrs Kelly says, "Even so, Amy, I could do with a memory like yours."

Kirsty says, "She's got a *phenomenal* memory. She writes poems and remembers them all."

I manage a laugh, try to look modest. "There are lots of important things I don't remember. Historical dates and stuff."

Mrs Kelly touches my hair. "I told you Shaun was good."

Chapter Eighteen

It's dusk, and cool air wafts across the back of my newly smooth neck. We're walking along The Promenade, which is a posh name for the paved roadway on top of the sea wall. *We* means Shaun and me. Mr Kelly insisted Shaun walk me home. Like I haven't walked it a hundred times before. Now, with the tide coming right up, it's *me* fussing about Shaun getting too close to the edge.

But neither of us plunges into the waves. And as we reach Dune Terrace, a car draws up outside our house.

I stop dead.

"What's wrong?" says Shaun.

"That car."

"What's the matter with it?"

"Nothing's the *matter* with it."

He says, "There might be, only it's getting darker and it's, like, maybe you wouldn't notice something wrong."

I hiss, "Shaun, shut up…" Then I remember my haircut

and feel sorry. He can't help stating the obvious. "Sorry. It's just – you know."

He says, "I don't know."

"No all right, you don't know."

The car headlights are switched off. The interior light comes on and the driver pushes open his door. Though I can't see much, I notice him sliding papers into a briefcase, which he locks before bringing it out of the car. He slams the door shut, goes round to the boot, slides the briefcase inside and clicks the remote. He looks at the house for a moment, and makes for our front door.

Shaun says, "He's going to yours."

"I can see that."

Shaun calls out, "Hey!" and I feel embarrassed. The man turns quickly and comes towards us. Shaun says, "Is there anything I can help you with?" Like he works in Currys selling fridge-freezers.

The man seems pleasant. "Help me? You might be able to." He's plump, nearly bald, wearing a smart suit and striped shirt, but no tie. He's nothing like as tall as Shaun, and has to look up to him. He points to the front door. "Do you two live here?"

"I do."

He eyes me. "Then I think it's you I need to talk to."

My mouth goes dry. It all adds up. The air of authority; removing confidential papers from public view; the decent car – more than a few steps up from Mrs Wickham's;

arriving without warning; wanting to see *me*. Somehow he knows. Knows about Robbie. In our silences on the way home, I've been thinking and thinking about my baby. About his tiny mouth, his wisps of hair, his brilliant blue eyes, the weight of his head, his beating heart, the little hand grasping my finger.

"Mind if I come in?" says the man.

Fumbling for my key, I turn to Shaun. "I'm okay now. Thanks for coming."

"You sure you're all right?"

"Absolutely," I say. The man smiles reassuringly, and Shaun walks away.

In those few moments, after the man said he needed to talk to me, I've made my decision to tell Mum. I hadn't wanted it to be this soon; it will be terrible for Mum and I've no idea what the outcome will be. I can't imagine I'll be allowed to look after – to keep – Robbie. Not after I risked his life. Abandoned him on a wet night.

I open the front door and call out, "Mum!" The man follows me into the kitchen. Mum, shifting in her chair, doesn't seem surprised to see him. But she's looking deadly serious. "Mr Jackson?"

"Call me Ken." He leans over, about to shake her hand, but she covers it with the left one. Perhaps he notices her twisted fingers. Whatever – he pats Toffee on the head several times. Nodding at Mum, he seems slightly nervous. "Very pleased to meet you," he says.

I swallow hard. "Mum, there are things to talk about."

"I realize that," she says, and her sad eyes lock with mine. I'm overwhelmed with guilt. What must she be feeling, knowing how badly I've let her down?

Mr Jackson glances at me. "Me and your mum, we spoke on the phone."

Toffee dances a couple of silly circles in front of me, then paws Mr Jackson's trousers. Mr Jackson bends down, takes Toffee's head between his hands. "Hi there, fella," he says, "how're you doing?"

My world stands still. *This isn't about Robbie.* Mr Jackson is the man Mrs Kelly saw at the post office.

And Toffee is his dog.

I find my voice. "You must have come about the card in the post office."

"I certainly have. Like I told your mum."

The three of us look at each other. I can't think of anything to say. Mum just looks resigned.

I pull myself together. "Who'd like a cup of tea?"

"That'd be nice," he says, "but first off, where's this brown dog?"

There's a long pause, while I stand with my hand out for the kettle and Mr Jackson looks towards the back door, then towards the door leading to the hallway and front room. Toffee sits back on his haunches and scratches his right ear. I leave the talking to Mum. She frowns.

"Mr Jackson, you're looking at him."

"This mutt?" The man's face is a picture. It would be funny if he wasn't so bitterly disappointed. "You call that *brown*?"

"It is a sort of brown," I say. "That's why we called him Toffee." I don't fill the kettle.

Mr Jackson feels for the inside pocket of his jacket. He pulls a photo from his wallet. "I brought this with me as proof of ownership," he says, and hands the photo to Mum.

"What a beautiful dog," she says, and passes it to me. The dog is about the same size as Toffee, with a glossy chestnut-brown coat and friendly face. I ask his name.

"Smartie," he says. "From a pup, you could tell he was super-intelligent."

I feel awful – him losing his beloved dog. "I hope you find him soon. Is he microchipped?"

"He certainly is." He runs his hand over Toffee's head. "I suggest you check to see if this one is. Or have you done that already?"

Mum says, "We haven't, though we ought to of course."

"Do that," says Mr Jackson, "and it's possible the owner might come forward." He touches the bare patch on Toffee's tail. "Though I wouldn't hold your breath."

I say, "We thought he could've been dumped. You know, out of a car or something."

I'm starting to feel relieved we can't afford a visit to the vet (until I remember the PDSA is free) when Mr Jackson – putting Smartie's photo back in his wallet – fishes deeper into it. Taking out three twenty-pound notes, he says, "I seriously doubt he's been done – I mean microchipped or vaccinated – so have this with my best wishes." Before Mum or I can say anything, he adds, "And no arguing."

I suspect the poor man's going to lose it if he doesn't get out of the house fast. I feel the lump in his throat like it's my own, and follow him to the front door.

Who would have guessed, fifteen minutes ago, that he'd be shaking my hand? "Take care," he says, and hurries along our uneven path to his car.

If Toffee could climb into Mum's lap, he would. As it is, his head is against her thigh and she's stroking him under his chin.

We don't say anything for a bit. Just look at each other, and at Toffee. We know what the other's thinking: how wonderful it is that we're not parting with him.

Mum says, "We mustn't look too far into the future."

"Try not to."

"I did notice straight away," she says.

"Notice what?"

She laughs. "You silly kid! Your hair, of course. It's absolutely lovely."

"Shaun did it."

"Really? Well, he's made a good job of it. He should go into business when he's old enough." She grapples with the glass of water beside her, and I realize she's due her medication. I push two pills out of the blister pack and drop them into her palm. "Thanks, love," she says and swallows one. Though not easily. Even with all the practice she's had, she can still get one stuck in her throat.

"Now then, Amy. Tell me everything."

It's like I've switched heads – back to my old one, still aching with its awful secret. I hesitate: "Well…there's quite a houseful at the moment. There's—"

She interrupts. "How about the doorstep baby?" She downs the second pill without too much trouble. "I can't begin to imagine," she says, "what the circumstances can have been…for a mother to—"

"He's fine, Mum!" I lose eye contact with her, and turn away to wipe the draining board. "He's fine. A lovely-looking baby. Very, very sweet." Next I make a little drama out of the kids bouncing on the furniture and Kirsty being horrified about Jordan playing with Lego. Mum laughs. And I giggle. Like it was the funniest thing.

There's a mirror on the window sill by the sink, but it's too small to see my whole head. I go upstairs to the bathroom, turn on the light and look in the mirrored-door of the medicine cabinet. I see the really great haircut, but try not to look too hard at the face it frames.

I feel so on edge I don't go downstairs immediately. I go

to my room, find a piece of paper and rough out the letter I've been thinking about. It takes for ever. But eventually I put down what I want to say:

Dear Kirsty,

I won't blame you if you think I'm cowardly and worthless. I'm the only one to blame. I hardly know where to start, except to say there's no way of telling this, except the truth. This afternoon, with your family being so kind, I'm finding it twice as hard to tell you what, for Mum's sake, I've had to hide.

I can't make this less awful than it is, so I'll come straight out with it. Robbie is my baby.

Please believe me when I say I had no idea I was pregnant. You'll say, how could I not know? Believe me, I didn't.

One of the things eating away at me is that I've not confided in you. I hope one day I can forgive myself for this, and that you'll also forgive me. I didn't tell you, mainly because I didn't want to put you under pressure. Like worrying about whether to tell your mum she's caring for my child. Also – to be honest – I've been afraid you might never forgive me. That you'll be ashamed of me. Ashamed for me. For abandoning my baby – though I knew, at the time, that taking him to your mum was the best I could do for him.

I'll completely understand if you feel I've failed you

as a friend. I know we've never felt we needed to swap details about every single thing – stuff we want to keep private – but it doesn't change the fact that I've lived a lie in front of you.

What I have to tell you is that seeing Robbie today was shattering, and I don't know how much longer I can keep up this pretence. Can you imagine what it's doing to me? If I didn't think you might still be there for me, I don't know what I'd do.

With all my love,

Amy.

I read it through for about the tenth time and look at my watch. Poor Mum, she'll wonder what I'm doing up here. I fold the letter, stuff it at the back of my drawer and wonder if I'll ever send it. I wish I believed in miracles. Like I'll wake up one morning and…

…And what? Find I don't have these feelings for Robbie? Find I don't long to feel the warmth of his little hand clutching my finger, don't want him to meet my gaze with his blue, blue eyes. I hope they stay blue. They're wonderful.

Snap out of it, Amy.

I run downstairs. Mum's dozing. Toffee looks up expectantly. I shake a few dried biscuits into his bowl, and take fish fingers from the freezer compartment. I say softly, "Mum?"

She opens her eyes. "I wondered where you were."

I say lightly, "On that other planet?"

She chuckles. "Situation normal, then."

"How many fish fingers?"

"Two?"

"You can't manage three?"

She shakes her head. "I don't think so."

I get busy grilling the fish fingers with a sliced tomato. I butter a slice of brown bread and arrange it all on her favourite plate: our last remaining one with a blue rim. I make it look appetizing by tearing up a lettuce leaf as garnish. I put the tray on her lap, and she smiles. "Thank you, love. It looks delicious."

Chapter Nineteen

Luckily there's no trouble finding a vet. Kirsty looks in Yellow Pages and off we go with Toffee and Mr Jackson's sixty pounds. I'm relieved Kirsty offered to come. I'd have been uneasy going on my own.

I don't tell Mum where I'm going, in case she convinces me of some ethical reason why I shouldn't go ahead. Like Toffee not strictly belonging to us.

There are "Lost" notices on the waiting-room wall. Two dogs, a cat and a tortoise. I force myself to read them and look at the photos. Kirsty looks at them too, though casually. I sigh with relief: neither of the dogs looks remotely like Toffee.

Now it's our turn to go in, and the vet, Mr Fulwith – sporty-looking and friendly – says, "So who's this nice chap, then?"

I tell him he's called Toffee. "He's a rescue dog, so we

don't actually know much about him. We've no idea how old he is, but I'd like him to have an identity microchip, please."

"Right you are," he says, and types my name and address into his computer. "First – let's see if he already has one." He reaches for a gadget on the shelf behind him and runs it over Toffee. I hold my breath. What if he is *already* microchipped? This could be the end. Just a phone call away from finding his owner.

But it's all right. No sign of anything!

Kirsty says, "Can you tell how old he is?"

Mr Fulwith takes hold of Toffee's wolf-like jaws with both hands and examines his teeth. "Hard to say." He touches the bald patch on his tail. "Not very old," he says, "even if he does look as if he's been through the wars."

Kirsty persists. "So what would you guess – about four?"

Mr Fulwith shakes his head. "Not even that. He's quite a young dog."

I find myself beaming, thinking of all the years ahead. The Toffee years.

One little click with a small hypodermic needle between Toffee's shoulder blades, and the microchip with its identity number slips under his skin. The vet tells us there's a special offer on this week, so Mr Jackson's sixty pounds pays for the microchip *and* the vaccination Mr Fulwith says Toffee needs. There's even a little cash left over, which

I can put towards dog food and a proper collar and lead.

When we're outside again and on our way home, Kirsty says, "Where did Toffee really come from?"

"He just turned up." I eye her. "You knew that."

"Yeah, just making sure."

"Like I spotted him in someone's garden and thought, there's a nice dog – think I'll nick him, along with a couple of gnomes."

Kirsty gives me a punch on the arm. "Don't be ridiculous."

I punch her in return. "Precisely."

We must look like a couple of kids.

On the way home we stop off at the post office. I really ought to get something as a thank you to Shaun for cutting my hair. I know Mrs Goodge has a shelf of cut-price chocolates. They're probably past their sell-by date, but Shaun won't curl up and die.

Kirsty stays outside with Toffee, and I go inside to look along the shelves for the best bargain. I choose a double-layer box of dark, milk and white chocolates with mixed centres. "Treating Mum?" says Mrs Goodge, and I think: Of course – I *must*.

I hesitate. "How long out of date are they?"

"Hardly at all," she says. "Less than a week past their best before date."

"Great. That's brilliant." I hand over a fiver. "I'll have another box of the same, please."

She puts the two boxes in a green and purple paper bag. "They're a right good buy, are these. It's not often you can buy two boxes of chocolates and get change from a fiver. When I were a lass there were all sorts you could buy for sixpence, and *still* get tuppence change."

I say, "Wow," though I've no idea how this compares with today's money.

She says, "Did he get in touch – the man who'd lost his dog?"

"Yes – wasn't his though."

Toffee jumps all over me when I come out of the post office. You'd think I'd been gone for weeks. Kirsty says, "What a shame. He had to hurry off."

"Who?"

"Mr Smith. He made a terrific fuss of Toffee." She makes a little face. "*She* was with him – the Ice Queen."

I give her a look. "What is it with you and Mrs Smith?"

"Nothing – I just think she's a bit stuck-up."

"Did you tell them we'd been to the vet?"

"Yes, Mr Smith thinks you've done the right thing, having him microchipped."

I say, "Oh, good."

She looks at Mrs Goodge's brightly-patterned bag. "So you got some."

"Two boxes. One for Mum as well."

By the time we're back at Dune Terrace, Kirsty is desperate for the loo. Toffee, mad keen to get indoors, charges ahead of us, and Kirsty runs upstairs.

Mum isn't alone. "Hello!" she calls. "Look who's here!"

Mrs Kelly is in the kitchen with Mum. And beside Mum's chair, Robbie's in a buggy, kicking his little legs.

I'm dizzy at the thought of Mum having no idea she's with her grandson for the first time. I kneel beside him, head down, my face on fire. When Mum touches Robbie's hand, it's like my thumping heart must visibly be shaking my body. I stay here on the floor, looking into his little round face. While I tickle him gently, Mum and Mrs Kelly chatter until Kirsty comes back down. Getting up from the floor, I realize I'm still clutching the chocolates. I put them on the table.

Mrs Kelly looks at me. "Mission accomplished?"

I assume she means the vet. "Yes."

Eyeing the colourful paper bag, Mum says, "Just what have you two been up to?" Which shows how seldom I come into the house with anything more exciting than eggs or milk.

Then the penny drops. Mrs Kelly has only just realized Mum didn't know where we'd been. Her shiny bob falls forward and she hides a smile.

Mum narrows her eyes at me. "What's the secret? You might as well tell me."

I stand up and retrieve the paper bag. "I bought you some chocolates, and had Toffee microchipped."

Mum tries to keep a straight face. "In what order?"

"Toffee first."

"Oh well, what's done is done," says Mum, and I think she's relieved. This way, she doesn't have to decide whether I was right to go to the vet.

Kirsty's mum says the tide's right out, so why don't Kirsty and I take Robbie out for a breath of sea air, plus Toffee can let off some high spirits.

I open the front door while Kirsty pushes the buggy over the step. A breeze whips up and we leave our mums' voices behind. Toffee, full of beans – and his invisible identity chip – heads for the dunes and the beach.

On the dunes the buggy acts up like a wonky supermarket trolley, so we carry it between us – Robbie making happy noises – until we reach the beach. Even here though, the damp sand is rutted from where the tide pulled out. Robbie is quite content; it agrees with him, being jiggled along, avoiding puddles and piles of seaweed. We've gone quite a long way, when Kirsty says, "How about we swap and you push the buggy?"

I keep my voice even. "Yeah, okay."

So here I am, pushing my baby son along the beach – like a young mum on holiday.

What if I was never allowed to do this again? I get a lump in my throat, thinking of not being there to help Robbie build sandcastles, or make him picnics for when he goes paddling. I think about him being old enough to collect shells, or lie on his tummy and gaze at reflections in rock pools. Who will answer his questions? It's so hard, not being able to share my thoughts – especially with Kirsty. So hard not to be able to say *my baby – my son – my kid*. I try not to look too far ahead, to a time when he might not be with Mrs Kelly.

Kirsty charges around, zigzagging in all directions, getting Toffee to chase her.

After a while I say, "D'you think we should go back?"

She says, "Okay," and I turn the buggy round.

Kirsty sees a stick, picks it up. I think she's going to throw it for Toffee, but instead she stops. "Look, Robbie," she says, "this is your name." And slowly, with sweeping lines and curves, she writes ROBBIE in the sand. I tip the buggy slightly so he can see what she's doing. His eyes follow her. "It'll stay there," she tells him, "till a ginormous wave comes along and washes it away."

Chapter Twenty

Last night I dreamed about Robbie. We were living with Mum in a house that was meant to be this house, yet wasn't. Robbie could talk – though not very much. Then, Mum suddenly went away and Shaun was there, hurrying towards me, smiling a big smile. In the dream I knew I was dreaming. But when I woke up it was as if I was still in the dream, trying to recapture the happiness I'd felt when Mum laughed at the way Robbie had begun to talk.

Whenever I'm over at Kirsty's I try not to seem too fond of Robbie. Sometimes – acting like he's not my favourite – I wonder if I pay too much attention to the other kids. It's not easy, because when I go round he's incredibly sweet – putting his arms out to me when I come in the room. One day, when Mrs Kelly said, "Go on, Amy, pick him up – he adores you!" I found it hard not to burst into tears.

Every now and again it comes up in conversation:

the fact that no one is any the wiser about Robbie's mother. Mr Kelly describes her as having "disappeared off the face of the earth". Then I remember it's me they're talking about and I think, *No she hasn't, she's here, standing right in front of you.*

Robbie's little arms and legs are starting to look a tiny bit podgy, and it's really getting to me: not him getting fatter, but me not knowing how much longer he'll be around for me to watch him develop. In twenty years' time I could sit next to him on a bus, or in a cafe, and not know he's my son.

I don't know how long the authorities wait before they assume "the birth mother" won't be claiming her child. Sometimes I'm so churned up I don't know if I can bear it. But I have to. I've got no choice.

It's nearly the end of exams. In fact, it's final English Lit revision this morning and the exam – *my* last one – this afternoon. I'm alone in the form room, thinking about Robbie, and trying to make sure I've got everything I need for the exam. This is the one where I ought to do really well.

I try out two biros. Make sure they're both working.

There's a touch on my shoulder. "Amy?"

It's Kirsty and I say, "What're you doing, creeping up on me?"

She's grinning. "I wasn't 'creeping up on you' – but, hey, listen."

I slip the pens into my bag.

She says, "You're to promise not to say anything."

"Okay."

"No, *really* promise."

"Cross my heart."

She says, "You'll never guess."

"Well, I won't if you don't tell me."

She looks round to make sure no one's come in. "Mr Smith and the Ice Queen have asked about adopting Robbie."

There's a pain in my chest.

She mouths in my ear, "Sounds like they're hoping the birth mother won't turn up." She's clearly waiting for something from me, but I can't speak.

It's a relief when the form room fills up and Mr Smith appears. I sit down and Kirsty slides in beside me. "Are you all right?"

"I'm okay."

She looks awkward. "Don't tell anyone, will you?"

I manage to look her in the eye. "Of course not."

"Mum'd kill me if it got out."

I take a breath. "When will people know?"

"They'll never know if it doesn't come to anything."

Not unkindly, Mr Smith says, "Amy?"

"Sorry, sir?"

"Is there something you'd like to share with us?"

If only he knew. "No, sir."

"What about you, Kirsty?" he says.

She tugs on her ponytail. "No, sir."

"Right then, shall we get on?" He opens *To Kill a Mockingbird*. "I think we've done enough practice papers, so let's just chat through the text before your exam."

Now it's like he's asking himself a question. "I wonder," he says, "why this is the only book Harper Lee wrote."

Kirsty puts up her hand.

"Yes, Kirsty?"

"Perhaps she put everything she knew into it – and... sort of drained herself."

Mr Smith considers this. "I've wondered about that," he says – and Kirsty blushes with pride.

Cherie says, "Perhaps she wrote other stuff but nobody liked it."

Mr Smith sighs. "We'll probably never know that for sure."

Half sitting on the edge of his desk, he stretches out his long legs. Zara, who's clearly got the hots for him, can't possibly know how silly she looks with her mouth hanging open. I look at him, imagining him as Robbie's father. It's like he reads my mind. "As the father," he says, "do we agree that Atticus comes across as pretty well perfect?"

I spot Neil Betts making a face like he couldn't care less about Atticus.

Atticus, the father, is great – always patient with his kids. (Mum's in love with him. She's seen the film with Gregory Peck.)

Mr Smith looks across at me. "Amy," he says, "how do you see Atticus? Any particular thoughts?"

I'm usually keen to join in, but right now my mouth's dry and it's like I've literally lost the plot. Kirsty elbows me as if I might have forgotten Mr Smith is waiting for an answer. "Well," I say, "nobody's perfect…" Then it starts coming back to me. "But even though Atticus works full-time as a lawyer, he seems to be coping well as a single parent. As far as we know, he's fair and straightforward with his kids and…"

I trail off, and when Cherie Dewhirst butts in with "Sir, sir!" I'm relieved.

Mr Smith says, "If you calm down, Cherie, we'll hear what you have to say."

As usual, her voice is breathy and excited. "I think he *is* pretty well perfect. But do his principles put his family at risk?"

Mr Smith says, "In what way?"

"Well," she says, "he stands up for people who have bad luck, or are born unlucky." She gets into her stride: "He doesn't mind making a show of himself."

"That's interesting," he says. He pauses for a moment,

and I understand him wanting us to get the most out of the story. "How do we mainly perceive Atticus?" he says. "As a father, or as a lawyer? Or do we find it hard to differentiate between the two?"

Shooting her hand up, Zara burbles on about Atticus Finch's brilliance until Mr Smith, tactfully cutting her short, draws Shaun into the discussion. Shaun, though he's not the greatest reader in the world, makes comparisons between today's racial attitudes and those in the book. Mr Smith nods vigorously. "Well done, Shaun."

This session ought to be right up my street. I only wish I could make the most of it, like I would if I could stop thinking of Mr Smith taking Robbie to his first day of school; taking him out at weekends; teaching him to swim. I'm starting to wonder what Mrs Smith is really like, when the bell rings and we all head for the door.

Mr Smith says, "Good luck, everyone."

Lunchtime. I hurry home as usual, but I can't eat a thing; it's like a membrane is stretched across my throat. And Mum – because she's not too well – doesn't feel like eating either. But I mix her a cup-a-soup anyway, because she must get some nourishment. If I don't eat, it won't matter, but with Mum, it's important she keeps up her energy, or at least hangs on to what little she's got.

If she doesn't perk up, we'll have to go to the surgery.

I hinted at this yesterday, but she won't have it. She insists she'll be better soon.

She's worried about me not wanting anything to eat. I can't cope with a "discussion", so I say I've been daft and ate a Mars bar Shaun gave me. I put Mum's soup and a small piece of bread on her little table, then go up to my room.

I sit on the bed. Try to get a grip. I go to the bathroom and sit on the loo – my arms round my knees – but that's no help at all. Coming back to lie on the bed, it's like I'm watching a film. Mr and Mrs Smith pushing Robbie in his buggy. Wheeling him up their front path, wherever it is they live. Giving him his tea, putting him into a cot in his cute nursery. Putting a teddy bear by his feet for the night. Switching on a wall night-light shaped like a crescent moon. Saying "sweet dreams" and creeping out of the room.

How am I going to cope with English Lit this afternoon? I think about staying at home but Mum would worry, so I have to go back.

Somehow, I get my act together. I have to, this exam is so important. Among the muddled thoughts spinning in my head, I know that even though Mr Smith wouldn't know I was the mother of his child, I can't let him down.

We're in the hall, sitting in rows behind each other. Mrs Hart, who's invigilating, says. "You may turn over your papers."

There's a moment's rustling, then utter quiet as we lower our heads and read through the questions.

They're good. Even the ones on *The Merchant of Venice*. I can cope.

Chapter Twenty-one

Each morning when I wake up it takes a few seconds to sink in – the fact that my GCSEs are actually over. The relief is enormous. Now, mid-afternoon, the mist that hung about until lunchtime has cleared and it's turning out to be a gorgeous, sunny day. But Mum's uncomfortable in the heat. It's rotten for her, not being able to go down to the sea on the spur of the moment. There are beads of sweat on her forehead. I dab them with a cold flannel. I wipe her hands as well, and leave the flannel on a plate with ice cubes to keep it cool. It's clear she's in pain, but she pretends it's nothing much. "Damn headache, that's all – but I've had my ration of painkillers until later." She smiles. "You go out. Get down on the sand with that hound." Toffee springs to attention. He knows exactly what she's said, even though she hasn't mentioned his name.

*

The sea is magic. It's sparkling, the tide's half-out and there's just enough air to ruffle my hair. Suddenly he's beside me. Shaun. How does he work out where I'll be? With one hand behind his back, he looks like he's hiding something. He nods at Toffee. "D'you know what I've got?"

In all honesty, I want to be alone. I need thinking time. I say, "I've no idea."

"It's a frisbee. I got it in a charity shop."

"Oh, Shaun, that's so kind – Toffee'll love it."

He says, "Shall I throw it for him?"

"Yes – go on!"

He flings the frisbee. It whirls higher and higher before landing quite a way off. Like a greyhound, Toffee races to bring it back. Shaun and I, we spend a good ten minutes giving Toffee the time of his life.

I look at my watch. "Isn't it nearly your teatime?"

Shaun says, "Yeah, better go," and hands me the frisbee. He turns, then looks back over his shoulder. "Careful you don't get sunburnt!" He walks a little way, then turns again. "Let me know if you want your hair trimming."

"Yes, I will. Thanks."

He's already jogging when the idea hits me.

"Shaun!"

He stops dead. Spins round. Comes running back. Skids to a stop in the sand. "What?"

"I just had a thought." *Am I mad?* "Shaun, do you think you could carry my mum?"

"Where to?"

This is typically Shaun – and strikes me as so daft that all my pent-up feelings dissolve in relief. I let out a giggly sigh. "Well, not to Newcastle. *Here*. Bring her here. Down to the sea. So she can feel the breeze."

"Yeah, course – let's go."

Oh, *Shaun*. All black and white. No greys. He doesn't say, *When, Amy? Today or tomorrow, Amy?*

But he's right. The sun might not shine tomorrow.

With Toffee leading the way, we hurry back through the dunes. I try not to lose my nerve, try not to change my mind. We go round to the backyard. When I push open the gate, Shaun seems to forget what we're here for. "Flipping 'eck, Amy, this gate's on its last legs. D'you want me to fix it?"

I look at the hinge that's worked loose. "Great," I say, "but not right now."

"Tomorrow?"

I can't commit myself. "Could be. Thanks." I stop at the kitchen door. "I'll just pop my head in first – we don't want to give Mum a shock."

Shaun says, "Shock can be extremely dangerous for an invalid."

As I open the door, Toffee pushes in front of me. Mum's asleep. It strikes me it's a shame to wake her, but all the same I touch her hand. She doesn't move, so I squeeze her fingers.

She opens her eyes. "Amy, love."

"Mum, I've got a surprise." I wait for this to sink in. "We'll have tea later – we're taking you down to the sea."

Wincing, she moves her left shoulder. "You and whose army?"

"What d'you mean? You're as light as a feather. Shaun and me, we're taking you down there now. It's so *beautiful*. The tide's out, the sand's warm – but not too hot. We can paddle."

Then it's kind of heartbreaking, because tears roll down her cheeks. "Really? You mean it?"

"Really."

Shaun is standing at the door. I nod to him. "Come in, Shaun. Meet my mum."

Mum wipes her eyes, and smiles. "Ah, the hairdresser."

"Stylist," he says.

"Whatever you call yourself," says Mum, "you're a living marvel."

I pick up the phone, and Mum says, "Who're you calling?"

"Kirsty – just to say Shaun won't be back for his tea till later."

Mr Kelly answers. I explain what's happening and he says to remind him to let us have some runner beans. If we're interested, that is. I say thanks, we'd love some, and ring off.

I whisper to Mum, to ask her if she wants a wee before we set off. She does, so it's a few minutes before we're downstairs again. I'm about to suggest the best way of carrying Mum, when Shaun – first making sure we don't forget the frisbee – picks her up like she's weightless, and we're off out the front door. Toffee thinks this is massive fun, and has to be persuaded not to jump up at Mum's bottom, which is sagging slightly between Shaun's arms. I'm closing the front door when I think, Hey, wait a minute – and dash back inside to get our moth-eaten tartan rug and Mum's sun hat from under the stairs.

I'd worried that managing Mum over the dunes could be a problem. But Shaun, like he's half man, half mountain goat, carries her as if she's his prize. His princess in a fairy tale. She looks wonderful, her dark silky hair swaying to the rhythm of his steady pace.

Shaun looks into Mum's eyes. "Where would you like to be, Mrs Preston?"

"Close to the sea, please."

I run on ahead and spread out the rug where the sand is still dry, yet near enough to the sea for us to paddle. I sit down as Shaun gently lowers Mum, and I pop her sun hat onto her head. I realize the only way she'll be comfortable, and still able to look out to sea, is if we sit back-to-back. I wriggle round – so now my view is the southerly curve of the shoreline and Croppers Rock.

We sit like this for about a quarter of an hour, Mum and me talking with our backs to each other. I don't need to see her to recognize the almost-tears in her voice when she says, "I'd begun to think I'd never come down here again."

"That's awful, Mum. We'll come often." I call out to Shaun, who's about to throw the frisbee. "Won't we, Shaun!"

He takes great leaps across the sand to us. "Won't we what?"

"Bring Mum down here often."

"Of course we will. It'll be my pleasure, Mrs Preston. We'll come every day."

Mum wouldn't dream of laughing at Shaun, but the giggle is there. "Every week would be lovely."

"Consider it done," he says. Then he moves round to face me. "You know your baby?"

How is it my body can freeze on such a hot afternoon? I try not to stiffen my back against Mum's. "My baby?"

"Robbie," he says.

I open my mouth to speak, but nothing comes out. I control my breathing. "He's not *my* baby."

Mum moves her head against mine. "Shaun doesn't mean *your* baby. It's just obvious you're very fond of Robbie." She pauses. "Aren't I right, Shaun?"

"You are right, Mrs Preston. Dead right."

"Shaun," Mum says, "you're a tonic." She eases her neck. "Anyway, what about Robbie?"

Shaun says, "I probably shouldn't say."

Mum says, "You've started now, so you might as well finish."

"Like *Mastermind*?"

156

"Yes," says Mum, "like *Mastermind*."

Toffee rushes off, barking at a seagull.

Shaun says, "Someone might adopt him. It's not for definite, but they might."

I say, "You're not supposed to know that," which makes it sound like I also know something I shouldn't. I hesitate before I add, "One day, someone will probably adopt Robbie, but there's no one in particular at the moment."

Mum says teasingly, "Are you sure?"

Shaun pulls a face. "Like Amy says, I'm – we're – not supposed to know anything." Then he looks at me, holding my gaze. "But there is something I know."

For the moment I don't want to think about Mr and Mrs Smith. Changing the subject, I tell Mum that of course Shaun *knows things*. (Despite being dyslexic, he's very bright indeed. He's what Mr Wilson calls "College material".)

"I don't need college," he says, "I'll be running a chain of salons."

I say, "You'd need to train."

"Not for long I wouldn't."

I force a laugh. "So it's a chain, eh? What will you call yourself?"

He frowns in concentration, and we spend a while thinking up silly names for hairdressing salons. I know Mum's in pain, but she still laughs at "Get Shorn" and "Shaun's Unisex Shampoo and Shave". Every now and then

Shaun nods vigorously at what he reckons is a good name for his empire.

I say, "Shaun, how about we paddle?" And he bends down, scoops Mum up gently and carries her into the sea. A little way in, still supporting her, he helps her to stand.

With the sea rolling round my ankles, I paddle beside Mum and Shaun. Toffee rushes to join us, and Mum laughs. Shaun sways her from side to side like she's a piece of seaweed. She's loving it.

I squint at my watch. We ought to be making tracks. It's nearly time for a bit of tea and Mum's early evening medication. But it's so lovely here I don't want to break the spell. Not for the next few minutes at least.

Chapter Twenty-two

It's been a great day. Such a different day, especially for Mum. We've had our tea. Nothing haute cuisine, but I cooked properly. Sausage and mash. Plus broccoli, which is full of healthy antioxidants. (I'm always on the lookout for nourishing vegetables that could help improve Mum's health.)

I'm wiping down the draining board. The TV is on – one of the soaps – but I'm not paying much attention. I've got my back to it. Sounds like the usual over-the-top stuff – someone breathing their last breath. Whoever it is gasps, and Toffee jumps up, catching a claw in a loose thread in my shirt. I half turn. He's not wagging his tail, and squeals when I release his paw.

I hear a whisper as if from far off. "Amy?"

I spin round. Something's the matter with Mum.

Dropping to my knees beside her, I force myself to stay calm. She's having a panic attack and can't breathe. I jump up and open the drawer where I keep paper bags. I hold one over her nose and mouth. "Breathe into the bag, Mum."

She tries, but her eyes are scared. I tell her I'm calling the doctor and take no notice when she tries shaking her head to say no. I know the doctor's number by heart; but it's after hours and there's only a message. The voice gives me another number to try. Hell, I've got no pencil. I go back to Mum. She's trying hard with the paper bag, but it's not helping. Hurriedly, I kiss her forehead, take the paper bag off her face, and put it back on again. "I've got to dial again, Mum."

I find a pencil, ring our doctor's practice and wait for the out-of-hours number. I hold my breath, ready to focus on the recorded voice – there's no time for making repeated calls. I listen to the number and write it down. I look back at Mum. Her eyes are full of fear.

I call the new number. A woman asks who I am. Who do I want the doctor for? When was Mum born? This is awful. I can't remember the year Mum was born and I'm not going to get her into more of a state by asking her to talk. I tell the woman it's really urgent. She asks if Mum's bleeding – and has she hit her head? I say no to both and give her our address. She says a doctor will be here very soon, and tells me to keep Mum calm.

I *would* try to keep her calm but suddenly she leans forward, clutching herself round the middle. She starts retching. I grab Toffee's bowl from the floor and put it under her chin, just in time. She retches again and is very,

very sick. More of it comes with more retching. She lets her head fall back, and I take the bowl away.

Moaning, she sounds as if she's in agony.

"Where's the pain, Mum?" But I can see where. It's the whole of her stomach area, and lower.

This is all my fault. If I hadn't had that crazy idea of Shaun and me taking her to the beach. If I hadn't had her sitting on the sand for ages. If I hadn't let her practically stand up in the sea. If I hadn't thought this would be good for her – which it obviously wasn't – she wouldn't be ill now. God, if only the doctor would hurry.

It feels like for ever but it's only ten minutes. There's a rap at the front door. I forget about keeping calm and rush to open it. I don't know her, the pretty woman on the doorstep, but she's got the confident look of a doctor.

"Hello," she says. "Am I right for Mrs Preston?"

"Yes. Through here."

She follows me into the kitchen and looks at Mum. It doesn't seem to surprise her that Mum's sitting with a paper bag over her face, which she now lets drop. I can *feel* Mum's relief at knowing we've got help.

She smiles at Mum. "Mrs Preston," she says, "I'm Dr Walker. You're having trouble getting your breath?"

Mum nods.

"And she's been terribly sick." I point to the bowl on the draining board. Dr Walker takes a quick look at the vomit, then picks up Mum's wrist to feel her pulse.

161

I say, "And she's got a lot of pain."

Dr Walker nods, takes out her thermometer and pops it in Mum's ear. She doesn't say anything, so I don't know if things are normal or not. I don't ask.

Dr Walker looks at Mum, then at me. "We'll want Mum to go into hospital." If Mum could shake her head and say no, she would. But she can't. It's only in her eyes I can see how much she doesn't want this. The doctor takes an oxygen mask from her bulky bag and fixes it round Mum's ears and onto her face. Then Dr Walker takes out her phone and calls for an ambulance.

She looks at me. "Is it only you and your mum?"

I check my watch; make it look – and sound – like this is a temporary arrangement. "At the moment, yes."

"Dad coming back later, is he?"

"No." My brain whirrs, and I tell a lie. One of many, but I can't risk Mum being taken into hospital and never coming back here. "My sister Lisa is due home any minute."

Mum's eyes widen above the mask. I say, "Her usual time, Mum? She should be here any minute." It's like my nose grows longer. "Unless she has to stay on at the shop." I look at Dr Walker. "She could get held up if there's a late customer."

The doctor says, "If your sister hasn't got back by the time the ambulance arrives, perhaps you can text her." I don't tell her I haven't got a mobile.

She smiles such a kind smile. "I expect you'd like to come with Mum?" she says.

"Yes, please."

At the hospital I trail along after Mum's trolley while she's taken from place to place. She ends up in the High Dependency Unit, where they ask me to wait in the corridor so they have a chance to make her comfortable. Although I don't see Dr Walker again, other people stop and talk to me. A nurse says they'll tell me some more when Dr Briggs has seen Mum.

When I see Dr Briggs – who is cosy-looking and the same height as me – he tells me he'll talk to a Mr Dorrington, after which he thinks they'll have a clearer picture.

I ask Dr Briggs, "Do you know what's wrong? I mean, I know she has rheumatoid arthritis, but she hasn't been like this before."

He says he can't be sure, but he'll be back to talk to me again. He's gone a few paces, but I can't keep it in any longer. I say, perhaps too loudly, "Dr Briggs?"

He comes back and sits down beside me. He seems a kind person.

"We're doing everything we can," he says.

To me, this sounds ominous. I pour out my guilty fear: "We – I – took Mum down to the sea this afternoon.

She was so hot – sweating, really – I thought it would cool her down. Me and my friend, we helped her paddle. We sat on the sand for quite a long while. On a rug. Would that have made her ill?" This sounds idiotic and I say, "I don't mean the rug, I mean the whole thing. The outing."

He pats my hand. "Tell me your name."

"Amy."

"Well, Amy, I can honestly say that letting your mum enjoy a breath of fresh air on a lovely day like today won't have been the cause of her trouble. It's far more likely to have been brewing for a while."

"She's seemed more tired than usual for quite a few days."

He stands up. "There's a cafe near the main entrance," he says. "Why not get yourself a coffee or a soft drink?" He puts his hand in his pocket, as if he might be going to give me some money.

I try to look like I hadn't noticed. "Thank you, I'll do that."

My sense of direction is zilch. Finding the cafe is going to be an orienteering exercise, minus the map. I hadn't taken any notice of how Mum and I ended up at the High Dependency Unit. We'd come up in a lift and only stopped once – for someone to get out for the Prem Unit, where it had hit me like a brick that I was probably a few paces from where the doctors had saved Robbie's life.

Now I'm off down a flight of stairs, and through a pair of swing doors and down yet more stairs. It's lucky I start spotting *Way Out* signs. Surely this means I'm near the main entrance? Unless I'm near the main *exit* – if there is one. No, it's okay, one more door and I'm beside the entrance.

I don't buy a drink straight away because I need to check my purse for the bus fare home. I try not to make it obvious that I'm counting my money. I don't want to look as pathetic as I feel. Anyway I've got enough, so I buy a cappuccino and take it back upstairs to where Mum is.

I'm still waiting outside the HDU, finishing my frothy coffee, when Mr Dorrington introduces himself. He's tall, thin and willowy – the exact opposite of Dr Briggs. Who now joins him. This somehow gives me confidence, though he looks to Mr Dorrington to speak first.

"We have two issues here, Amy." He pauses, and I soon realize Mr Dorrington pauses a lot. I wonder if this is just habit, or whether it's more significant. He says, "Your mother is really quite poorly." My heart pounds. What does that mean? *Your mother is seriously ill. Your mother is very seriously ill. Your mother is…dying?*

Dr Briggs says, "We think it's safe to say Mum has a condition called pancreatitis."

This doesn't sound any safer to me, even when Mr Dorrington explains: "Put simply, this is an inflamed pancreas."

Dr Briggs says, "In addition, she may have gallstones."

I can relate better to this because there are some in a jar in the science block at school. He adds, "Though these shouldn't pose too great a problem."

I have a sudden thought. "Would my mum's arthritis have caused this pancreas—?"

Dr Briggs helps me out. "Pancreatitis?" He shakes his head. "This is something quite separate. Though your mother's poor health won't be helping matters."

Mr Dorrington says, "Your mother will be in hospital for, well—"

"As long as it takes," says Dr Briggs. "By which we mean, unfortunately she won't be coming home just yet."

Mr Dorrington says, "Your mother has explained she is not in touch with your father, and that you and your sister are known to Social Services."

He stops there. A long pause. And I wait. This could be it. The beginning of the end. Mum in residential care, me on my own and Robbie adopted. Suddenly I'm on the point of tears at the thought of how Mum met my baby without having any idea who he was.

Dr Briggs says, "If we need to be in touch with your sister, can we assume she's on the same number as you?"

I nod. "But she's out more often than me."

I know what I have to do. And I must do it immediately. Even so, I don't want to look rude, like I'm not grateful for their help. Fortunately Mr Dorrington has to hurry off, and when Dr Briggs asks if I'd like to see Mum, I say, "Do you mind if I find a toilet first?"

"Of course not," he says. "There's a visitors' loo round the corner, then to your left." He touches me briefly on the shoulder. "When you come back, let the Ward Sister know who you are. She'll take you to your mum…" He hesitates. "Who, by the way, is a bit wired-up, so try not to be too alarmed when you see her."

I let him get out of sight, then I run. I amaze myself because I easily find my way to the cafe, which is where I'd seen the phone. And in my purse – actually *in my purse* – is Lisa's mobile number. *And* I've got the right change for the phone.

I punch the number, put my money in and wait. I can't believe it, I *can't* believe it – she answers immediately, sounding quite lively. "Hello?"

"Lisa, it's me. Now listen. Really listen. I've not got long. Mum is in hospital. She's in the General."

"Why?"

"She's very ill – and you've got to get here to see her. Plus you *have* to say – if you're asked – that you live at home permanently. *Permanently*. Do you understand?"

"Yeah, okay."

God, is that all she can say?

I speak clearly, so there'll be no misunderstandings. "Come tonight. To the hospital."

"I hate hospitals."

"I know, but you've got to come. Mum'll be desperate to see you."

"Yeah, but… Is she really ill?"

"Yes! She's in the High Dependency Unit."

"I will come – though…"

"Are you still there?"

"I'm worried about Darren. I thought you were him."

"Well I'm not. *Now listen—*"

"For God's sake!" she says. "I *am* listening."

"Just give everyone the impression you'll be at ours tonight – and every night."

"Okay."

"Is that all you can say – *okay*?"

"Well – this is a bit of a shock—"

"I'll say this once more, Lisa: *you live with me and Mum.*" I hesitate for a second. "And for the time being, we'll let Mum think you've moved back in." She sighs, and I add, "*Right?*" But my money runs out. There's not much more I could have said. If that doesn't get through her thick skull, nothing will.

I've got my bearings, and with only one wrong turn find my way back to the High Dependency Unit. I'm not sure if the nurse at the nurses' station is actually the Ward Sister. I don't like to look too closely at her badge – it might look as if I'm fascinated by her enormous bust. She's notices me anyway. "Yes?" But then a phone rings, and it sounds like whoever's at the other end is annoyed. The nurse – or Ward Sister – says it's not strictly her responsibility, and puts the phone down. But it's like she's forgotten me. I clear my throat. She looks up. "Can I help you?"

"I'm Amy Preston. Is it all right for me to see my mother?"

There's this lovely smile. "Of course you can, pet. Follow me." She tells me Mum is quite seriously ill and that for the time being she has a specialist nurse caring for her. We stop outside a door with clear glass at the top. It's opened by Mum's nurse who says, "Ah, you must be Amy."

My stomach churns. Why am I nervous of seeing Mum? From where I am, I can't see her because another nurse blocks my view. But then the nurse moves, and there's Mum's bed – the only bed in the room. She's surrounded by wires and tubes, a drip on a stand, and a monitor close by. There's a movement, her hand lifts a little. I go to the bed, touch her fingers.

"Amy, love," she says, "are you all right?" Typical of Mum – forgetting herself, and worrying about me.

"I'm fine," I say, "but how about you?"

"They've given me something for the pain. It's wonderful – I'm imagining myself beside the sea."

"We'll go again," I say. "I promise."

"Just thinking about it," she says, "makes me believe in a future."

I tell her I've been in touch with Lisa. Her face lights up, then she says, "I hope you didn't worry her."

"Of course I didn't. She's going to try to get in to see you this evening."

As her eyes start to close I lean over her and whisper, "Toffee sends his love." She's already half asleep and probably can't hear me. All the same, I stroke her hand and say, "Night, night, Mum – sleep tight."

Chapter Twenty-three

I'm back home. Alone – apart from Toffee, who'd like to go out. Sorry, boy, you'll have to make do with the backyard. (I don't dare leave the house in case there's a call from the hospital.)

I jump as the phone rings. My ribcage squeezes inwards, but it's only Lisa. Amazingly, she's already been to see Mum. "I thought I'd go as soon as possible," she says. "It must be good for her, mustn't it, to know we care?"

"Absolutely! It'll do her the world of good, knowing we're *both* rooting for her." I'm so relieved Lisa's made this effort. "Was she awake?"

"Yeah."

"And pleased to see you?"

"She didn't talk a lot, but she smiled." There's a pause before she says, "By the way, did they say what's wrong with her?"

"Yes – pancreatitis."

"Is that serious?"

"Yes, Lisa, it is. That's why she's in the High Dependency Unit, *with her own nurse.*"

"Okay, okay," she says, "there's no need to get—"

"Get what?"

"Like you're the only one who knows anything. I mean, I *am* your sister. Plus I'm older."

There's a lot I could say in reply to that. Instead, I say, "Sorry, Lisa, it's been a difficult day." I pause. "And don't forget, if anyone brings it up – you live here with Mum and me."

"For heaven's *sake*, Amy—"

"It's *important.*"

"Okay."

And that's the end of the conversation. I wait for a second, then she turns off her phone.

I stand in the kitchen, listening to the silence. It's strange. Eerie. Usually at this time I'd be sorting out Mum's medication, making sure her pills and capsules are in order. But I haven't got them; the doctor wanted them taken with her to the hospital. I go upstairs to her room. I tidy stuff lying about and put her nightie from yesterday in the bathroom wash basket.

I go back to her room. Sit on her bed. Worry about her. And about Robbie. And the dreadful sadness of Mum not knowing she has a grandson. Of her and Mrs Kelly, sat in our kitchen – neither of them realizing the baby in the buggy has a mum and granny in the same room. Tears trickle down my face.

I'm still sat here – miserable – wishing for all sorts of things that can't come true, when the phone rings in the kitchen.

I spring off the bed and dash downstairs. Oh God – is it the hospital?

I snatch up the phone. "Hello?"

I wait, listening to the sound of breathing. I know who it is before he speaks: "This is Shaun Baxter."

Shaun *Baxter*. How many Shauns do I know? "Hi, Shaun—"

"Are we taking your mum to the beach tomorrow?"

"Listen, Shaun. She's in hospital."

He says nothing, but I can tell he's still there. I say, "She was sick and I had to get the doctor. Next thing I know, he calls an ambulance and she's in the General."

"I'd best tell Mrs Kelly." The phone goes down on a hard surface. I hear a baby crying in the background. Is it Robbie?

Mr Kelly comes to the phone. "Hello, Amy. What's all this then?"

"It's Mum, she's got…pancreatitis."

"She's got what?"

"Pancreatitis – it's an inflamed pancreas. And she probably has gallstones." I'm starting to cry again, but try to hold it in. "It's serious."

"Don't upset yourself, love… Is your Lisa there? Can you get her to the phone?"

Hating myself for lying, I take a deep breath.

"Lisa's with our mum at the hospital. She'll be back later." I wipe my eyes with a corner of the tea towel. "Can I speak to Kirsty?"

"She's at the cinema with Jordan. Let me get Susie for you."

"Thanks."

"She won't be a second," he says, "she's just cooling young Robbie down."

"He's not poorly, is he?"

"No – just a slight temperature."

I long to be two people at once: one holding Mum's hand, one with Robbie.

It's a huge comfort hearing Mrs Kelly's voice. "Amy, sweetie, tell me everything. When did all this start?"

I tell her most things, including taking Mum down to the sea – which I'm sure Shaun will have mentioned. And he has.

Repeating my lie, I feel sick. "Lisa should be back any minute. She's been visiting Mum." (At least that bit's true.)

Mrs Kelly asks which ward Mum is on. When I tell her about the High Dependency Unit there's a short pause before she says, "I think that means it'll be family visiting only... I'll call in to see her the minute she's moved onto a general ward."

I say, "Thank you," and she says she'll call me tomorrow, but that I must *promise* to call if there's anything they can do. Day or night. She repeats that: *day or night*. And I'm to tell Lisa the same. It's so good to have her at the end of the phone. I know how lucky I am.

I say, "I'd better go, in case the hospital calls."

"Of course. Now listen, you're not to worry. Mum will be all right. She's in a marvellous hospital – we know that, don't we?" she says.

I say yes we do, and ask if I can come round tomorrow to see Kirsty.

She says, "Of course. We'd love to see you."

Chapter Twenty-four

I'm thankful yesterday is over. I don't want another day like that. Thank God exams have finished. I walk up the Kellys' path. Kirsty's waiting; she opens the door wide. "Hi. How are things?"

I step inside. "Mum's still poorly, but they're wonderful at the hospital. *So* kind."

When Mrs Kelly comes out of the kitchen carrying Robbie, I have to cross my arms to keep myself from reaching out to him.

My heart sinks. Suppose in the future it's not me and Robbie together, but Mrs Smith who'll kiss and cuddle him; brush the top of his head with her lips? It's unbearable – the thought of Robbie being adopted: the finality of not being able to run along the sand to see him whenever I want to.

Mrs Kelly tickles him under the chin. "Say hello to Amy!" Looking at me, his mouth changes from a mint-with-a-hole to a quivering smile. It's amazing, it's like he understands.

Mrs Kelly says, "And how's Mum today?"

But I'm staring at Robbie, transfixed. "Oh, sorry. Yes, they say there's not a lot of change and she's comfortable."

Mrs Kelly says, "That sounds very encouraging."

Kirsty draws attention to Robbie. "Look at him, Amy. There's no doubt he knows you."

I touch his cheek and Mrs Kelly says, "Don't you think he's filling out?"

I look into his forget-me-not eyes. "Oh yes, definitely." I take his tiny hand. "You are, aren't you?" He pokes out the tip of his little pink tongue – and my heart nearly breaks.

Chapter Twenty-five

It's a week before they move Mum. She's on Castle Ward now, in a side room on her own. After such a serious illness she needs as much care as possible. But the fact she's no longer in the HDU is helping me – knowing she's making progress.

Mrs Kelly has been to see her. She took magazines and grapes. Mum says grapes might sound boring, a bit of a joke because it's what visitors usually bring, but they're exactly what you want, sweet and juicy.

Though the staff say Mum's improving, it seems very slow to me. Mrs Wickham visited. I hope she doesn't feel she ought to visit me too. Mum says there's no reason why anyone from the Social should turn up. They think Lisa and I are very capable. Telling me this, Mum had given my hand an extra squeeze. When I leaned over to kiss her goodbye she whispered, "We'll make it through the rain."

As soon as they moved Mum I called Lisa, urging her to visit again soon. It would be good if the nurses on Castle

Ward got to know her. If she *does* visit, everyone's more likely to believe she actually lives on Dune Terrace.

There's still the possibility Mum might have to face a gall-bladder operation if, like Mr Dorrington said, the stones continue to cause trouble.

Being on my own, except for Toffee, gives me too much time to think. Day or night, even watching telly, I think about Mum. And Robbie – and about Mr and Mrs Smith wanting to adopt him. I see him often, but I do wish I didn't see Liam each time I look into those blue eyes. Kirsty asks me round and Mrs Kelly's being very kind. Which she always is, but right now she's going out of her way. Mr Kelly too. And Shaun, he'd do anything for me, though I don't think he totally understands how I feel about Mum. I think his strangeness might be to do with not having been loved by a parent, and not having one to love. Poor Shaun – it doesn't help that he doesn't see what effect he has on people. It can be something quite ordinary, like standing too close, not realizing he's crowding you; or giving that explosive laugh when there's nothing funny to laugh at. Perhaps it's the result of having folk play pass-the-parcel with him all his life. Being Shaun – great big Shaun – must be like living on an emotional roller-coaster. Still, maybe the way he can't quite connect gives him some sort of protective shell.

*

179

This afternoon I walk Toffee over to Kirsty's. It turns out she's not in – she's gone into town with Jordan to help him choose a suit for a cousin's wedding – but I stay behind to help Mrs Kelly with the children. Mr Kelly's at home – on duty in the garden with the little ones. Clean sand has been delivered and they're "helping" him refill the sandpit. There's an awful lot of squealing and shouting. Looking out of the window, I can see Toffee, lying down, not too close to the activity. He likes the kids but he's sensible about keeping his distance.

This leaves Mrs Kelly and me with Robbie, who's lying on a changing mat on the kitchen table. I'm dealing with his nappy. I've already wiped him with baby wipes and wrapped up the *very* dirty nappy. Now his little bottom's pink and clean and the only smell is baby. Fresh and sweet. Mrs Kelly hands me a new disposable nappy, which I smooth out. It has teddy bears on the front so you know which way to fasten it. I shift it under Robbie, while he kicks his feet in the air. I have to hold his ankles together with one hand while I fasten the front with the other.

Mrs Kelly says, "Well done, Amy. It's not easy when he's this lively. Wait till I tell your mum, she'll be proud of you!" It's great, the way she's so positive about Mum. She never lets on she was worried, which I know she must have been.

I tickle Robbie and he gurgles. It's funny that such a messy chore has made me feel so happy, and I love it that Mrs Kelly lets me change him. After I've washed my hands, she asks if I'd like to make up his bottle. I've done this a few times before, and though I feel stabs of sadness – thinking that if things were different I could still be breastfeeding him – I'm glad I can help with the next best thing.

To keep pace with his healthy growth, Mrs Kelly has upped his number of powdered formula scoops. First I put the cooled, boiled water in his bottle, then measure out the number of scoops and add them to the water before screwing the lid on the bottle. If it wasn't for this – doing small things for Robbie, and keeping my hopes up for Mum – I don't think I'd be coping at all right now.

Mrs Kelly finishes folding a pile of towels she brought in from the line. Checking the kitchen clock, she says, "Is that really the time? Andrew and Gina Smith should be here soon."

I didn't know they were expected and my heart thuds uncomfortably. My hand feels sweaty on the bottle as I give it a shake. I clear my throat. "They seem rather interested in Robbie."

"What makes you say that, Amy?"

I mustn't drop Kirsty in it. "Well – haven't they been round before?" I dribble a little of the milk on the inside of my wrist to check the temperature.

"They have, yes." She adds a towel to the growing pile. "Actually," she says, like it's not a big deal, "Mrs Smith is interested in knowing how fostering works."

Though I can't imagine Mrs Kelly telling me a fib, I'm not sure I believe Mrs Smith can be *that* interested in fostering. I keep my voice light. "Well," I say, "you're the expert. You've had loads of experience."

Mrs Kelly chuckles. "You can say that again." She puts Robbie's tiny vests neatly together. "As a matter of fact," she says, as she pulls a sleepsuit out of the wash basket, "Mr and Mrs Smith have been approved as adoptive parents."

I wait for a moment. "You mean, so they could adopt Robbie?"

"Well – not necessarily. At this stage, it's just general approval."

"They must be glad." I wait a few more moments. "How do people get to adopt?"

She sits down and reaches out to stroke Robbie's feet. "With a fair amount of difficulty." She looks thoughtful. "Though I admit I've been tempted myself a couple of times."

I ask, "What makes it difficult?"

"For a start," she says, "it takes months to be approved. Sometimes more – what with counselling and visits to a child's possible future home. And reliable folk providing references."

"It all sounds very businesslike."

"Well actually, it needs to be." Then she adds, "The adoption authorities call on people who are prepared to recommend the potential parents. Friends of the couple, for example. Though it's not always a couple, of course – sometimes it's a single person hoping to adopt."

I say, "Lots to think about then."

"My word, yes." She pauses. "A reference might also be given by a person respected in the community."

"You mean like a vicar?"

"Yes, possibly." She looks serious. "It's a big responsibility – saying you believe someone is fit to take on a child for life."

I think of Mr Smith filling out forms because he wants a child. "Sounds like a whole lot of hoops to jump through."

"There certainly are." She pauses. "It's also pretty rigorous with fostering."

There's a louder than usual squeal from the garden, followed by a yap from Toffee. Mrs Kelly stands to look out of the window.

I say, "What are they doing out there?"

She chuckles. "It's okay – just excitement at so much sand."

I'm shaking the bottle again – every movement clocked by Robbie's bright eyes. I decide to scare myself: "Do you think Mr and Mrs Smith would like to adopt Robbie?"

Like I hadn't asked something so specific, she says, "Someone's going to want to." She pauses. "I'm hoping for good things where the Smiths are concerned. They haven't had it easy."

The doorbell rings. "Ah!" says Mrs Kelly. "Talk of the devil!"

I have to sort myself out. The minute Mrs Kelly is out of the room – opening the front door and chatting – I sit down ready to give my baby his bottle. My arms tighten round him for a moment and I kiss the tip of his ear. Such a natural thing to do, yet fear hits me in the stomach: how would I bear it if he was adopted, and these little ears weren't mine to kiss? Footsteps come along the hallway and I push the teat into his eager mouth.

Before they reach the kitchen door, I hear Mr Smith's soft laugh. As the three of them come into the room, I look up, efficient and confident. You know what they say about swans – all calm above the water but their feet paddling like crazy underneath? That's me.

Mrs Smith is tall, nearly as tall as her husband. I suppose at first glance she could fall into Kirsty's "Ice Queen" category: elegant, and kind of beautiful. She doesn't seem cold or aloof though. She's quite freckled and I wonder if Mr Smith likes this. Her chin-length hair is mid-brown and shiny. I bet she washed it this morning. Her eyes are the lightest blue. The brown eyeshadow and carefully smudged eyeliner make me think of moths. Her jeans show off her narrow waist, and her bright-white T-shirt reveals a dip of cleavage. Round her neck there's a little gold charm. It's one of those that, if you spin it, says *I love you*. I used to wish Liam would give me one.

Mr Smith says, "Hello, Amy."

I say hello, leaving off the "sir" because it might sound out of place in this situation.

"This is my wife, Gina," he says. For a quick moment she smiles at me, but really she's only got eyes for Robbie. Mr Smith asks how Mum is.

"She's coming on all right, thank you."

He says, "That's good. Toffee not with you this afternoon?"

"He's in the garden, I say, "helping Mr Kelly with the little ones."

Mrs Kelly smiles. "Gina, would you like to finish feeding Robbie?" Gina's fair skin turns pink, and I notice how the freckles merge. Robbie hangs onto his bottle so tight I almost have to unscrew the teat from his gums. I hand the bottle to Mrs Kelly, then stand up with Robbie. Mrs Smith sits in my chair and I put Robbie in her arms. Still flushed, she crosses her legs, then tries them uncrossed. Mrs Kelly hands her the bottle. When Robbie's hands reach out like he wants to grab it for himself, Mrs Smith looks up at all of us. "Did you see that? Isn't he clever?"

I think of other clever things he'll do. And it's suddenly all too much. My mind rushes ahead. Me not there to hear Robbie's first words, watch him take his first steps. Not there when he runs out of school with a swimming certificate. Not there when he gets ten out of ten for spelling.

With Mrs Smith's head bent over him, he sucks away. But she's holding the bottle awkwardly and he's sucking air. I don't think she's got the experience to notice. Mrs Kelly hasn't noticed either, unless she just doesn't want to say anything in front of me.

She goes to the window. "Amy, love, would you mind popping into the garden? Ask the kids which they'd rather have with their fish fingers – baked beans or spaghetti hoops? Oh – and give Frank a hand for a few minutes." *Frank.* Funny that, I mean, I do know he's called Frank but to me he's always been Mr Kelly.

She wasn't exactly subtle, Kirsty's mum. It's obvious they want to talk confidentially. About fostering. Or adoption?

I wander over to the sandpit. Toffee leaps up, pleased to see me. The two boys and a girl all choose spaghetti hoops. I help with the sand, tipping bucket-loads into the wooden-sided pit. The kids chatter non-stop, showing how bright they are; or they ask questions – which Mr Kelly only answers if they seriously seem to need an explanation.

Slowly pouring sand and smiling, but with cold fingers clutching somewhere inside me, I wonder what sort of mother Mrs Smith would make for Robbie.

Chapter Twenty-six

I saw Mum earlier. She's not too bad, but there's no definite date for her coming home. The blood tests seem never-ending.

It's been dull all day. Nothing like the gorgeous day when Shaun carried Mum down to the sea. I'm watching TV, hardly noticing what's on. Mum's constantly on my mind – added to which, I can't get *that image* out of my head: Mrs Smith with Robbie in her arms.

Tears wet my cheeks. I don't ask Liam to come into my head, but he's suddenly here. Me without Liam, me without Robbie. Me without *Mum* is so unbearable I scramble out of my chair, go into the backyard and take deep breaths to release some of the tension.

Indoors again, I flop down and blow my nose. On the second blow, looking away from the TV, I nearly jump out of my skin! Someone – ginger-haired – is walking past the kitchen window. Toffee barks like a mad thing. It's a bit of luck, him sounding like something the Dangerous Dogs

Act wouldn't stand for. I lean across the sink, craning my neck to see if I can spot where they've gone.

Now there's banging on the front door, and my heart's bursting in my chest. I slip into the hallway. If only we had a spyhole…especially now I'm on my own. Toffee charges ahead of me.

The voice is raucous. "Amy! I know you're in there! For God's sake open this bloody door!" It's Lisa, and my knees go weak with relief.

"Hang on!" I push up the latch.

She's dyed it ginger – her short, spiky hair. It looks dreadful. She bends down to pick up two of the plastic bags at her feet. Toffee sniffs the third, and I bring it inside. I can't stop staring at her hair.

She eyes me like I'm poison. "Don't look like that."

"I'm not looking like anything."

"Yes you are."

"Honestly, Lisa, I'm not. I'm pleased to see you. It's just you gave me a shock, skulking about like that." I lead the way into the kitchen. "Are you stopping?"

She chooses one of her smiles, the one she uses when she realizes she could have been nicer. "I thought with Mum in hospital you might want a bit of company."

It's enormous, the relief flooding through me. No more lying. Lisa's really here! I say, "I'd love it if you'd stay." It's easy to guess the real reason she's here. I reach for the kettle. My heartbeat settles down and I give a little laugh.

"Darren's not on his way too, is he?"

"He's gone."

So I'm right. "I'm sorry."

"Don't be," she says, "He's a shit-faced filthy liar."

"Oh well, you're better off without him."

"That's something we can agree on."

I make tea for me, and a mug of coffee for Lisa. Since I was nearly caught out by Mrs Wickham I've stocked up on instant.

I ask Lisa how many times she's been to see Mum. Though really I know. She says she thinks it's twice. Then again it might be once. I say wouldn't it be a good idea if she goes tomorrow afternoon and I go in the evening? I'd go as late as possible, which I like because I can help settle Mum down for the night.

She says, "I'll think about it...I told you I hate hospitals." I tell her Mum's not wild about them either, and – to be fair – she looks guilty for a moment. But then she says do I think the way I forced Mum to paddle caused her collapse. I'm not rising to this. Instead I fill Toffee's pie dish with fresh water.

"I can have Mum's room," she says, and I say, "Just so long as you leave it really nice for when she comes home."

She says, "Then I suppose we'll have to share again." She opens a cupboard and makes a face at what's not in it. "I'll go to the chippy."

"Have you got any money?"

Surprisingly she has, so she goes out and comes back with fantastic fish and chips and two bottles of Fanta. Our mood takes a turn for the better and she talks like a train, mostly about how horrible Darren is. How he's double-crossed her and how nobody, but nobody, is ever going to do that to her again.

I practically have to force Lisa to visit Mum. But she does, which I know will make Mum so happy. When she gets back I ask how Mum seemed. She doesn't answer at once; just fiddles with her ginger spikes in the tiny kitchen mirror. Eventually she says, "Good, yeah, she's good. D'you think I suit this colour?"

"I asked you how Mum is."

"The nurse with the big boobs says she's doing okay."

"She's the Ward Sister. She's nice – very kind."

"Right."

Later on this evening, I visit Mum. There's a sparkle in her eyes. Seeing Lisa has made all the difference.

Today is brighter than yesterday, and I think it would be a good move to take Lisa across to Kirsty's. I have to bribe her: if she comes with me I'll cook tea for the next two days.

She says, "Do we have to take the tatty mongrel?"

I ignore her, and fetch the collar and lead I bought for Toffee last week.

We could do with washing up before we leave, or at least wiping the crumbs off the table. But in Lisa's eyes the mess doesn't matter. Or doesn't exist.

With the front door clicking shut behind us, I say, "When we're at Kirsty's do *not* forget you live with me and Mum. You always have done."

"Since when?"

"Li-*sa*. Since for ever."

I've reckoned without Shaun. We run into him outside the Kellys'. He doesn't wait for me to say who Lisa is, just pats her on the head, flicks a ginger spike, and says, "Not good on you, that tone. Too harsh."

She backs away. "Who are you, for God's sake?"

"Someone who knows a disaster when they see it."

I say quickly, "Lisa, this is Shaun – who lives with the Kellys. You know? Shaun who carried Mum to the beach and—"

She gives him a look. "So we've got you to thank, have we?" She turns to me. "Do we really have to go in?"

Kirsty opens the door. "Hi!" she says. "And hi, Lisa! Great to see you!" She's only saying this for my sake. Still, she leads the way indoors.

I say quietly to Lisa. "Shaun's got a few problems, but he's *fantastic* with hair."

She raises an eyebrow at mine. "Is that right?"

Kirsty says, "Everyone's in the garden. Come through."

Toffee accepts the invitation and races towards the back door. Because I don't like him rushing up to the little ones, I call, "Toffee! Stay!"

The same three kids are here. The girl, Sammie, runs up to me. "Amy! Amy!" I tell Lisa to say hello to her. "Hi," she says, like the kid's seventeen.

Kirsty's mum makes out she's thrilled to see Lisa. Perhaps she is. I don't know. I can't tell what Mr Kelly's thinking, though he nods pleasantly. "Susie went to see your mum yesterday – says she's coming along nicely."

Lisa says, "Yeah, she's good."

Kirsty brings out a large sponge cake and a tin of biscuits, and Mrs Kelly goes back indoors for mugs of tea and drinks for the children.

There's no sign of Robbie. I look back at the house. What if he's not here? What if the authorities have decided it's all right for the Smiths to have him on a trial basis or something – and not wait until they're certain the birth mother won't turn up. Make certain *I* won't turn up and wreck everyone's plans.

I say casually to Mrs Kelly, "No Robbie today?"

"He's gone down for his sleep. A nap around this time seems to suit him best." I feel the grin spread across my face. Lisa doesn't ask who Robbie is. Why would she? She's not interested in anything much, except the sponge cake. Me, I need to talk about him. I tell Lisa that

Robbie's been here for quite a while. Looking at me like I'm a saddo for mentioning it, she curls her tongue to catch a mouthful of strawberry jam oozing from the sponge.

Shaun says, "Found on the doorstep. Middle of the night."

Lisa licks her jammy lips. "In a shoebox, I suppose."

Mrs Kelly raises an eyebrow. "Yes, as a matter of fact."

Lisa says, "Funny how there's always one handy."

Kirsty says, "Actually, most babies – even newborn – wouldn't fit into a shoebox."

It's time I said something. "Unless it was for very big shoes. Pippa Chislett's dad takes thirteens."

Kirsty hands milk to Sammie and one of the little boys. She says to Lisa, "Robbie was premature. Everyone was dead worried – he was in hospital for a few weeks."

Mrs Kelly asks Lisa if she'd like more cake. She says she would, and no one notices when Taylor, the other little boy, sneaks into the sandpit; not until he gets sand in his eye and starts screaming his head off. For the time being, Robbie and the shoebox are forgotten.

So I don't get to see Robbie today. It leaves me feeling rather down, makes me realize how much it means to me: having him close, giving him a cuddle. Plus, nowadays, changing him and giving him his bottle.

We get back home and Lisa turns on the TV. There's

something she likes – a game show where contestants nearly win a huge sum, but usually don't.

I snap my fingers. Toffee wags his tail. "Right, Lisa," I say, "I'm off out." Then I add, "I told Mum you'd visit soon."

"Okay...anyway, this is only a repeat." To my surprise she stands up and switches off the TV. "Where are you going?" she asks.

"Nowhere in particular – just out," I say.

But there *is* somewhere in particular. I take the frisbee with me and choose a stick from the dunes on our way. Once on the sand, I let Toffee off the lead. Like Mr Jackson said, it doesn't look like our "mutt" is going anywhere. I throw the frisbee and stand, watching Toffee tear after it.

The tide is a fair way out, with the sea looking perfect for the sailing boats rising and falling on the blue-green swell. They could be starting a race, but Croppers Rock blocks my view. I won't be able to wait and see. I'd have to be here for ages to watch them go behind the rock and come out the other side.

Toffee is a long way off, just a dot in the distance. Waving my arms, I call him. He knows to come back, and starts careering towards me.

The sand is just right. I take my stick and draw a large heart pierced with a cupid's arrow. Under it I write AMY

LOVES ROBBIE. Crazy to get back to me, Toffee puts on an extra spurt, nearly reaches me, splays his legs out like a dog in a cartoon and skids to a stop just short of my artwork. "Okay," I say, "feeling left out?" I write AND TOFFEE. He sniffs it and sits back. It's like we're both thinking about it. I hunker down beside him, pull him close. He licks my ear and I laugh: "That tickles!" Pushing myself up, I look at the love heart once more before kicking over the traces.

Chapter Twenty-seven

I can see Mum's a whole lot better today. Great news – she's not going to need the gallstone operation after all.

She's fed up of being in bed, and sits in a chair as often as possible. She's reading a thriller Mrs Kelly brought her. Showing me its lurid, fake bloodstained cover, she says, "This is absolutely gripping!" Then, though there's no one within earshot, she lowers her voice: "If I can't sleep tonight I'll be reading it under the bedclothes."

"Aren't you allowed to read whatever you like?"

She laughs. "Of course you can, but they probably think someone as poorly as me – as I *was* – shouldn't be risking nightmares."

We start giggling – which makes me feel ridiculously happy. Mum gives a little gulp. "Oh dear, we really must learn to behave." I'm on the opposite side of the bed from her chair, and walk my fingers across the bedspread.

"Lucky you've got a room to yourself." I pause for a few moments. "When d'you think they'll let you come home?"

Teasing, she says, "Have you got room for me?"

"Room?"

"With our Lisa back home?"

"We'll share again. It'll be perfect. The three of us – not worrying about anything."

Mum looks serious. "Don't let her take advantage of you. Make sure she does her own washing."

I think of the load I've already done. "No problem."

"Well – just so long as she does." She reaches into the locker for her purse. "Can you get me half a dozen second-class stamps, love? I'd like to thank folk for sending me cards."

I take the coins. "I'll get them tomorrow." I look at the Get Well cards. I've seen them before but I look again. There aren't many – I suppose because we pretty much keep ourselves to ourselves. There's one from Mr and Mrs Kelly, and a separate one from Kirsty. And one from Shaun! Today there's a new one that wasn't here yesterday. Mum says, "Look who it's from." I open it. Quite a flowery poem, and a note saying, *Good to see you looking so much better. All best wishes from Irene Wickham.* Mum says, "Nice of her really."

The nurse I think of as the shouty one comes into the room. She beams at Mum. "Hello, my love!" She's wheeling a machine for testing blood pressure and taking temperatures. She clips something onto Mum's middle finger and presses a button on the machine. Numbers appear – and change – on a screen. They don't mean anything to me, though I'd like to know more. I ask the nurse if they're normal. "They look fine to me!" she says, and puts a thermometer in Mum's ear for a second. She makes a note of the result, leaves two painkillers on the bedside locker and shouts, "See you later!"

In the corridor, afternoon visitors are on their way out. It's time for me to go too. I so hate leaving Mum, even though I know she's well looked after. Plus she has a good book. If you like that sort of thing.

I lean over her, support myself on the arms of the chair, and kiss her on both cheeks.

"There's no need to come again today," she says.

I grin. "Don't you want me to?"

She says, "That's not the point. You need a bit of time to yourself."

I walk to the door and, after I've closed it, take one last look through the glass pane. She blows me a kiss, and I mouth, "See you tomorrow."

I start walking towards the *Way Out* sign, but I've only gone a few steps before I stop dead. Mr and Mrs Smith are stood at the nurses' station. For a moment I think of saying hello. But I don't, because the Ward Sister – the one with glasses, not the busty one – has on a sad face and is saying something Mr Smith is clearly finding upsetting. He glances briefly at Mrs Smith, who puts her arm around him and, listening to what the sister says, nods several times.

I slide quietly behind them, but then I look back and catch sight of Mr Smith. He looks devastated.

Back home Lisa takes one look at me and reckons I'm in a mood. "What's that face for? Something up with Mum?"

"Like you'd care." I know I shouldn't have said it. Now I'm not the only one in a mood.

I tell her Mum's all right, and suggest we go out together: take Toffee for a walk. But she'd rather watch another time-wasting TV show. This one's about people having their stomachs stapled, so they won't want to stuff their faces. I thought she didn't like hospitals, and can't think why she wants to watch this.

I only need to raise an eyebrow for Toffee to come running. I don't bother with a lead. I walk fast, only slowing for a minute when the dunes hold me up. When we're both down on the sand, I throw the frisbee. Every minute though, with the tide coming in, we've less beach to play on. Play? The way I'm feeling at the moment, I don't count myself as part of Toffee's happy world. The sky has turned to a purplish violet, painting the last strip of sand an eerie mauve. Even Toffee looks a different colour.

I can't get to sleep. I keep seeing Mr Smith's face. Finally, I drift off, but I wake late with Toffee pawing at my door.

I can't get into the bathroom; amazingly, Lisa is up and washing her hair. I don't care too much. I need to call Kirsty, and with Lisa splashing about it gives me time.

I dial, and Kirsty picks up. "Hello?"

"Hi. It's me."

"Hello you – how's your mum?"

"She's okay – looking better."

"That's good. I hope—"

I interrupt. "Kirsty."

"What?"

"I saw Mr Smith and his wife at the hospital."

She says, "His mother's very ill."

"Right… He looked terribly upset."

"Yeah, well…they've been back again… Mrs Smith's been confiding in Mum."

"What about?"

I hear Kirsty's slow intake of breath. "You won't tell anyone?"

"Do I ever?"

"Just don't say anything."

"I promise."

"She thinks that because Mr Smith's mother is so ill they ought to let her go."

"*Die*, you mean?"

"Yes—"

"But that's dreadful—"

"No, listen, Amy. They know she wouldn't want to be resuscitated if—"

I say, "It sounds as if it's more what Gina Smith wants… You've never liked her, have you?"

"Well…" She pauses. "But that's not what this is about. This is about Mr Smith's mother having another heart attack, or a stroke. If she did – and apparently it's highly likely – it could be massive and her life might not be worth living."

"Only *might* not? Has anyone thought what Mr Smith might want?"

"That's part of the problem. He's not ready to let his mother go."

"Doesn't that just go to show what a lovely man he is. Sensitive and caring." I swallow – try to moisten my mouth. "Would you let your mum go?"

"Of course I wouldn't, but she's not old…or seriously ill."

We're both silent for a moment, then I say, "Well, I think it's appalling." My voice sounds shaky and I wish it didn't. I don't think I can say much more without bursting into tears.

"You all right, Amy?"

"It's just that…well, you only get one mother." Thinking of my place in Robbie's life I'm unable to speak.

Kirsty says, "Are you still there?"

I turn away from the phone to take a breath. "Sorry – yes. What d'you think's going to happen?"

"I don't know. Mrs Smith might come round tomorrow. She's here an awful lot. Dad says she might as well move in."

We say goodbye and Kirsty's phone clicks off. I feel weak and sink into Mum's chair. While Lisa's hair-washing water gurgles upstairs, my eyes follow fast-moving clouds through the window. Thoughts chase around in my head. The one frightening me most is Mrs Smith as Robbie's mum. The last day or two I'd begun to talk myself into this possibility, consoled by the certainty that Mr Smith would make a fantastic dad. But now, hearing *she* is actually going against his wishes, I don't know what to think.

Lisa's used all the hot water, so I have what Nana Kathleen called "a lick and a promise". Next I take Toffee out, and waste what's left of the morning torturing myself with what it would be like if Mum didn't get better after all.

I lighten up a little when I decide to run along to the post office for Mum's stamps, until I remember I haven't brought any money with me. I glance at my watch. If I run home, I could get there before lunch. Just. Then I think of Lisa agreeing to do some ironing, and panic in case she scorches my one decent top. I yell for Toffee and we head on home.

Lisa has forgotten about the ironing; says she'll do Welsh rarebit to make up for it while I watch the lunch time news. I look at her fiddling about with bits of cheese and wish I could talk to her.

I can't say more to Kirsty – though I long to tell her everything, and imagine the two of us sitting cross-legged on her bed, me pouring my heart out, even having the courage to show her the letter I wrote.

Right now I miss Mum desperately. How I wish Lisa was the sort of sister I could look up to. Who'd understand, who'd be able to put herself in my place. Who I could talk to.

It's while I'm having an imaginary conversation with this "other Lisa" that a voice in my head says, *Shaun*. Of course… Shaun, who's already dealt with so much in his life. He even *looks* like there's a box in his head marked "Secrets". Not that I want to confide in him; anyway that wouldn't be fair. It's just I need to be with someone who's easy to be with and who, if ever I *did* want to say something, would probably listen. Which is funny, when you think how awkward he was when we first met. How he could only relate to Toffee.

After we've eaten the Welsh rarebit, which is stringy but quite nice, I call the Kellys, and Mr Kelly puts Shaun on. "Amy!" he says, and I hold the phone away from my ear. "Hi, Shaun."

"Hi, Amy."

"Shaun?"

"Amy?"

"Shaun, d'you think you could help me do a bit of weeding?"

"Where?"

"Round at ours – the bit of garden at the front. It's a right mess."

I tell Lisa Shaun's coming round. She says, "What for?"

"We're going to do some weeding."

She laughs. "I hope you're not expecting me to help."

I say, "Of course not. Isn't it your programme?" I'm safe with this; there's always something she wants to watch, or needs to catch up with.

There are times you'd think Shaun's got wings. Not because he's angelic, but because he arrives at such speed. He's knocking on the door before I've had a chance to put old clothes on – well, even older clothes. I open the door. He fills the space. He's got his back to me, looking at the front. I won't say "front garden" because it's hardly that. It's just a small flattened patch. More weeds than grass.

He swings round. "Better crack on," he says, "look at it!"

"Yeah, it's a disgrace. I don't know how I let it get like this."

We've not got any proper gardening tools, so I've raked around in the kitchen drawer and come up with two old forks and a vegetable knife. "Sorry," I say, "we'll have to make do."

"S'okay," he says, and soon we're on our haunches,

digging around, making little piles of weeds. He's so strong we'll have it done in no time.

My head is bent over a patch of chickweed. "Shaun?" I say, and he tugs on a tough-rooted dandelion.

"Yep?"

I come out with it. I have to. "Are Mr and Mrs Smith still interested in Robbie?"

"Yep." The dandelion comes up, root and all. He shakes the dry earth off it. "Mrs Smith likes the idea of fostering kids." He looks at me for a moment. "They lost a baby. It died."

It's as if the breath is knocked out of me. How dreadful. What could be worse? After a moment I say, "How do you know that, Shaun?"

"I overheard stuff." He pulls a face. "I'm not supposed to know. You won't tell."

"Of course I won't."

Not looking at me, he wiggles the old fork about. "You're good at keeping quiet."

What does he mean? That he knows I won't repeat things?

He says, "Little Robbie might do okay," and waves a weed at me. "Groundsel, this."

I'm shaking at the thought of Mrs Smith's baby and hardly trust myself to speak. "Oh?"

"Yeah. Rabbits like it. I was with a family kept rabbits."

I say, "Were you?" but I can only think of the baby dying.

"Yeah. Not for long, though." He tickles the root until the earth falls off. "Not every kid strikes lucky." He chucks the groundsel aside. "Can you imagine how good it would feel, having someone like Mr Smith for your dad?"

While he pulls the blade of his knife across a stone, I pile up my straggly pieces of chickweed. I take a controlled breath. "Mrs Smith might not be the mum you hoped for." Then I add, "Not that I'm talking about you personally."

He wipes sweat from his forehead. "Mr Smith'd not marry anyone who weren't dead nice."

"Some folk may seem very nice, Shaun, but they can sometimes have another side to them." I force my fork into the ground and the prongs bend.

His eyebrows knit together. "How d'you mean?"

"Well, they're not always lovely – and nice."

"She's lovely, is Mrs Smith. Beautiful."

"Being beautiful doesn't necessarily make her a good person."

Shaun stands up. Rubs his back. "How d'you mean?"

What do I mean? I think hard. "She's not like us – or at any rate, not like me. She's prepared *not* to save a life." I take a deep breath. "For her, life's not sacred."

"She's not a Buddhist then."

"This isn't about religion, Shaun. It's about Mr Smith's mother."

"You mean the business about not resuscitating her." He gives me a long look. "Some people, like Mrs Smith, send out the wrong vibes. Me, I'm like that. I'm not great at showing my feelings. To be honest, I'm often confused about them myself."

We scrape and scratch in the earth, till what little grass there is stands more chance than it did before.

Lisa's watching *Embarrassing Bodies*. I can't stand another minute of it, and fetch Toffee's lead.

She says, "You'll walk that dog off its feet."

"You mean paws. Anyway, he doesn't mind how often he goes out."

She sighs. "If you say so."

Though I'm tired, I walk fast, trying to shake off my mood. I feel bad about Shaun, who'd love to have a dad like Mr Smith. I take deep breaths; try to relax. But I only end up more tense than ever. I let myself think of Nana Kathleen, and how different it would be if she was still here. This chokes me up like it always does, and I start to cry.

Chapter Twenty-eight

Robbie is larger. Much too large. Gross, even. He's in a state-of-the-art buggy. I'm chasing Mr and Mrs Smith. They're racing each other. She's pushing the buggy and winning. Mr Smith can't catch her up, and my legs won't move fast enough to run beside him. Robbie bounces up and down in the buggy. But he's not strapped in properly. He's laughing, but Mr Smith doesn't think it's funny. Neither do I. We both fall further and further behind. Mrs Smith is sprinting like she's going for gold. She heads for the harbour. Mr Smith calls out, "We don't want your kippers!" and waves at the man in the smokehouse behind the harbour wall. Mrs Smith whips the buggy round, nearly tipping Robbie out. Three people come running. One of them grabs Robbie. Now he's half in, half out of the buggy. I'm nowhere near him—

I wake up, my heart pounding. I lie still, dry-mouthed. The house is silent so I can't have been shouting, which I sometimes do when I'm dreaming. If I'd called out or made a noise, Toffee would have barked.

There's a howling wind in the chimney, and rain spitting huge drops onto the fan of pleated newspaper in the little grate. As usual I left the window open last night. I rush to shut it before the curtain gets any more soaked. Toffee gives a stretch, and exercises his funny early-morning voice. It's like he says "Hello" – which usually I laugh at and say hello back. But this morning I'm still half in my nightmare. I look at the alarm clock. I hadn't thought it could already be morning. But it is. It's the weather making it so dark outside.

I wash and dress, and think how life will be when Mum's back and I'm making her breakfast again.

I go into her room. It's already a tip. Even worse this morning, with Lisa dead to the world on top of the bedclothes. I don't bother about being quiet. I pull back the curtains – dry because she didn't open the window. She moans, "Do you have to? It's the middle of the sodding night."

"No it's not – it's half eight."

I run downstairs and let Toffee out. I force down a piece of toast and leave bread and cereal on the table for Lisa. There isn't much left in the packet. I'll buy cereal when I get Mum's stamps. Toffee comes back in, wet already, and I shake food into his bowl. He gobbles it up.

It's still bucketing down, and I probably wouldn't go out at all if I wasn't determined to bring Mum her stamps this afternoon. I leave the house, hood up, and for once – though he's whining to come – I don't take Toffee because of having to dry him off when we get back. I feel mean.

The teeming rain and near-black sky don't do anything to cheer me up. Dark thoughts and the nightmare are still fresh, like a horror film you knew you shouldn't have watched. It's frightening, all this vile stuff sloshing around in my head. What are dreams for? Do we hope we can dream our way out of trouble? Or do they flag up how awful our lives really are?

My dream can't help me. It only showed what I already know. That I'm worried to death over Robbie's future. What made fate decide to sling all this at me? Like the shock of giving birth to Robbie and having to leave him at the Kellys'. And splitting with Liam, though I knew that had to happen. Weighed against all this, the possibility of Mr Smith becoming Robbie's dad had begun to look like something I could live with.

Not much comfort in that any longer, though. Not with Mrs Smith giving me nightmares. Literally.

There's hardly anybody about. Seems I'm almost the only human being crazy enough to come out in a monsoon. I turn my head, wanting to see how rough the sea is, but my hood doesn't move and I'm left staring at the lining. I'm wet through when I reach the post office.

Little Mrs Goodge isn't behind the counter, or anywhere else. The place looks deserted…until a man with a thick neck, bushy eyebrows and a frown comes from the back and stands behind the glass post office screen. His frown deepening, he eyes me. It's clear he sees me as a total nobody. Or is *he* the nobody – who needs me to think he's important? I don't care either way.

I remember Mrs Goodge is on holiday; she's gone to stay with her daughter on the west coast of Scotland.

Before asking for Mum's stamps I try to dry my hands under my parka. I say, "Six second-class stamps, please."

He makes a point of peering at the floor, over on my side of the counter. "Do me a favour."

"Sorry?"

"Go back and wipe your feet on the mat."

I can't believe he's so rude, but I go to the door and make a show of wiping my feet before I come back to pay him and take the stamps.

I resent giving Mr Beecroft – his name is on a little plastic stand – the satisfaction of selling me anything else, and if there was somewhere else to go for cereal I would. Then I think of Mrs Goodge needing to make a living, and I feel a bit better.

In front of the eggs and milk, there's an abandoned box on the floor. It says *24 x Salad Cream*, and I nearly trip over it. I still can't shake off my sickening dream. Uninvited images swim into my head: Mrs Smith with the real

Robbie, not the oversized version in my dream. Mrs Smith, hard-hearted, telling him his granny is dead. And at the funeral, her face stony while Mr Smith's is wet with tears.

I pull a packet of bran flakes off the shelf and turn it over. I check for vitamins and minerals. Will this brand be as good for Mum as her usual cereal? I want to have everything right for when she comes home. Which has to be soon. It *has* to be. Having her live in my head, giving me answers I can't hear her speak, is nothing like enough. The medics can't rush things, I know that – and they're fantastic – but I need her here. To be wise for me.

The post office door opens. I glance sideways. A woman with rain running off the hood of her mac wheels a buggy up to the post office counter. I turn away because I notice Neil Betts and Jez Calvert on the pavement, looking like they might follow her in. The way I feel this morning, they're the last two on earth I want to talk to. I pull my hood right down. The next time I look they're still outside, dripping wet, reading Mrs Goodge's ads in the window. (*Found – Brown dog* isn't there any longer. We never put it back up after Mr Jackson took it down.)

Mr Beecroft leaves the post office area. Puffed up and smug, he points to the buggy. "I'm afraid you can't bring that in here. I'm expecting a delivery." You can hear the pleasure in his voice – letting the woman know he's got the upper hand.

I feel for her until she says, "Oh, sorry," and hurriedly pushes the buggy to the door. *Sorry?* I'd tell him to stuff his delivery. Is Mr Beecroft going to help her with the door? No. He goes back behind the post office counter and the parcel he's weighing, and lets her struggle as she manoeuvres the buggy over the step. She parks it close to the wall. I watch her make sure the brake is on – which she's doing at the same time as a Shop-For-Food lorry pulls up outside, darkening the window. Now she's back in the shop looking like she's heading my way towards the cereal. She pushes back her soaking-wet hood. I feel ill – it's Mrs Smith.

I think she'll spot me, but she stops at Baby Products. While she dithers, reading the labels, I pull my hood right down and plunge round the top corner of the aisle. I'm clearly not thinking straight, and as I run towards the door Mr Beecroft barks, "I hope you're going to pay for that!" God – Mum's cereal. Keeping my back to Mrs Smith, I put it on the main shop counter and, my hands shaking, fish out the change from my purse. He checks the coins slowly, so slowly you'd think it was deliberate. My heart is thudding. *That has to be Robbie outside.* I glance through the window at a beefy delivery man hoisting a towering pile of boxes onto his shoulder. Mr Beecroft slides my money into the till. The door opens and the delivery man is inside, seeming to fill the front of the shop. "Where d'you want it?" he says.

"Stockroom at the back," says Mr Beecroft.

I'm desperate to get out, but the man and his goods are blocking the way. Though I try to get round him, there's not enough room. He's huge, taller even than Shaun. He looks down at me. "That your kid out there, bawling its head off?" He flicks a look at Mr Beecroft. "I wouldn't leave a dog out in this," he says, and that hypocrite Beecroft raises his eyes to the ceiling.

"Shocking," he says.

My heart's still hammering. Has Mrs Smith heard these comments? It doesn't look like it – she's still at the back of the shop. Beefy Man steps aside for me. I keep my head right down because I know what I'm going to do, and I also know there's CCTV in the shop. It'll have caught me before, when I bought stamps and chose the cereal. That doesn't matter. It's now that matters.

At last I'm outside, leaning over Robbie, who's buffeted by the wind and crying his little heart out under the plastic buggy hood. I don't risk looking round to see if anyone's watching. Grabbing the buggy, I let the brake off and start running.

I'm already past the rear end of the Shop-For-Food truck, but the buggy's wheels have a mind of their own, and I get so close to the road I nearly send both of us careering into the side of a white van. I'm splashed head to foot with spray. With rain hitting my eyeballs, I run until the van – hooting at me – disappears.

I don't know how my brain keeps ticking over, but it

does. It tells me there's no one nearby. No one's following me. No one's staring at me. I spot someone in the chemist, but it's just the pharmacist reaching up to a shelf. We only have a few shops, and I leave the last one behind – a wool shop that's closed more often than it's open.

Water rushes down the road because the drains can't cope. One's had its cover forced off. A fountain of water shoots up. It's like me. Me with my head blown off.

Bumping into a pothole, I'm out of control. The buggy swerves sideways. For a second it's on one wheel, but I can't slow down. I daren't. I'm hanging on for dear life. For Robbie's life. No way am I letting Gina Smith have him.

Chapter Twenty-nine

Toffee is ecstatic to see me; and to see Robbie – who seems fine after his bouncing ride, and whose bright eyes follow every tail wag. There's no sign of Lisa. The breakfast table is the same as when I left. And here's me with a packet of cereal, six second-class stamps and my baby son.

I unclip the see-through hood and lift Robbie out of the buggy. Toffee makes excited noises; he's discovering he's mad about this tiny person. Or perhaps he knows it's the baby he's seen before. I stand here, brain-dead, like I need winding up but can't find the key.

Or can I?

Taking a steadying breath, I look into Robbie's eyes. They lock with mine and it hits me with a glorious soft thud: *I'm at home with my baby!* Mine, not anyone else's. I can do this…

…Or I could if I knew where to put him. Somewhere Toffee won't lick him to bits.

I keep calm. Think for a moment. Of course – the front

room. I slip him back in the buggy and wheel him through. When Toffee makes to follow I push him back into the hallway, but he's not having it and barks non-stop. Robbie stiffens and screams. I look down at the back of the buggy, at a space underneath for shopping. There's an Asda plastic bag. It's not just a spare, there's something in it. I bend down, pull it out. This is almost too lucky – like the last half-hour happened for a reason. Why else would I find a disposable nappy wrapped round a bottle of ready-to-warm formula?

I come to my senses. This isn't fate. This is Mrs Kelly giving Gina Smith time alone with Robbie. It's probably all part of the adoption plan.

But where does only one feed and a nappy change leave *me*? I'll need stuff, and someone has to get it.

It's pretty obvious I don't have an option: she's not reliable, she's selfish, she's lazy – but she's okay at shopping.

Lisa.

I leave Robbie yelling in the front room, and half fill the kettle. I need to heat up water to stand his bottle in. I turn on the kettle and switch on *The Jeremy Kyle Show*: I want to drown the manic noise of Robbie crying, just so I can think straight while I get his bottle ready. Waiting for the kettle to boil and shoving Toffee from under my feet, I run in and out of the front room – each time picking Robbie up to give him a quick rock. It must be time for his feed because with every second he's getting more and more hysterical.

217

Nothing I do – rocking him faster, kissing him – has any effect. Tears spurt from his tight-shut eyes. You'd think all this screaming would tear the skin off his throat. He must know things aren't right. Does he think *I'm* not right? No – I *was* right. I *am* right. He was desperate out there in his buggy. I had to bring him home.

The kettle boils. I pour water into a mixing bowl and stand the bottle in it. I fetch Robbie and walk round the kitchen with him. I'm frantic, in case the shouting match between the teenage couple on TV – her with hardly any front teeth – will upset him even more. But it's strange, something in the girl's voice stops him dead, and he starts watching the screen. All the same, I switch channels to a quiet programme about a family moving to the country, and sit at the table to give him his bottle. I make sure the milk is warm enough, and let him suck. And suck and suck, while his eyes roll sideways towards the TV, like he's hypnotized by this family moving into a converted chapel.

The whole time he sucks and swallows, I'm more sure than ever I was right. It's a crazy thing I've done, but I had to do it.

I look up. Lisa's stood in the doorway. Raising a freshly plucked eyebrow, she looks at Robbie. "I'm not imagining it then – I did hear something."

She picks up the cereal packet, looks at the picture on the front and bangs it down. "I don't like this stuff."

I force a smile. "If you hang on, I'll make some toast."

She pulls two slices of brown bread from the wrapper. "I'll do it," she says. Gives me a look: "Seems like you're a bit busy." She struggles with our awkward grill pan. "I hate brown bread."

She's determined not to actually look surprised. On and off she stares at me, waiting for the bread to toast. She turns it over, then gazes out of the window until it smells burnt. She fishes it out, blows on her fingers and flips a piece onto a plate. She nods at Robbie. "You'll give it indigestion."

"No I won't."

"You bloody will, you're shaking like a jelly. What's the matter with you?"

"Nothing."

Robbie burps. Casually, she looks more closely at him. "Anyway, whose is it?"

I don't answer, and she gets out the margarine. For a moment or two it seems she might not ask again.

She makes a mess spreading jam on her toast. "Does it have a name?"

I pretend I haven't heard; make it look like I'm too occupied checking the bottle to see how much Robbie's drunk.

She licks jam off her thumb. "This is well weird, Amy. I come down for something to eat; you're giving some baby its flippin' bottle – and you're not even bothered what it's called."

Suddenly I'm crying. "…*Lisa…help me.*"

She stops, the toast halfway to her mouth. "Help you?"

My nose is running and I give a big sniff. "I need you, Lisa."

"God, you look revolting. I'll make you a brew."

While she turns on the tap, I try to work out what I most need from her. "Promise you won't lose your rag?" I watch her fill the kettle. "All I want is for you not to say anything."

"About what?" She nods at Robbie. "Like I need ask. Anyway, who's wanting to know?"

"Everyone will want to know." I tug on the bottle to stop Robbie swallowing air. "I…" I search for the words and come out with the truth: "I snatched him."

She stares at me, her mouth open. "You *what*? Have you gone completely off your trolley?"

"I didn't have time to think. It was something I had to do."

"*Why?*"

"You wouldn't understand."

"So nobody knows it's here," she pauses, "except me." I can practically hear the cogs grinding. She fumbles for tea bags. Drops one on the floor. Finally she gets one in each mug. She half turns. "I don't have to stay, you know."

"Lisa – you've got to. You're going to have to visit Mum instead of me." Her eyes avoid mine. "Lisa, look at me – *please.* You have to stay…" My voice breaks: "If you don't, how can I look after the baby?"

She shrugs. "I can't see the problem – seeing as it's not yours to look after." She chews the inside of her cheek. "Anyway, what is it – boy or a girl?"

"A boy."

"Are you *ill* or something?"

"No."

"There must be something wrong. Nobody snatches a kid for nothing."

"This isn't nothing. This baby…" I desperately want to tell her the truth. "Lisa—"

She cuts me off and reaches for one of the mugs. "Here – drink your tea," she says and pushes it towards me. She takes a gulp from her own mug. "Okay, so you need me here."

Does this mean she'll stay?

She says, "I'm not promising anything definite."

"Stay until I've got things sorted." (*Until I'm certain Gina Smith can't ever be Robbie's mother.*)

She fixes me with a stare. "I'll want to know a few things. You needn't think you can keep me in the dark while I run your errands—"

I stop her. "I'm not expecting that!" I pick up my purse from the table. "But right now this is urgent – can you go into town, please? Get nappies and formula." I glance at the bag of dog food and decide we've got enough to be going on with.

"How will I know what to get?"

I look at the spare nappy, at the number giving its size – one up from when I last changed Robbie. He's growing so fast! I know what formula Mrs Kelly uses and tell Lisa I'll write it down for her.

She shuts the front door behind her. The phone rings. I worry Robbie will cry, but he's falling asleep, satisfied after his feed. Before I pick it up, I let it ring another couple of times. "Hello?"

It's Kirsty. "Amy. Something *terrible*—"

"What?"

"It's little Robbie – someone's taken him."

Careful. "How d'you mean, *taken* him?"

"Last week Mum arranged for Mrs Smith to take Robbie to the shops today. And what does the idiot do this morning? Leaves the poor little thing outside for someone to run off with! Mum's beside herself. Well, everyone is."

"Mrs Smith left him *outside*?"

"She's mad."

"God, Kirsty, this is awful." And then I say – because Mr Beecroft is bound to describe me, and anyway I'll be on CCTV – "I was in the post office first thing."

"Did you see anything?"

I'm wobbling, feeling for the chair behind me. *What the hell have I done? I'm the mad one – they'll never let me see Robbie again.* "No, nothing."

"The police are here – trying to get some sense out of Mrs Smith."

I hear talking in the background and she says, "Sorry, Amy, I'll have to go—" And her phone goes down.

I picture the scene at the Kellys'. The police wanting a description of Robbie. Everyone sick with worry. Mrs Smith a gibbering wreck. Thank God she didn't see me.

I want to change Robbie's nappy, but it would wake him. I wish I'd remembered to ask Lisa to get baby wipes.

Toffee is keeping me sane. I talk to him all the time. Forcing the words aloud – even softly – is like a pain around my heart. I tell him how awful the Kellys must be feeling. And Mr Smith. He'll have heard by now, and be feeling terrible for Mrs Smith. I don't like to think of him suffering again. He's had enough sadness.

Lisa's made record time. She's back with the nappies and formula. Another thing I forgot is something to sterilize the bottle. The *one* bottle. From now on, I'll boil it.

It's like she's enjoying the drama. "Buying all this stuff – I'm dead sure they were onto me in Boots."

"Don't be daft, how could they be?"

"Bad news travels fast. Everybody's talking in town." She takes a deep breath, hangs onto my quick glance. We're eye to eye. "This baby's the one they found in the shoebox. This is Robbie, isn't it? The one on the Kellys' doorstep." She narrows her eyes. "But you knew that, didn't you? Why didn't you tell me?"

How can I feel physically sick and sound almost normal at the same time? "I'm sorry, Lisa, I wasn't ready."

"Wow," she says, "we gotta watch the local news. It's bound to be on." She's bought a bottle of cider and pours us both a glass. I don't usually drink but I can do with something right now. Lisa says, "How did you nick him without anyone noticing?"

I drink some of the cider. "I don't know. It was easy."

"And no one saw you?"

"I had my hood down. There were some lads outside. It could've been one of them."

She shakes her head, like she thinks I'm dead thick. I say, "Lisa – Robbie'd been left outside in the pouring rain. I acted instinctively!"

"If you were that worried about him getting wet, why didn't you take him back to the Kellys'? Why bring him here?"

I don't answer.

"Why here, Amy, and not the Kellys'?"

I drink quite a lot of the cider. "There's this woman who wants to adopt him. *She* put him outside the shop. She's not fit to be a mother. I can't let her have Robbie."

Lisa pretends to look thoughtful. "And you reckon," she says, "if she doesn't see him for a bit, she'll go off the idea."

She's putting me through it. I look helplessly at her. "I don't know."

She drains her glass and pours herself some more. She raises the glass. "Okay – I'll help you."

She digs deeper. Why *did* I bring Robbie here? When I tell her more – how Mrs Smith wants to let Mr Smith's mother die – she can't see the connection. "Amy," she says, "you've got to stop spending your life worrying about other folk. Start thinking about Number One for a change."

"That's what I am doing."

"No, you're not." She pauses. "Plus, you're sticking your nose in where it's got nothing to do with you."

"It's got everything to do with me!"

"Like what?"

I hesitate. "You wouldn't understand."

"Too right I wouldn't." She sighs heavily, like she's doing some serious thinking. "Let's look at this one more time," she says, "before you come to your senses and give the kid back to Mrs Kelly."

"I've done it now, Lisa. I abducted him."

"No you didn't, you took pity on him because he was out in a storm."

"It wasn't exactly a storm."

"Near enough," she says, "and afterwards – realizing what you'd done, you just…" She trails off.

"Panicked and forgot to give him back?"

"Yeah, exactly!" she says. "Look – you did what you

thought was right, and now you're in shock." She scratches her head. "Whatever happens, you'll only get a caution."

"I can't let Robbie go."

She takes a swig of cider. "For God's sake, you sound like a bloody song!" She leans over and prods Robbie. "Anyway, what's the kid to you?"

I pull him closer. "He's mine."

She starts using exaggerated, measured words. "You... mean...because you're keeping this baby out of Cruella de Vil's clutches...you're starting to believe he's yours to keep." She sniggers. "Like, a baby is for life – not just for Christmas."

I take a slow breath. "He's mine, Lisa. I gave birth to him. In my room, in my bed. On June the third."

"You what...?"

"You heard me, Lisa."

"But you..." She dries up like she's forgotten how to speak. A muscle twitches in her jaw. She's not sniggering now. Her mouth opens like a fish. It's as if she wants to carry on, but invisible bubbles come out instead of words.

We're silent. I look out of the window. Two seagulls surf the wind.

She sits down, looks at me like I'm bound to say something if she waits. But my mouth's as dry as dust.

Eventually she finds her voice. "...And you never said anything to Mum?"

"No."

She starts burbling, wants to know everything. When did I realize I was pregnant? When I tell her I didn't know, she pretends to explode with disbelief: how can anyone be that simple?

She wants every detail, again and again – until I remind her about afternoon visiting; she'll have to take Mum's stamps.

I can't eat anything, but Lisa washes down a bowl of cereal with the last of the cider. I worry about her breathing cider over the nurses, tell her to suck mints from the hospital shop before she goes up to the ward. She can tell Mum I'm not well. Nothing serious; a bug or something.

I make her swear she won't say a word to Mum about Robbie. I promise her she's the only one who knows.

"*They'll* all know what happened," she says. "The whole friggin' hospital."

Desperation grips me. "But they don't know Robbie is *my* baby. And they won't, unless you shoot your mouth off."

She says, "Okay, keep your wool on," and runs her tongue round her lips. "Does the father know?"

"No."

She says, "Who was it?" I shrug and she says, "Like I can't guess. That soft kid, Liam."

Okay, so she knows. But I'm not ready to say his name out loud.

Chapter Thirty

Lisa's back. Mum has heard about Robbie and she's deeply upset. Who could do such a terrible thing? Guilt piles up on me. How could *I* do such a terrible thing? How could I, in the heat of the moment, without stopping to think, do something that's causing so many people such pain?

Lisa says, "Mum sends her love – says she knows how you must be feeling about Robbie."

I feel awful all over again. "Poor Mum."

"Poor Mum nothing, she's coming home soon."

"Oh – what a relief!"

"Yeah – well, she can't stay there for ever."

Then it all hits me. Robbie and me. Me and Mum. Mum, me and Robbie. It's like I'm up against a stone wall with Gina Smith sat on top, laughing. If only she'd climb down and walk out of our lives and… And what? That's the trouble: I don't know.

Lisa's not too bothered. If it all comes out, it all comes out. And I should stop worrying because there's nothing

I can do about it. I don't think I ever wished I was Lisa before. But I do now. Well, almost. For once, she's the one with a clear conscience.

She's gone upstairs to the loo. Robbie (asleep in his buggy), and I are having a quiet moment. I wait for the cistern to flush, but it doesn't. Instead, Lisa's footsteps fly down the stairs – until she trips, swearing, on the last two. "Friggin' police car heading this way!"

My voice is just a squeak. "How d'you know?"

"Saw it from upstairs."

"How near?"

"Too near."

Now we both hear it. A car slowing down outside.

"Oh my God, Lisa." My heart's on a trapeze. "Take Robbie out the back. Keep him out of sight."

She freezes like she'll never move again. "It's still raining," she says, "he'll get wet." I'm about to hit her when something switches her on: "I can pull up the plastic hood," she says and whips the buggy round and out through the back door into the yard. A moment later I hear the rickety gate close.

I check the kitchen. Stuff the empty cider bottle under the sink. Then, just as there's a knock at the front door, I spot the tin of formula on the draining board and shove it in the oven.

Looking round one more time, I go to the door with Toffee. I don't rush, I need to look calm. There are two police officers, one a woman PC – quite pretty – and a tall man with a pudgy nose and glasses. They show their identity cards. For me their uniforms are enough, but they tell me their names and the police station they work from. Which I immediately forget. They smile. The woman PC bends down to make a fuss of Toffee. "Have we got the right house for Amy Preston?" They know my name. They've come for me.

"I'm Amy." My heart's still thudding – with the worry that Lisa won't disappear fast enough in her stupid stilettos.

The policeman says, "It's a bit wet out here, all right if we come in?"

I step back and they stand in the hallway, looking around. The woman says, "Are you alone?"

"Only for a minute. My sister's popped to the shops."

"You won't mind if we ask you a few questions?"

I wonder if I ought to say I've guessed what it's about. That Kirsty called me. But before I can make up my mind, they tell me – like I won't have heard – about a serious crime at the post office; that I'm recorded on CCTV and they hope I might have seen something that could help. Telling them I bought a couple of items, I lead them through into the kitchen.

To say I'm on edge doesn't begin to describe it. Toffee makes it even worse by sniffing at their trouser legs. I pull him back by the collar and twiddle his ears. The woman

PC brings out a photograph. "This baby boy is missing," she says, and holds out the photo. "He was last seen in his buggy outside the post office." She pauses. "Did you see him at all?"

I don't want to take the photo from her, but she seems to expect it. My hand shaking, I take hold of it. The shiny paper quivers as I stare into Robbie's little face. I say, "I only saw the buggy." I swallow hard and look her in the eye.

I'm about to tell her about Kirsty calling me, but she's talking again. "It's shocking, isn't it? A little scrap like this—"

I butt in. "Robbie is *such* a gorgeous baby." Then, because I think I might get trapped in a corner, I say, "Actually...my friend Kirsty Kelly called me earlier."

"Ah," she says, "two of our colleagues have been with the family this morning."

Somehow I think it's good these two aren't the same officers. I give the photo back. She says. "You're clearly very upset," she says, "would you like to sit down?"

"No, it's all right. It's just I see Robbie quite a lot when I go to Kirsty's. It's awful to think of no one knowing where he is."

The policeman's voice is flat, expressionless. "Except whoever took him, of course."

The woman PC says, "With you being in the post office this morning, it's possible you can add something to information we already have."

I have to ask. It seems natural. "I realize I must have been on CCTV, but how did you know it was me?"

"Strangely enough," says the policeman, "the woman looking after the baby – Mrs Smith – recognized you."

I say, "Really?" and pray I don't look as frightened as I feel. "That's funny – I didn't realize it was her. Was it really Mrs Smith?"

He looks over his glasses at me. "Oh, yes. No question of that."

I say, "You see, she had a mac on. You know – with a hood?" I chew my lip, like I'm sorry for not being more helpful. "If I'd known it was her I'd have said hello." I pause. "Not that I know her very well. I know Mr Smith better. He's my form tutor."

The woman says, "Oh, right," then adds, "she spotted you when you almost forgot to pay."

The policeman takes a notebook from his breast pocket. I'm surprised how calm I sound, telling them how I bought stamps from Mr Beecroft, then cereal. I don't ask, of course – but I'm wondering if the CCTV followed me round. I decide it's best to seem as open as possible. "I nearly fell over twenty-four bottles of salad cream."

"Ah, we didn't see that," says the policeman.

Toffee, relaxed, has flopped down with his head on his paws and I feel slightly less like I'm falling apart. "I was looking for cereal. We were clean out of it."

The woman PC says, "Did you find some?"

"Yes."

The policeman says, "Did you notice anything unusual?"

"Like what?"

He coughs. "Just generally. I'm not referring to the cereal."

Does he think I'm daft? "Only that Mrs Goodge wasn't there today." I pause and frown a little. I'm gaining confidence. "Wait a minute. Yes, there were lads outside – probably from school – though I didn't see them too clearly."

The woman this time. "How many?"

I pause again. "Three, I think. I'm not totally sure."

She says, "Did you see anyone with a buggy?"

I nod. "Only the woman – Mrs Smith. She came in with a buggy, but after she was told to take it out I didn't see it again. I was kind of concentrating on who was outside."

The policeman says, "So – even though you were concentrating, you're not sure how many lads you saw."

Is he trying to trip me up? "Well – perhaps I wasn't *exactly* concentrating. Maybe I just noticed them. Like you spot things going on around you."

The woman nods, while he writes in his notebook. "Right. So you saw Mrs Smith come into the shop with a buggy—"

I risk interrupting him. "Though I didn't realize it was Mrs Smith."

"Agreed," he says, "and next you saw her park the buggy outside—"

"I didn't actually *see* her park it—"

"Okay." He pauses. "Did you see her come back in without the buggy?"

"Er – yes." I frown hard, like I very much want to help, and the woman PC nods in an understanding way. I say, "It was unfortunate, really. The guy standing in for Mrs Goodge – she's away on holiday – didn't want the buggy in the shop. He told Mrs Smith he was expecting a delivery."

The policeman says, "So you overheard the conversation?"

"It wasn't a conversation as such. She just did what she was told and put the buggy out in the rain." I give a little shrug. "I wasn't eavesdropping."

The woman PC says, "That's not implied."

The policeman ticks something in his notes. "I think we understand."

I say, "He *made* Mrs Smith take the buggy outside. I thought he might help her over the step with it, but he didn't."

The woman says, "How old are you, Amy?"

"Sixteen."

"Still at school?" she says.

"Yes, I'm going back in September."

"Starting to think about your A levels, eh?" She grins.

"Ever thought about joining the police force?"

"I haven't, no. I don't think I'm the type."

Toffee must feel his short rest is long enough. He yawns and pushes up onto his haunches. And I notice what he's been lying on...

...The Huggies wrapper Mrs Kelly must have folded round Robbie's spare nappy.

They musn't see it. I have to make them look somewhere else. The cooker, the door to the hallway, anywhere. The window...

Taking a step towards Toffee, I say, "Looks like the rain's letting up."

It's too easy really, the way they follow my gaze. "You've got a nice location here," says the policeman.

I say, "Yes, we're very lucky," and slide my foot under Toffee's belly. Bending down to stroke him, I scrunch the wrapper up in my hand. I'm putting it casually into the bin when the woman PC says. "Mum at work, is she?"

"No, she's in hospital."

Her face creases with sympathy. "I'm sorry to hear that."

"She ought to be coming home before long. Actually, I was about to do out her room."

"Well then," she says, "we'd best be getting out of your hair."

They're making for the hallway when Lisa comes through the back door. She laughs, all vivacious. "Now then, our Ames!" she says. "You didn't tell us you were entertaining."

Although I'm thinking, *For God's sake, where's she left Robbie?* I say, "This is my sister, Lisa."

The policeman looks like they've done the job they came for, but the woman says to Lisa, "I hear your mum's in hospital. I'm sorry to hear that."

"Yeah," says Lisa, "she's been dead poorly, but she's on the mend."

"Good," says the policeman. He turns to me. "Thanks for your help, Amy." Is it my imagination, or is he looking at Lisa like he's beginning to think he might have seen her somewhere before – like sloshed, with too few clothes on? Whatever, he doesn't say anything and ushers his colleague to the door.

Waving goodbye, I manage to smile.

And they go.

I shut the front door, and hiss at Lisa – who's followed me into the hallway – "*Where's Robbie?*"

"Out the back."

"Lisa, for God's sake—"

"It's okay, he's dead to the world."

I run to the back door. She's right, he's fast asleep. I wheel him into the kitchen, where I suddenly feel so weak I collapse into Mum's chair. I look at Lisa. "You took one *hell* of a risk."

"Kind of calculated."

"You could've wrecked everything."

"I'm sorry," she says. "If it's any consolation, I'm starting to feel a bit shaky."

"Join the club," I say, but my mouth's too stiff to smile. I'm in deep, deep trouble.

Chapter Thirty-one

Later, when I put Robbie upstairs – safely wedged on the bed with pillows, so there's no risk he'll suffocate – it's like he's meant to be here. I come down and turn on the TV. Lisa is in Mum's chair, leaning forward like her favourite film's about to start. I sit on a stool. Toffee settles at my feet.

This is it… The local news – with Robbie's dear little face filling the screen. Mr and Mrs Kelly are sat behind a table with a police officer – a lot more senior-looking than the one who came here. His account of what happened this morning has a lot to do with what I said earlier, though they don't mention my name.

Lisa's eyes bulge. "They don't know nothing, do they?"

Now it's Mrs Kelly's turn. She straightens her shoulders. "Whoever you are, please come forward. Bring Robbie back. Please think carefully about what you're taking on: a young baby who needs expert care. Are you able to cope?" She pauses. "If you are Robbie's mother – all the more reason to get in touch. We need to talk urgently. There are people waiting to help you." Another pause. "If you're Robbie's mother, or a friend, or anyone with information – don't waste another moment. The number to call is here on the screen. Just pick up the phone."

The police officer thanks the Kellys. It's over, and now there's the weather forecast.

Lisa says, "Where was the damn CCTV tape?" She looks genuinely disappointed. "You've been robbed of your film debut." She's silent for a moment, then stretches out a foot to prod me. "They really want the kid back. If this Mrs Smith was that bad, she wouldn't be in the running to adopt him."

"He's mine."

"Okay – but you can't look after him. Not for much longer. I mean – what have you got? One packet of nappies and a small tin of milk powder." She stops, and it looks like she might actually be trying to sort her head out. "What would this do to Mum," she says, "her knowing you had a kid? She's been very ill, Amy. What would it do to her?"

Her comments hit me so hard I start crying. Worse, I *wail*. Toffee jumps up, barking.

Lisa grabs my shoulders. "Amy – shut *up*!" She lowers her voice. "There's someone at the back door."

I pull myself together. "Quick, get upstairs to Robbie and please – *please* – keep him quiet."

She runs from the kitchen, while I hide the buggy in the front room. There's another knock, but I wait – making sure Lisa's safely in my room. I'm the one Robbie knows: should I have made Lisa answer the door? Should it be me checking on him? Too late now though, and I open the back door.

Shaun fills the doorway. "Hi, Amy." He's carrying an old leather tool bag. "Now the rain's stopped I'll fix your gate."

I step outside. "Oh right. Good. Thank you."

Head bent, he eyes me closely. "You all right?" He pauses. "You know – what with everything?"

"I'm okay."

He's noticed I'm puffy-eyed. "No worries, then?"

"I'm fine, Shaun."

He pulls open the bag. "Top man, Mr Kelly. Lending me his stuff. He even went out to get a new hinge."

There's still a stiff breeze; I brush a curl out of my eye. "You look like you know what you're doing, Shaun."

He starts prising off the old hinge. "Shocking, isn't it?"

I say, "The latch looks rusty too…"

He looks at me oddly. "I'm talking about baby Robbie."

My heart lurches. "Yes – it's just been on telly."

"I couldn't watch." He pauses. "Poor Mrs Kelly. It's hard on her, is this." He looks down for a second, scrabbles in Mr Kelly's bag and finds what he wants. He glances at me. "Who'd do a thing like that – walk off with a kid?"

"Shaun – whoever took him today must have wanted

him." The hinge comes away from the gate post, and I add, "Probably desperately."

Shaun says, "D'you reckon?"

"They must have done, mustn't they?"

He positions the new hinge. "Mrs Kelly thinks it could've been a lad fetching him back for the birth mother. You know, the girl who—"

"I know who you mean."

He stops what he's doing. Holds my gaze; won't let it go. "It could have been her, Amy. She could've wanted Robbie so much, she…" He trails off and swaps one screwdriver for another. "What do *you* think?"

"I don't think anything, Shaun. I left before the buggy disappeared."

He holds two screws between his lips, then takes one of them and starts screwing it through the new hinge. At least it stops him talking. But it doesn't stop him looking from me to the screw – and back again.

He tightens the screw with a final twist, takes another from his mouth. "I saw you."

My stomach turns to water. I manage a little laugh. "No one saw me, Shaun. I dashed home like mad, it was chucking it down. There was no one about – I didn't see anyone, let alone you."

He fishes in the bag again, finds a tool with a sharp point and starts making a fresh hole for the next screw. "I'm not talking about today."

Memories clutch at me. I feel the pain of that night, squatting behind the hedge, holding Toffee down. The small window upstairs at Kirsty's. A single light switched on. Which I'd thought must be Mr Kelly in the bathroom because he'd been the one to come to the door so fast. Mr Kelly who saw Robbie first. Who picked him up and called out to Kirsty's mum.

I watch Shaun give the screw a little shove into the hole. He screws it firmly home, then locks eyes with me. I can't look away.

Oh, how I want to tell him. "Shaun—"

He opens and shuts the gate, testing the fit. "Would you like me to tell someone? You know, about…"

This could be a life-changing moment. I swallow. But I can't string the words together. He's looking at me. Hard. At last I speak. "Who would you tell?"

"Mrs Kelly?"

We're silent for a few moments, then there's a cry from upstairs. It's very faint, but Shaun hears it and looks up at the bedroom window.

I say, "Yes, all right. Mrs Kelly."

Did I really say that?

He says, "I'll say I saw you leave Robbie that night, and you've got stuff to tell her. Is that okay?"

"Yes."

*

Shaun stayed for a bit, then went back to the Kellys'. That must be almost an hour ago, and I'm sat here with Lisa and Robbie, waiting for something to happen. A car stops outside. I say to Lisa, "Will you look – see if it's her?"

"Okay."

I'm holding Robbie. Toffee trots after Lisa. She opens the front door a crack, says over her shoulder, "Mr Kelly's here as well."

I go to the door.

They get out of the car and come up the path. Lisa moves aside, and I wait on the step with Robbie in my arms. It seems quite natural, the way things happen: Mr Kelly takes Robbie from me and hands him to Lisa. Mrs Kelly takes me in her arms and holds me close.

Mr Kelly follows Robbie and Lisa into the hallway. Mrs Kelly says, "Frank, why don't you and Lisa take Robbie into the front room?"

Mrs Kelly leads me into the kitchen. She says, "I'll put the kettle on, shall I? Make a brew." There's already water in the kettle. All she has to do is switch it on. She turns round. "So blood's thicker than water, eh?"

I think, yes, it definitely is.

"You're a courageous kid," she says. "There's not many would go to such lengths."

I'm confused: surely she can't be pleased with me. "How d'you mean?"

Slowly, she shakes her head. "She had me well and truly fooled."

"Who did?"

"Your Lisa...I didn't have an inkling. I would never have guessed, not in a hundred years. She didn't give herself away for one single second, not even when you both came over for tea in the garden."

"Mrs Kelly – Lisa didn't know anything. Not until today. It was Shaun. He worked it out because he'd seen me. That night, outside your house."

The tea's forgotten, she looks at me in disbelief. "You're not telling me Lisa had no idea *where* you were taking her baby?"

I can't go on. I'm floundering. Drowning. "Mrs Kelly—"

"Yes, love?"

"Robbie's my baby. Not Lisa's."

The kettle switches itself off. Mrs Kelly's voice is a whisper. "*Yours*, Amy?"

"I never looked pregnant. I didn't know I was. It was a shock, a terrible shock."

There are tears in her eyes. "Oh, my dear girl."

"You were the only one I could think of that night. To take him to... I'm sorry."

"Thank God, Amy. Thank God you thought of me." For several seconds we look at each other, then Robbie cries in the front room. I use the water in the kettle to warm the bottle I made up earlier. Mrs Kelly watches me. Is she remembering how she taught me to do this? I make for the door. "I'll ask Mr Kelly to feed him, shall I?"

When I get back, Mrs Kelly is refilling the kettle. What is it about kettles? There are always kettles. Needing to be filled, needing to be poured.

We sit down. Mrs Kelly says, "Would you like to tell me about it?"

"Everything?"

"If you like," she says. "If it would help."

So I tell her everything. Except about Liam; though she's bound to have realized. I tell her about this morning. I tell her how – running through the rain – I was more sure than ever that I had to keep Robbie away from Gina Smith.

She asks the big question, the one I'm waiting for: "Amy – your mum. Does she know?"

I squeeze the word out: "*No…*" And take a shaky breath. "She saw Robbie when you brought him here… She has no idea who he is."

Mrs Kelly looks around. "Where d'you keep your tea bags?" I show her, and where we keep the teapot we hardly ever use. She pours boiling water on the tea bags. "It'll be very, very hard for your mum," she says, "but she needs to know. She'll want to support you – with whatever you decide."

"I want him with me." I can't stop the tears. I feel like a kid. "I stole him though. They'll take him away, won't they?"

"Amy, love – I don't know." She comes over, takes my hands in hers. She speaks slowly, quietly. "You're not in the best position, are you? Still at school. And your mum… Well…with the best will in the world she wouldn't be able to cope with a baby all day."

"There's Lisa."

"Mmm." She hesitates. "…I take it young Liam's the dad." I nod, and she says, "And so far away."

"I don't want him to know."

She says nothing. And I say nothing. I'm hoping she feels like me, that telling Liam could be a massive mistake.

I hope she'll understand what I have to say next. I look into her eyes. "I can't bear it – the thought of Mrs Smith adopting Robbie. I *can't* let that happen. If it wasn't for her, I wouldn't have run away with him this morning. She's awful – I know what she's like." I gulp through my tears. "She actually thinks it would be best if Mr Smith's mother was dead." Then I remember promising Kirsty I wouldn't say anything. I need just one more lie. "Someone overheard her at the hospital."

Mrs Kelly raises her eyebrows. "Or a little bird told you? …Amy, love, I think you may have got Mrs Smith all wrong." She sighs. "She's supporting her husband through a very sad time… One way or another, I see her as a young woman who badly needs something to go her way at last. Between you and me, it's been tough for her over the past few years. It's been tough for both of them." She touches my cheek, finds a tear to wipe away. "Until yesterday they were facing the most difficult decision of their lives. Then, last night, it was virtually taken out of their hands."

"How?"

"Mr Smith's mother suffered another stroke – and as their last kindness, he and Gina let her go."

"And *all* she can do, the day after his mum dies, is think about taking Robbie out. Couldn't she have waited?"

"It was prearranged, Amy – and Mr Smith, particularly, didn't want to take this special time away from Gina. We felt it would help them both."

I'm quiet. I'm still finding it hard to see where kindness comes in. "If they truly loved her, wouldn't they do everything in their power to save her?"

"Amy, she was already very sick."

"But you're always hearing that if strokes are treated early, people can lead happy lives."

"In her case, Amy—"

"And how parts of the brain step in and take over from the damaged parts. People recover their speech. There are TV ads telling you what to look out for and how you should act quickly. Wouldn't you have thought – being in hospital – she'd have stood every chance?"

Mrs Kelly shakes her head. "Of course we can never be a hundred per cent certain about anything – but I don't think so. Last night's stroke was…" She frowns. "The deciding factor." She puts out a hand to me. "I understand the way you feel, Amy – absolutely – but I'm as sure as I can be that the Smiths have done the right thing. And knowing what I know about Gina, I'm certain it will have been terribly hard for her, helping Andrew come to the right decision."

While she takes the others their cups of tea, I sit quietly – listening to them talking. I'm glad I'm alone. I have to think. I'm not thinking differently about Robbie, I want him as much as ever. But I'm thinking differently about Mrs Smith – partly after everything Mrs Kelly said. And even more, though I'd been trying to forget it, because of her baby that died.

Mrs Kelly comes back into the kitchen, and while Mr Kelly and Lisa stay in the front room, she asks if I've thought how I'm going to break it to Mum – that Robbie is my baby.

Would I like her to help me? I don't know what to say. I don't know which will be worse for Mum: having me or someone else telling her. Mrs Kelly asks if I'd like her to come to the hospital with me. When I say I need a little while to think about this, she says, "Tomorrow, I think, don't you?" and I realize tomorrow is only a few hours away.

The Kellys get ready to take Robbie back with them. Apart from him, there's not a lot to take. Only his buggy, his bottle, a packet of nappies and the tin of formula. Just as I'm beginning to get a sinking feeling at seeing him go,

Mrs Kelly says, "Amy, you come with us. I'll have to contact Social Services and talk to the police again, which means you may need my support. I think it would be as well if we were all together."

It's clear Lisa doesn't want any part in this. Doing a vanishing act with Robbie has probably stopped feeling like a scene in a TV soap. "I'll stay behind," she says, "and look after Toffee."

Chapter Thirty-two

When we arrive at the Kellys', Kirsty is out with Jordan. I'd been dreading facing her, so it's like I've been given extra time...though I know this is only temporary. I don't know how Mrs Kelly keeps so calm. She's incredible, dealing with Social Services and the police – telling the sergeant who came round that she's only thankful Robbie is back with her, safe and sound. She even manages to plant the idea that this evening isn't a good time to add to my worries; that there'll be time for explanations soon enough.

I've been worried to death Mum might hear about Robbie before I get a chance to talk to her, but the police say they won't release information of any kind until tonight. Mrs Kelly asks their permission to call Mr and Mrs Smith. She says she's sure she can trust them to keep the news to themselves.

Now, I have to get my head round telling Mum.

The police say they can't "condone" what I did, and it's

lucky I'm not older. If I was, they'd be dealing with me a lot more firmly. It's odd: they seem to have the idea that I don't understand the meaning of responsibility. I think it's exactly the opposite: it's being utterly committed to Robbie, to his care and happiness, that made me act like someone gone mad.

Mrs Kelly is understanding enough to let me come home for the night. So – okay – I'm a coward: I don't have to see Kirsty just yet. Luckily, Lisa's indoors with Toffee and acting like a reasonable human being.

Next morning, when we get to the hospital, Mrs Kelly attracts the attention of the sister at the nurses' station. "We'd like to speak to Mrs Preston – in private, please."

The sister nods, puts a tick on the paperwork she's dealing with, and strides off to the ward.

I say to Mrs Kelly, "Mum was in a side room before, they must have moved her."

Mrs Kelly frowns. "That's a shame."

The sister returns. "You can go in, there's no one with her." She smiles. "All being well, she'll be able to go home tomorrow."

Mrs Kelly says, "Oh, marvellous."

I say, "Is she well enough?"

The sister looks serious. "Let's keep our fingers crossed." Tears prick my eyes – which she notices. "Of course she's well enough," she says, "we wouldn't let her go if she wasn't." As I move away, she pats my arm.

We stand in the doorway to the ward. There are six beds, three on each side. Mum's is on the left at the end, nearest the window. She spots us and smiles happily. I feel like the biggest traitor that ever lived. I hurry to the bed and kiss her. "So you're coming home!"

"Yes, tomorrow, all being well – I can't wait. Mind you, by the time the doctor's been, and all the forms have been filled out, it won't be till the afternoon. They say getting out of here takes for ever."

Mrs Kelly says, "Lindy – d'you mind if I pull the curtains round?"

Mum smiles. "Not if you'd like to."

Mrs Kelly draws the curtains. "Amy," she says, "bring that chair over. I'll sit on this one."

I bring the chair across and sit down. The three of us are in a cocoon of pink and green tartan, and I have no idea how we're going to tell Mum about Robbie. I'm still waiting for Mrs Kelly to start, when Mum says, "What's this then, a mothers' meeting?"

Mrs Kelly says, "Lindy. I've come with Amy…because we need to talk about something important… Something difficult."

Mum's face loses its brightness. "Have Social Services been nosing about?"

Mrs Kelly looks puzzled. "No. Why would they?"

Then – just in time – Mum remembers Mrs Kelly believes Lisa lives with us permanently. Mum says, "Don't mind me, it's just my imagination running riot."

I take a breath, and when I say, "…Mum?" something in my voice alerts her.

"What is it, Amy?"

I look at Mrs Kelly. Her eyes are saying, *Be brave, go ahead,* and I say, "Mum, it's about little Robbie—"

Mum interrupts. "Oh, Amy, he's been found! Hadn't you heard?"

"Yes – I—"

"Safe and well. Isn't it wonderful? I felt absolutely sick—"

"Mum—"

"Do we know *where* he was found?"

My mouth's too dry to let me swallow properly. "…On Dune Terrace—"

"Good heavens! Whereabouts?"

"…At ours."

She's mystified. "Surely not at our house?"

I wish there was a less shocking way of telling her. "Yes, at our house." My heart thumps like it's trying to find a way out. "Mum…Robbie's…a special baby."

"Every baby's special, Amy." She frowns. "However did he get to be at our house?"

"I took him there."

She says, "I don't understand."

"It was me. I took him from outside the post office."

I want to tell her why, but there aren't the words.

Mrs Kelly feels for Mum's hand. She clears her throat. "Amy took Robbie home because…"

"Because what?"

"Because he's mine, Mum."

"*Your* baby?" Mum looks at Mrs Kelly, like there's a private joke between them. "I think we all know how fond you are of him, but—"

I stop her. "Mum – I really do mean *mine*. Robbie's my baby." With my next breath my voice cracks: "I didn't know I was pregnant. I'm sorry, Mum. So sorry. I know this is terrible for you." Tears sting my eyelids. "Terrible for everyone."

Mum opens her mouth to speak, but no sound comes out.

Mrs Kelly strokes Mum's hand. "Lindy – Amy is a wonderful girl."

"No, I'm not."

"Amy, you are."

"I'm *not*."

Mum takes a proper breath again. She says, "Make up your minds." And…we kind of laugh. This is hard to believe, but we do. All three of us. Not happy laughs, just nervous relieved sounds, like we're letting air out of a balloon that would have burst any second.

Mrs Kelly says, "I'll say what I was going to say. Amy is a wonderful girl, a girl who's come through the most difficult time imaginable."

Mum says, "When was…" She falters. "When was Robbie born?"

"June…the third." I can't help tears running down my cheeks. I lick them off my upper lip. "He was born at home, Mum. In the night. I left him at Mrs Kelly's." I crumple. "I'm sorry."

Mrs Kelly passes me tissues from the box beside Mum's bed.

I blow my nose. "I didn't know what was happening. I thought I'd got a bug. I didn't know there was a baby."

Mum leans forward, her head in her hands. I'm scared. Could she be ill again? No, thank goodness; she lifts her head, looks at me. "I suppose I'll look silly if I ask who's the…?"

I say, "Mum, it was Liam. I—" But I can't go on. Thinking of everything I've kept from her makes me go numb.

Mrs Kelly says quietly, "Shall we leave it there for now, Amy?" She looks at her watch. "If you trot along, you'll catch the half-past bus. I'll stay – spend some more time with Mum."

Mum reaches for her purse, but I say, "I've got change."

Mrs Kelly says, "Is it all right if I stay for a bit, Lindy?"

"I'd appreciate that. Thanks."

Mrs Kelly touches my arm. "Give Kirsty a call."

"She knows, doesn't she?"

Mrs Kelly nods. "Yes, but I'm sure she'll want to hear it from you."

Mum's eyes are like a magnet. I go to her. Put my arms round her. She pulls my head onto her shoulder. "I'm with you, sweetheart." Her lips brush my ear. "Every inch of the way."

Running down the stone stairs I'm already worrying about what I'll say to Kirsty, and thinking about Mum coming home tomorrow. I'll have to put pressure on Lisa, nag her into having Mum's room clean and tidy by the afternoon. I can manage the rest of the house. But I don't care, I'll need something to take my mind off the mess I've made of my life.

I barely notice people getting on and off the bus. My mind acts like a cinema screen. I rewind: watch myself telling Mum the enormous secret I never imagined I'd share with her. It's like my heart, just below my throat, is skittering with a strange kind of relief. As if I've jumped an enormous hurdle and landed safely. That's how I feel at the moment, though I'm not expecting it to last.

I'm right: even as the bus takes a sharp bend, the few minutes of calm start to evaporate and I'm wondering how Mum will cope with this bomb I've lobbed into her lap. In my mind, half of me sees her looking at me in shocked disbelief, while the other half sees Robbie in Mrs Kelly's arms, and I realize all over again how desperately I want to watch my child growing up.

Chapter Thirty-three

At the very instant I'm jumping off the bus, thinking of how I'm going to face Kirsty – a car draws up. The driver's window rolls down. "Hi, Amy!" My heart plummets. It's Mrs Smith.

It's no use pretending I haven't seen her; she's only a couple of metres away. She leans across the passenger seat and opens the door. She smiles widely, and I wonder how she can be feeling inside. "What a nice day," she says, "Better than yesterday!"

I think of her leaving Robbie out in all that rain.

She says, "Actually, Amy, this is a bit of luck…" The smile falters. "I badly need to talk to you." She makes sure the car door stays open.

I don't respond like I'm too keen, but I get in because I need to know what she thinks she's going to do – now she knows I'm Robbie's mother.

Before I've had time to think any further, she puts the car in gear and we pull away from the bus stop. I hadn't reckoned on us *going* anywhere else to talk, but before I know it we've passed Dune Terrace, driven into town and out again, and are passing through a sprawl of local authority houses.

Now we're in open countryside, and I'm getting worried. "Where are we headed, Mrs Smith?"

"You'll see," she says.

I'm exhausted. I'm not up for a mystery tour, and I wish she'd turn round and go back. To be honest, she scares me.

We're speeding along roads with high hedges. Now past fields of stubble and others already ploughed up. So far she's said nothing, and it makes me jump when she says, "How's Robbie?"

There's no hint in her voice of me being the cause of what she suffered yesterday, and it's a second or two before I say, "He's fine."

"How many bottles a day is he having?"

I wish I actually knew. "I'm not sure – as many as he needs."

"I've been thinking about how he's growing out of everything. Vests and babygrows, and so forth…"

"He's all right, he's got loads of stuff." My God, I sound like a sulky kid.

She says kindly, "I don't suppose your mum knits, does she?"

"Not much." Mum was never a knitter. Nana Kathleen was. If she was here she'd be knitting day and night.

"I'm knitting him a little waistcoat," she says. "It's red, in a blackberry stitch. Very sweet."

I feel sick. I ask her to stop the car. She slows down. Stops. I get out and lean against the door.

Looking worried, she switches off the engine. "Are you all right, Amy?"

"I'm not too good in cars. I sometimes get sick."

"Poor you – take a few deep breaths."

Staring through trees at a wildflower meadow, I tell her I'll be okay. Then I get back in the car.

"Better?" she says, and lets the handbrake off.

We leave the shady lane behind, and now there's open country with just a cottage here and there. We pass a church; now we're into a village – quite small. "Here we are," says Gina. "Won't be a tick." And she gets out to unlatch a gate. She swings it wide open, gets back in the car and parks up in front of a double garage.

She comes round to my door. "Welcome!" she says. "*Chez nous!*" I think this might be the name of their pretty house with lattice windows. (Rather like Nana Kathleen calling her bungalow *Bide-a-While*.) But it's not. The name over the door says *Orchard Cottage*.

I get out. There's nothing for it – I have to follow her to the house. She unlocks the front door. "Come in, Amy," she says, "there's something I want to show you."

All this is more than strange. Not telling me why I'm here, *and* she's acting odd – like she can't decide what voice to use. One minute she's edgy and tense, the next she's relaxed and happy.

"First though, come into the kitchen and I'll make some coffee."

I wait while she fills a kettle. She presses the button, then says, "Come upstairs, Amy." She smiles. "I've been longing to show it off... I'm so glad it's you."

She leads the way and I guess, from the number of doors on the landing, there must be three bedrooms. One of the doors is open. She says, "You'll love this," and I follow her inside. She waves an arm round the room. "The minute we moved here," she says, "we knew this was the right room for a nursery. It's not finished of course." She hesitates. "We played safe with colours." She gives a little laugh, looks me in the eye. "We started before we knew the sex of the baby."

Pots of pastel-coloured paint are stacked up, and rolls of nursery wallpaper lean against a wall. One is partly unwound and I see pictures of Jack and Jill and Little Bo-Peep. I'm not sure who I pity most. Me or Mrs Smith. Does she think this room will make me change my mind?

She smiles. "Don't you think any baby would be happy in here?"

You're not talking about any baby. You're talking about Robbie.

"Have a look," she says, "there's a lovely view from the window." I look out at a lawn, flower beds and, at the end of the garden, a small orchard. Beyond it there's a wood.

"Come downstairs," she says, which I think is a bit odd as we haven't been up here long. Still, perhaps that was all. She's shown me the room and I have a good idea of how it'll look when it's finished.

"We'll have a cafetiere for two," she says, and runs down ahead of me. She glances over her shoulder to make sure I'll follow. She smiles like she's a bit nervous, and I start coming down. In the kitchen she warms the glass jug and spoons ground coffee into it.

She lowers her voice. "I bought a carrot cake," she says, as if this is especially significant. She pauses. "Andrew's simply mad about it, but he won't begrudge us a couple of slices." She places pottery mugs ready on a tray, and pours hot water onto the coffee. Next minute, I'm following her back upstairs.

In the nursery, she puts the tray on the floor. "Would you close the door, please, Amy?" I do what she says, and we sit side by side on a roll of blue carpet. There's a brightly-coloured paper bag beside her. When she feels inside it, a jack-in-the-box jumps out. It's like one on TV that used to frighten me when I was little. She laughs. "Cute, isn't it!" she says, and pours me a mug of coffee.

When she starts cutting the carrot cake, the sight of the frosting makes me nauseous and I don't take the slice she offers me. However I have to do something, and though

261

there's no sugar on the tray, I start sipping my coffee.

Like she's read my thoughts, she says, "Oh, sorry! Do you take sugar?"

"It's okay, thank you. I quite like it without."

We're silent for a few moments before she says, "Amy, I know this is difficult for you."

I want to tell her my mind's made up – as much as I'm allowed to make it up. But I know she won't want to listen. She confirms my thoughts: "I've asked you here," she says quietly, "to what would be Robbie's nursery, to show you what a happy, tranquil start in life he'd have with me and Andrew." She looks around the room, then at me. "How does this feel?"

The midday sun fills the room, making diamond patterns on the floorboards. I imagine it shining on the nursery-rhyme wallpaper. I can hardly trust myself to speak. It's all I can do to say, "It's a really sweet room, Mrs Smith—"

She says, "Please. Call me Gina."

"It's lovely."

Her hand is on my arm. "Amy, I want to make you a solemn promise." She takes two slow breaths. "Andrew and I would *love* your little boy for the rest of our lives."

"Mrs Smith, I—"

Her beautiful eyes are fixed on me. I can't speak. She says, "Andrew and I – we'd never blame you. Not for anything."

"I had to—"

She shakes her head. "You don't have to explain."

I need her to understand. "I took him because I love him!"

She puts an arm around my shoulders, turns me to face her. "Of course you did. That and the love you've shown him on your visits to the Kellys' will stay with him for ever." Her eyes don't leave my face. "What better gift could you pass on…" She pauses. "…Before you give him up?"

This is more than I can cope with. Tripping over the jack-in-the-box, I stumble across the room and out onto the landing.

"Amy, love! I didn't mean to—"

I don't care what she did or didn't mean. I'm out of here.

I'm halfway down the stairs, and she's leaning over the banisters. "Amy—?"

I reach the bottom and try the front door but it won't open. I turn back and hurry along the hallway into the kitchen.

She's coming down the stairs. "Amy—"

I'm already on the back step. "I'm sorry – I need to get some air."

"That's all right," she says. "Of course. Have a look round the garden, it's Andrew's pride and joy. It'd be fantastic for Robbie. We'd put up a swing, and—"

Cutting her off, banging the kitchen door behind me, I want to *run* and keep on running, but I don't want to let her into my head, so I walk steadily across the lawn. I force myself to look at a vegetable patch and two compost heaps. I stop for a moment, take a deep breath of air – full of the scent of grass cuttings – then I walk, quite slowly, through the small orchard. Before I reach the wood at the end, I turn to look at the house. Mrs Smith is standing at the kitchen door. Even from here I can see the tension in her body.

She calls, "Amy! I—" but then I'm into a copse – running, and out of earshot before I hear what else she has to say. I swish through long grass, damp from yesterday. On the edge of the actual wood, the huge trees and ferny ground draw me in. Low-growing branches whip my jeans as I push my way through. I don't care if it's cool and sunless; it feels good here – away from Mrs Smith and her promise of Robbie's perfect future.

There's a rustle of leaves, but I can't see any sign of a bird and wonder what small animals live here. I imagine the wood coming alive at night with owls and badgers. The earth smells of walks I had with Liam – one especially, where we climbed a tree and sat hand in hand with our backs against a knobbly trunk. I was wearing a thin blouse, and sore marks showed up on my skin. Which afterwards he kissed. Remembering this blurs my eyes with tears.

I walk a little way along a barely visible narrow track. It's muddy, as if the sun never reaches it. When it comes to an end I stand still for a moment.

Just as I'm starting to wonder if I've been stupid enough to get lost, I hear Mrs Smith calling. Her voice is thin, like it can't find its way through the trees. "Amy! Where are you, Amy?" I stand stock-still and she stops calling. No way am I letting her take up where she left off; I can't cope with another word on the subject of my love for Robbie. Or his future with her and Mr Smith.

I push my way forward. The wood is getting darker, like the sun might have gone in. Brambles scratch my hand and I suck at beads of blood I can hardly see. For a few moments, while I don't move, it's wonderfully quiet. So peaceful. Until – quite close, though I can't see her – Mrs Smith calls again. "Amy! We need to talk!" Her voice causes a bird, high up, to squawk in panic and flap wildly in the treetops.

I hear her again, though not what she's saying. She's talking in an undertone. Twigs snap underfoot. Footsteps, but not *my* feet. Now, dammit, I've got something in my eye, and the footsteps keep on coming.

I squint with my good eye, and she appears in my line of vision. "Amy!" Holding back waist-high branches and lit by a freak ray of sun, she would look – if it wasn't for the mobile phone clamped to her ear – like a statue growing out of the greenery. She talks into her phone. "It's all right, I've found her."

I blink, and my eye clears.

She shakes her head at me. "You had me worried."

I try to smile. "Sorry. I lost sight of you. I had something in my eye."

"Let me have a look."

"It's okay, it's gone now."

"Good, then let's get you back to the house."

I've got no choice, and follow her back through the wood while she talks excitedly about rabbits and foxes. I traipse after her, hoping she won't tell me she's bought Robbie a box set of Beatrix Potter tales.

We sit at the kitchen table, and she tells me she just spoke to Mr Smith. "He's been to the funeral director's," she says.

"I'm sorry. It's very sad."

After a moment she says, "His mother had looked forward to grandchildren for years. She would have loved Robbie."

I think of Mum and how fond she is of Robbie. And how, for his sake, she might be unselfish enough to let another granny take her place. Grief wells up in me, and I feel my face distorted by hot tears. Before I know it Mrs Smith is behind me, her arms falling over my shoulders and her hands turning my head so my nose is pressed into her breast.

She strokes my hair back from my face. "Amy – dear Amy – I promise you faithfully – Andrew and I..." Her arms stiffen and she trails off, listening. My neck hurts, and just as I have difficulty taking another breath,

I hear it. A key in the front door.

I want to speak, but I can't. Someone else does, though – and he's standing in the doorway. "Oh, Gina," he says. She lets go of me and he comes across the kitchen to take her in his arms.

Holding her close, Mr Smith looks at me over her head of shining hair. His voice is full of pain. "Amy, I'm so sorry."

I can't quite believe I'm with Mr Smith, in his car, on my way home. It's almost surreal and I wonder if I've been given this space to think again. He and Mrs Smith in each other's arms in the kitchen. Robbie's nursery, the lovely garden. What am I doing, depriving him of this kind of life? Wouldn't everyone's troubles be over if I let go? Mum's, Mr and Mrs Smith's, Mrs Kelly's? Mine? And Robbie's – though for now he's perfectly happy and doesn't know the meaning of trouble.

Unexpected rain hits the windscreen, and I glance at Mr Smith's tanned hand flicking the wipers on, and at his clean-cut profile. I think how distressed he was for his wife. How loyal. Could I give Robbie up? Could I make this sacrifice?

We're home. He stops the car and comes round to open my door. I say, "Thank you for the lift, Mr Smith." Our eyes meet for a moment; his are so kind.

"You're welcome, Amy…and I'm sorry you've had

what must have been…" He gropes for the words. "…A stressful time."

He doesn't say anything else, but I can sense him watching as I turn my key in the lock.

Chapter Thirty-four

Home at last, and indoors I make a sandwich each for me and Lisa, then I call Kirsty to say I need to come over. She doesn't say much – just, "Okay then, see you in a bit."

I tell Lisa where I'm going, and ask her to keep an eye on Toffee. The tide's coming in, and it's quite blowy. I wish it would clear my head of Gina Smith and the pretty nursery. I'd love to talk to Kirsty about it, though I don't know if I'd be able to put into words how I feel. How painful it is.

Shaun's in the garden with the kids, helping Mr Kelly clear up after a messy picnic lunch. Robbie's having a nap upstairs and Kirsty and I are in the kitchen. For a time it's awkward. She sits down at the table and carries on with what she was doing when I arrived – pinning a paper pattern onto some blue and white striped material. I ask what she's making.

She pulls a face. "A blouse. I hope."

"You don't do sewing."

"I know, but I thought I'd give it a try. Jordan likes blue."

I can't meet her eye, but I touch the material. "It feels nice."

She says, "Why didn't you tell me?"

How can I ever explain? I rub my forehead, like I can rub out my frown. "I wrote you a letter." I pause. "But I didn't send it."

"Why not?"

"Mostly because I didn't want to put you in a difficult position. You know, feeling you had a duty to tell someone." I pause. "I wrote it after I saw Robbie here. The afternoon Shaun cut my hair... I didn't think you'd ever speak to me again."

"You should've known me better than that. We could have talked about it. You might have felt better."

I'm with my best friend, yet my mouth is like sandpaper. "I know. I'm sorry." I watch her sticking pins through the paper pattern into the stripy stuff. "I lied from the beginning. I had to, because of Mum. Then somehow, I don't know, I couldn't undo them – the lies."

Kirsty pricks herself. "Ouch!" She sucks the speck of blood off her finger. She takes a breath and says, sounding almost like her mum, "D'you want to talk about it?"

I'm not sure if I do, and the next thing I know I'm

losing it. Tears squirt out of my eyes and I start making silly squealing noises. Kirsty leaps up, her chair crashing to the floor. Her arms go round me. Arms I know and love. Not Gina's.

I lick the tears off my lips. "I was such an idiot."

She lets go of me, pulls sheets off a kitchen roll, stuffs them into my hand. "Robbie's dad…" She puts her head on one side. "I don't have to ask."

I very nearly smile. She rights her chair and we both sit at the table. "Amy – you and me, we don't have secrets. Why didn't you tell me when you first knew you were pregnant?"

"I didn't know."

There's disbelief in her eyes. "You must have."

"I knew what I'd done, of course I did; I'm not that stupid. I even thought afterwards how mad I'd been to let it happen, that I hadn't meant to do it until I was on the pill. It just kind of happened. You know – in the heat of the moment?" Our eyes meet. "You think you're in control…" She waits for me to go on. "It's… overpowering."

"Didn't you wonder, when you missed a period?"

"No, because I'd been all over the place for ages. And anyway I thought—" I stop there; I don't want to admit how thick I must have been. "You know? I just didn't think I could get pregnant… Not the first time… How daft was that?"

"Amy?"

"Yes?"

"Mum was out when I got back." She glances out of the window. "Dad hasn't given me any details." She pauses. "So who knows about Robbie?"

I feel awkward, take a breath. "Well – your mum and dad, of course... The Smiths. Lisa, Shaun, my mum. Probably Mrs Wickham by now. Bloody everybody."

"*Shaun* knows?"

"Honestly, Kirsty, it's like he's got some sort of sixth sense." Then I think, *no more lies*, and say, "He saw me leave Robbie here."

The back door opens and Mr Kelly looks in. "Ah – I thought I heard voices." He looks at me. Perhaps he notices my eyes are red. "Everything all right?"

Kirsty says, "Fine. We're good – just talking."

He nods and goes back into the garden.

We're quiet for a moment, then Kirsty says. "That was quite a list of names...but no Liam."

I shake my head. Chew my cheek and break the skin.

She frowns. "Shouldn't he know?"

I shrug, though her question deserves more than that. Then I say – like I've told myself a thousand times – "I bet he'd rather not know."

"Amy, you can't be sure."

"One thing I *am* sure about: I don't want Robbie ending up in Australia."

She looks thoughtful, then voices my dread. "They might want to come back if they knew about Robbie." Clearly, my face says it all, and she touches my hand. "Would that be so terrible?" She pauses. "Apart from anything else, doesn't Liam have rights?"

"Don't I have rights *not* to tell him?"

She says, "Won't Social Services want to contact him?"

"Even if they do, they're not likely to recommend him as a better parent over me." A weight settles in my chest – how unsuitable we both must look.

I let my forefinger doodle on the table. With every second it gets clearer. Robbie has to stay with me... Though if anyone wants to fight me for him, I suppose Liam might have rights. But would he want to parent a child he'd known nothing about? I'm more or less dead certain he wouldn't.

Kirsty looks sad. "Liam was so *nice*."

I pick up the envelope of her blouse pattern, blink back more tears and put it down again. "I know, and I want to remember him that way." Thoughts that have lain quiet bubble to the surface. "Later on – if Robbie asked me about his dad – I'd want to tell him the good things."

"Of course you would."

"Like he was—" I can't help it: my shoulders start shaking. I put my head on the table and sob.

I feel Kirsty's hand on my back. "Like he was...?"

I grab enough air to speak. "That he was very young,

that he *tried* to understand about Mum and me... That he was a lovely guy."

Kirsty says, "I suppose your mum realized Liam's the dad."

I nod, then tell her how her own mum shocked me rigid by assuming Robbie was Lisa's baby. She lets this sink in, then folds her fabric pieces and puts the loose pins in a small blue box.

I tell her Mum's coming home tomorrow and that I need everything to be calm.

She sighs. "Your poor mum." She gets up, goes to the fridge and takes out a carton of fruit juice. "Amy, I don't want to sound unkind or anything, but if you don't have Robbie adopted or – God forbid, and I hate saying this – see him put on a plane for Australia...who'd look after him? *You* can't, because of school and your mum and – well, you just can't."

I swallow hard. "Thanks for reminding me."

She slowly pours orange juice into two glasses. "Did you know, if there's someone in the family who'd like to look after Robbie, they could apply to be a special guardian, and you'd be able to—"

I cut her off. "There isn't anyone. No one except Lisa, and I can't see that working out..." I watch her replace the top on the juice.

She turns to me. "There's something Mum and Dad were talking about last night after you'd gone home. Mum's friend knows about a kid in Morpeth whose gran has applied to be his special guardian."

"Can't she simply look after him without being a guardian?"

"There's more to it than that. I think the mother's a bit unreliable."

I give a short laugh. "Like she's sixteen and a complete mess."

Kirsty says, "Actually, she's fourteen."

I ask if she knows why the kid's not being adopted, and she says the family wants him to stay with them.

Something happens inside me. An explosion of hope. This sounds so perfect, it's like I'm suddenly on a high after too much black coffee. Pictures crowd in on me, and I imagine Mum and me looking after Robbie together. And as well – because it can't only be Mum – the guardian: someone, a vague figure – who only takes a moment to morph into Mrs Kelly. The thought – the fantasy – moves me so much I'm almost blubbing again.

Kirsty pushes a glass into my hand. It's icy cold.

When I get home, Lisa's faffing about, making a big deal out of washing up a couple of plates and a bit of cutlery. For once I'd rather she left it to me. I ask her if Mum's room is ready.

"I'll do it in a minute."

I shout at her, "*Do it now!*"

"Okay, okay," she says, and goes upstairs. Very slowly. To be fair, when I check, she's tidied up properly and moved her piles of stuff into my room. (Our room.) All I have to do is remake Mum's bed with clean sheets.

Later, I tear up my letter to Kirsty.

Chapter Thirty-five

When Mum arrived home, and almost before she'd had time to get used to it, Mrs Wickham called to say she'd like to come round for a chat. I worried like hell, praying she wouldn't sway Mum towards it being best for Robbie to be adopted. One minute I was in the depths, preparing for a life without him; the next I was on cloud nine, thinking about the baby in Morpeth staying with its family – and praying something like that could happen to us.

As it happened, Mrs Wickham didn't want to talk about Robbie. Not her department, she said. She'd come to talk about getting more help for Mum. At first this freaked me out. What did more help mean? Here in the house, or in a care home where nurses dispensed drugs and I'd get on a bus to visit Mum with an armful of library books? It was an enormous relief when Mrs Wickham – getting me sat down first – said there'd be no question of Mum living anywhere else.

"Amy," she said, "you've got a lovely little house here.

With a bit of extra help – someone coming in, say, once a day – you and Lisa would manage that bit easier than you are at the moment."

When I collapsed in tears, embarrassingly, she put the kettle on, then went upstairs to tell Mum I was happy with the idea. *Happy!?*

A really nice person started this week – Mrs Dundas, who lives ten minutes away by car. She's friendly, but I can't help wondering – when we chat about how Lisa and I (ha!) help Mum – what she secretly thinks of me. Whether she goes home and tells her family I look quite ordinary. Not the sort you'd think would have the town in an uproar by running off with her own baby.

Now the dust has settled, I feel most guilty for being such a disappointment to everyone. I feel awkward with Mum, even though she's acting like I haven't done anything wrong. Funny really – Lisa's the only one I'm almost relaxed with.

With Mum so relieved to be home, and more than happy to have help in the house, I'm looking for a time when I reckon she can cope with knowing more about everything. Leaving her in the dark makes me feel like I'm treading on eggshells in a maze of dead ends.

We're in the kitchen, and out of the blue she says, "Amy, love, there's no need to pussyfoot around. I'm back, I'm better, we've got help. I don't need special treatment."

"I didn't want to worry you with stuff."

She puts out a hand. "Is there something you want to tell me?"

"It's just I need to talk about Liam." She waits. I can see she doesn't want to put pressure on me. I take a quick breath. "He didn't know I was pregnant."

She almost smiles. "If *you* didn't know, it's hardly surprising that he didn't." She closes her eyes, takes long moments to voice her thoughts. "I suppose you're worried about telling him. About Robbie, I mean. Or does he already know?"

"No, he doesn't, and that's what I'm afraid of." I sink to the floor, put my head in her lap. "I'm terrified of losing Robbie. I don't think I could cope."

Letting her in on my worst fear, I think of those months with Liam and wonder if I should have been more open with her. Had she felt left out? Thinking back to how I felt at the time, I was probably afraid of her guessing how much our feelings were deepening.

It's a bit late but I start making excuses. "You know, I used to worry when I was out with Liam. I worried that you'd be upset if I was late home."

"I'm a mother," she says. "We're put on this earth to be upset."

Then I tell her how perfect it felt, being with Liam. I smile, remembering the happiness: "You know – walks on the beach and in the woods... But, Mum – it had to end. Australia's too far... Anyway, he'll find someone else."

I glance up at her for a second. "I'm not kidding myself."

She strokes my hair. "Oh, Amy. When did you get to be so grown up?"

"Doing what I did doesn't seem very grown up."

Her hand moves down to the nape of my neck. Massaging me gently, it's like her crooked fingers are untangling my lies, breaking down my pent-up feelings. It's an enormous relief to tell her even the smallest things, and to know she understands.

I kneel up, gently pull her towards me. "You don't know what it means, talking to you like this." I look into her eyes. "It means everything."

I feel practically light-headed, until she says, "Liam and his parents will have to know." She pauses. "It's probably something best dealt with by Social Services."

It's left like that – in the air – with neither of us saying any more about Australia.

I'm dying to talk to her about the baby in Morpeth and the guardian idea. I keep thinking how Mrs Kelly would be the ideal person to be Robbie's special guardian. It's so obvious. Or that's how it looks to me. She's already caring for him, she really loves him. Wouldn't it be the perfect solution?

After Robbie had been checked over by a doctor – I suppose they have their reasons – he was allowed to stay with Mrs Kelly, and I've been seeing him every day. Kirsty and I have been to the cinema with Jordan. Shaun nearly came, but at the last minute thought the film might not be for him. Mrs Kelly warned him it was about a kid doing a runner to punish his parents for splitting up. All through teatime he thought about it, but in the end he came across to see Mum and Lisa instead. More Mum really, because Lisa has started taking Toffee for walks. There's an ulterior motive, of course. She goes to the smokehouse where she's keen on a lad. We now have kippers for breakfast, dinner and tea. Mum says we're in danger of smoking ourselves to death.

I'm filling every minute of the day – hoping it'll help me get through. I'm looking after Mum of course, plus I'm still going out with Kirsty every now and then. Even if she's with Jordan, she asks me to come. I thought she was just being kind at first, but I'm starting to wonder if she's been asked to keep an eye on me.

There have been official meetings about Robbie and me, and our future. I was asked to attend one, where we all sat at a long table. Though I was prepared for almost anything, I felt sick when they said they hoped I understood that if Mr and Mrs Smith adopted Robbie he would have excellent opportunities in life. I said I realized this, and that I knew Mr Smith would make the best dad in the world. After I said this, a bald-headed man next to Mrs Wickham said, "Do you know Mr Smith well?"

"Yes," I said, "he was my form tutor." Then it occurred to me he might have some crazy idea about me and Mr Smith. Laughable, really. Mrs Wickham whispered something to him, after which he looked relieved, rubbed his hands over his gleaming head and sat back.

It's Saturday morning and I'm taking away Mum's breakfast tray. I don't get further than the door. "Amy," she says, "we need to talk."

"Okay."

"Put the tray down for a minute, love."

I end up sitting on her bed with the tray on my lap. She says, "Look at me, Amy," and I realize I've been avoiding her eyes. She says, "We can't put off talking about Robbie."

"What is there to talk about? I'll either be able to keep him, or someone's going to tell me I can't."

She eases her position and stretches out her arm.

Her voice is quiet, steady. "It's not that simple, Amy." She won't let me look away. "There are still choices to be made." She lifts her hand. I take hold of it, and she says, "Sadly, you've not got the sort of choice you'd have if I was well. If that were the case, it would be a very different story. I'd be looking after Robbie, leaving you free to get on with your life."

I imagine a more hopeful vision of me in three or four years' time. "Mum – if someone could look after Robbie

I'd be able to go to college." Her hand is just bones. No strength in it. I say, "D'you think that can ever happen – me going to college?"

Instead of answering, she asks a question of her own. "Who is the most important person in our world?"

"Robbie...of course."

"Exactly." Her fingers move in my grasp. "It's Robbie's future we have to think about. Which doesn't mean I don't understand the huge importance any decision will make to your life."

There's a lump in my throat the size of a rock. "Don't you think his mum's the right person to look after him?"

"Under normal circumstances, yes. But they're not normal, are they? And above everything else, we have to think what's best for Robbie." She begins to bite her bottom lip, and I think I know where this is heading.

She says, "Amy, love, how do you feel you'd cope with putting Robbie up for adoption – hopefully giving him a really good start in life?" She licks the dent in her lip. "Once he was settled, you'd be able to carry on with AS and A Levels."

Who is this about – Robbie or me? Has stuff been going on behind my back? Has Mum been onto Social Services? Are they so bloody blind they can't see what's best for Robbie?

I let go of Mum's hand. The tray tips on my lap. Milk left in the cereal bowl spills onto the duvet. I start to cry.

Mum says, "Please, love, don't cry."

But I can't stop, and through a film of tears I see the torture ahead of me. Robbie – not mine, but Mrs Smith's. Me in an empty world, wondering what he's doing, what his favourite toy is. Whether he likes music. Or football.

I swallow hard. "Are you saying I *should* give Robbie up?"

"Sweetheart – I'm trying to take the long view. I'm looking at the situation purely and simply from the point of view of what's best all round for everyone."

I want to look away, but she won't let me. "Amy, love – Robbie's my grandson and, believe me, it's dreadfully hard for me to say this...but would it be best if you made a clean break?"

"No!"

The tray crashes to the floor. Lisa comes flying up the stairs. She pushes open the door. "No!" I yell, and shove her back onto the landing. "Not *now*, Lisa!" I slam the door in her face, and listen to her running back downstairs.

I drop to my knees beside the bed. "*Tell me I can keep him.*"

"Amy, I wish I could. You don't know how much I wish I could."

It's like I've used everything up. I push my face into the duvet, feel the damp from the milk. The only sound is the TV downstairs.

Mum's weightless hand touches the top of my head.

"Robbie will be able to stay with Mrs Kelly for a while," she says. "Well…until something definite…"

She winds my hair round her fingers. It's soothing. Positive thoughts about the Morpeth baby float into my head. I don't voice them – not this second. I want to give the idea a chance. I don't want Mum to say it can't happen. But if I don't say it now, when will I say it?

I lift her hand from my head, pull myself up and go to the window. "Mum?"

"Yes?"

I turn round. Take a breath. "Kirsty's mum really loves Robbie… Do you think she could be his guardian?"

Mum frowns. "Guardian? What do you mean?"

I steel myself. "Mum, there are people called special guardians. It might mean Robbie could live with Mrs Kelly." I pause. "There's an arrangement Kirsty told me about."

Shocked, she pushes herself up in the bed. "Don't get me wrong, I appreciate what the Kellys do for us – especially for you – but that's a *big* decision, Amy. Have you discussed this with anyone? Does Mrs Kelly have any idea what—"

"I haven't discussed *anything*! It was just something Kirsty said… Apparently her mum knows about a kid whose grandmother is his guardian."

"*I'd* do that if I could… And for heaven's sake, I wouldn't need to be Robbie's guardian." She controls her trembling mouth. "I'd only need to be me."

I can see she's getting upset, but I have to go on: "Mum, this is some different kind of arrangement, for when a kid's mother can't look after her baby, but the family doesn't want it to be adopted."

"Well, I've never heard of that."

I pick up the tray. "Can you ask Mrs Kelly about it?"

She's still uptight. "What exactly am I meant to ask?"

It comes back to me: the day I sat in the Kellys' kitchen – the day the Smiths visited. Mrs Kelly clearly so fond of Robbie. Stroking his toes.

I say to Mum, "Ask if she'd consider being Robbie's special guardian."

"Don't you think she's got enough responsibilities?"

My heart sinks. "I don't know – perhaps."

But what I do know is, I want something decided by me. Robbie is my baby. What happens next is down to me. Or should be.

One minute I'm telling myself I mustn't get too hopeful about the idea of Mrs Kelly being Robbie's guardian, the next I'm excited when I remember her telling me she'd once been tempted to adopt. I think about the first time I saw him at their house – when she called Robbie a little star. It was obvious she thought he was special.

For what seems ages, Mum and I are lost in thought: me looking out of the window, Mum leaning back with her eyes closed. Then she agrees to call Mrs Kelly. We don't say much while I help her dress and take the damp duvet cover off the bed. There's not much *to* say at this stage.

Once we're downstairs I give Mum the phone so she can call Mrs Kelly. I'm such a big coward I hunch up on the settee in the front room and pull a cushion round my ears.

Eventually, when I risk listening, it's gone quiet and I go back into the kitchen. "Well – did you ask her?"

"Partly."

"How d'you mean – partly?"

"She wouldn't give much away, though I get the feeling she and Frank have been discussing Robbie." She sighs, like everything's too much effort. "I found the whole thing extremely awkward."

"You mean you didn't actually ask her."

"I touched on it…but it's such a huge thing to ask of anyone. To find the right words."

"*Mum.* Having Robbie adopted would be a huge thing."

"Oh, sweetheart, I know that." Tears fill her eyes. "Susie – Mrs Kelly – admitted she's very fond of Robbie."

This is getting nowhere. "Mum," I say gently, "d'you think she'd mind if I go across to talk to her. Would *you* mind?"

She looks relieved. "No I wouldn't. I think that's the best idea, then you can ask her yourself."

I let Toffee out into the yard, have an argument with Lisa about soup for Mum's lunch, check my purse for money, and set off to see if Mrs Goodge has any bargain-price chocolates I can give Kirsty's mum.

Chapter Thirty-six

Mr Kelly answers the door. "Amy, hi! Come in." He leads the way to the kitchen. "Sit yourself down, love."

I've brought orange creams for Mrs Kelly, and put them on the table. "Those for me?" he says, but I know he's kidding. He reaches for the kettle. "Would you like a coffee?"

"If you're having one. Thank you."

He takes mugs from the shelf, and biscuits from the cupboard below. It's suspiciously quiet, and when I ask where everyone is, he says, "Kirsty and her mum have taken the kids for a breath of air. Shaun, too."

I'm a bit confused. With him on his own, it feels like he was expecting me. He spoons instant into our mugs. "Your mum rang earlier and spoke to Susie."

"I thought she'd be here, and—"

He picks up the kettle. "And you wanted to ask about a special guardianship for Robbie?" He pauses. "And you can do. First though, I thought you and me could look at it on our own."

"Right."

"It's like this," he says slowly, and pours water into the mugs. "If Susie were granted a special guardianship order for young Robbie, it would last until he's eighteen." A clock ticks in the silence. "You didn't realize that?"

"No."

"It's a fair few years, isn't it?" He waits for me to agree, and I nod. "But even so, my wonderful wife would like to go ahead." Hearing him say this, I have to remember to keep breathing. "Me," he says, "I'm Mr Sensible, and I want to make sure any decisions made now are the right ones."

I nod again.

"Milk?" he says.

"Yes, please."

He puts the mugs on the table and sits opposite me. "Can you see where I'm coming from?"

"Yes, I think so."

"What we decide at the present time – and that includes you – might look just the job. But we still have to guard against misunderstandings cropping up in the future."

He pushes the sugar towards me. "Help yourself." I take a spoonful and he takes two heaped ones. "Biscuit?" he says, and opens the tin. I shake my head.

He takes two digestives. "Don't tell me you're watching your weight." He crunches on a biscuit. "Last night me and Susie were chewing all this over – the question of Robbie's future."

I wonder where they were when they were talking about me and my child. In bed? Or still up, emptying the dishwasher and putting things away.

He's looking at me intently, and I wonder if it shows – how my insides are playing up. I say, "I just love it – the way the kids here are so happy. I know how hard Mrs Kelly works – and you – and there must be times you want to put your feet up and tell them to get their own tea."

He laughs. "Not while they're still at the Lego stage."

"I meant, I so love the life the kids have with you."

"It's not all happy families, Amy."

I relax. "Well, it can't be – but you know what I mean."

I think of Robbie's sweet face – his blue eyes and the funny smile he gave me yesterday when I visited – and I think that if I'm not able to bring him up, I would like him to be here. Until he's eighteen, though? This is a bit of a shock. It's more than my whole life so far.

I drink more of my coffee and Mr Kelly drains his. "Apart from the timescale," he says, "you'd have to understand that Susie would have complete control."

"How do you mean?"

"She would be the decision-maker." He makes sure I'm listening. "On the other side of the coin," he says, "Robbie would grow up knowing you're his mum; he'd see you often, see his grandma, see Lisa. He'd know he's part of your family, as well as part of ours." He pauses. "But you'd need to understand that decisions would be down to Susie."

"What kind of decisions?"

"It could be anything. Routine stuff like what Robbie has to eat, his bedtime, who takes him out – where to, and for how long. Later on there'd be other decisions, which hopefully you'd all agree on. Though if you didn't, Susie would have the casting vote." He pauses. "For instance, deciding where Robbie should go to school, or possible health problems… You and your mum would always be in on any discussion; it's just that if there were serious disagreements, Susie would have the last word, not you or your mum."

I sit, taking this in. Mr Kelly asks if I understand. Have I any questions?

"I can't think of any. Not at the moment."

He says, "I'll put my cards on the table, Amy. *All* our cards, because you have to realize that if Susie were granted a special guardianship order there'd be no going back, and that's a big, big undertaking. One that would affect me, too. And Kirsty, of course."

I feel I should say something, but I can't think what. Besides, it doesn't feel right to interrupt. The look on his face says there's more going on in his head.

"No disrespect, Amy, to you or Robbie – but I won't pretend I jumped at the idea immediately. My first consideration, as always – where the kids and fostering are concerned – is my wife and family."

"But this isn't fostering."

"Precisely. And it isn't adoption either. I'll cut to the chase... We're all very, very fond of Robbie. It's not going too far to say the little guy's eaten his way into our hearts. And we think a lot of you, Amy—" He rolls his shoulders, like he wants to release tension. "Though I have to remember I'm looking at a young lady who's done some pretty crazy things. A bit of a wild child, eh?"

"I never used to be."

"Some crazy things we don't need to go into – that personally I don't think you're likely to repeat."

"I wouldn't, I wouldn't." I need him to believe me. "I'd be able to finish school. I might even go to college."

"Yes, you might. With hopes of getting a good career going."

"Really?"

"Well, of course. You'd have time for all that while Robbie's with us." He pauses. "And we'd help you look into the question of care for Mum. It's something she wouldn't want you to worry about. She knows you've got your own life to lead." He looks me in the eye. "But getting back to the present..."

"Yes?"

"You're a busy girl," he says, "we know that—"

I interrupt. "Our Lisa helps..."

"I think we'll take that with a pinch of salt, shall we?"

I feel the blush rising up my neck.

"I respect your loyalty, Amy. Let's just say your sister's input looks to be a bit sporadic." He pauses. "I don't think we need a crystal ball to get an idea of life on Dune Terrace."

Hearing him say that makes me wonder if Kirsty guessed more than I realised. It's like he reads my mind. "Our Kirsty," he says, "never says a dicky bird...your secrets are safe with her."

I'm keen to reassure him about Lisa. "Lisa lives at home now. She's helping quite a lot."

He crosses his arms and I notice he's getting a bit of a pot belly. "I want you to realize," he says, "that if things go ahead, you'd be expected to lend a hand."

"Of course! I'd do anything."

"Babysitting. That sort of thing."

"Of course I would. I'd love to. Mrs Kelly knows I'm familiar with all sorts of things now." I reel off my skills: "Changing nappies, mixing formula, bathing Robbie." I pause. "I'd be able to see Robbie often, wouldn't I? And Mum – she would, too?"

"Definitely. It's not the purpose of the guardianship order to take the child away from its family. Quite the opposite. The only hard-and-fast rule is the guardian having rights over the parent."

I say, "I can't imagine disagreeing with Mrs Kelly."

He chuckles. "You'd have plenty of time to put that to the test."

I smile, and look at the clock. I want to get home and talk things over with Mum.

"Before you go," he says, "in case you're fretting over the Australian question…"

I swallow hard. "I've been kind of sticking my head in the sand."

He cracks his knuckles. "Susie made enquiries about residency being awarded to Liam, should he apply for it, and has been told, unofficially, that it would be unlikely to be approved. They say that in view of Liam's family background, a special guardianship order for Robbie in the UK is likely to be looked on as a better option."

I can't think what to say. I'd like to kiss him, but I don't think I ought to. Instead I say, "Would you give Mrs Kelly the orange creams, and tell her they're to say thank you."

He pushes back his chair. "No problem," he says. "She might let me have one."

Glancing at the chocolates, I think how they're nowhere near a big enough thank you for what Mrs Kelly's prepared to do for me. For Robbie.

Chapter Thirty-seven

When I get in, I'm relieved to find Mum alone. Lisa's out with Toffee – doubtless taking him past the smokehouse.

While I get a snack ready, we talk and talk.

I don't leave anything out. I'm as accurate as I can be – though of course I don't know every last detail. Mum's eyes fix on me as I list conditions attached to a special guardianship, particularly that they would last until Robbie is eighteen. For me, pouring it out like this underlines how tough the arrangement would be. But I'm happy to pay any price. Robbie would belong to me. We'd be close, emotionally and physically, and I'd see him grow up.

The change in Mum is extraordinary. The worry cloud hanging over her head looks ready to disappear. A shiver goes up my spine when I ask her what she honestly thinks. She takes a deep breath, and lets it out slowly: "I think it's the way forward."

I want to run out of the house right away. Race along the beach to the Kellys' and tell Robbie myself. Instead, deciding we won't wait for Lisa, I dish up two plates of baked beans on toast and peel a banana for Mum.

"Won't you have one?" she says.

"Mum," I say, "it'll be hard enough forcing down the baked beans!"

"Amy, you must *eat* properly."

I'm about to tell her I'll have a banana later, when the phone rings. It's Mrs Kelly, wanting to talk to me and Mum. By the time we've had what amounts to a three-sided conversation – Mum and I taking turns to speak to her – Mrs Kelly has promised to apply to be Robbie's special guardian. Which, when everything is in place, she would become in a few months' time. For me, each moment I think about this is like a glow of pure joy flooding through me.

Sunday, and I'm getting Mum's breakfast. I'm on autopilot – kippers again, then leaving her to have a lie-in. Later I'll help her dress before I go to see Robbie. Kirsty called to say we can take him out. We'll have *such a lot* to talk about.

In my head, I keep going over yesterday: my hour with Mr Kelly, then Mrs Kelly calling Mum and me.

But also, how can I forget the makings of that perfect nursery? And Mrs Smith in her husband's arms.

With my mind darting from one thing to another, I barely notice Lisa slopping about in her pink dressing gown. Apparently she can't find her copy of *Heat*. She goes into the front room to look behind the cushions. The next minute she's charging back into the hallway like a pack of wolves are after her.

She tears off the dreadful dressing gown. "He can't see me like this! Don't you dare open the door till I'm upstairs!"

I can see why she wouldn't want anyone to see her – she's a total mess. I ask, "Who can't see you like this?"

She pounds up the stairs. "I don't know! But he's bleedin' gorgeous!"

There's a knock at the front door. Toffee barks. I open it.

"Morning, Amy."

"Mr Smith…"

"All right if I come in?"

I open the door wider and he steps into the hallway. He looks serious. "Is there somewhere we can talk?"

"We can go in the front room."

"Are you on your own?"

My heart thumps hard. Is he here for his wife's sake – confirming her promise to love Robbie all their lives? Is it down to me to tell him that, almost certainly, this won't happen? For a second it crosses my mind to ask Mum to tell him, but I know this would be unfair all round.

If it's not about Robbie, why does he want to know if I'm on my own? I tell him I'm not alone. "Mum's upstairs, and Lisa's coming down any minute."

He sniffs the air. "Delicious smell of kippers."

We make for the front room. I can see Lisa's *Heat* sticking out from under the settee. She'll be up there, trying to make herself look good. It's obvious Mr Smith hears her padding backwards and forwards over our heads. Now she's in Mum's room, maybe hoping to find something half-decent to wear.

There are raised voices – mostly Lisa's. Mr Smith says, "D'you suppose we could take Toffee for a walk?"

I'll be grateful to get out of the house before Lisa puts in an appearance. "He'd love that," I say.

Mr Smith laughs at Toffee's antics in the dunes, and – like it's something he does every day – takes the frisbee out of my hand and throws it. Toffee hurtles after it, and we amble off in the same direction. The tide's coming in, but there's still enough sand for a walk.

Mr Smith says, "How are you?"

"I'm okay."

He looks out to sea while he tells me that for my sake, and Mum's, he's relieved to hear my news. He says, "Mrs Kelly came to see Gina and me last night, to let us know that in all probability she'll take up the reins as Robbie's special guardian. It won't have been easy for her. She knew how we'd feel." His Adam's apple moves as he swallows hard. "Gina was – still is – very upset."

So this is why he's here: to tell me he knows about Mrs Kelly's decision. He looks tired, and I say, "I'm sorry, really I am." I wish he'd look at me. I add, "All your hopes built up like that."

Now he looks at me. He has to, so his words aren't snatched away by the wind. "I'm sorry, too," he says. "Extremely sorry…about the time you spent with Gina."

We walk along together. Toffee comes back with the frisbee and Mr Smith hurls it again.

My voice has to fight the wind. "I'd been trying to convince myself I could part with Robbie." I hesitate. "If he had you as his dad."

His hair is blowing in his eyes. He pushes it back and says, "Amy – Robbie belongs to you."

Toffee comes bounding back to drop the frisbee. Mr Smith says, "Good boy," and keeps hold of it while we carry on walking.

In the distance, high up, I notice a kite. Yellow and red. I'm still watching it when he turns to face me. "Make the most of these next few years, Amy. You've got a lot going for you."

"I'm just beginning to realize what it could all mean."

He says, "You know that if you go to college, your mum will get more help at home."

I think of how encouraging Mr Kelly'd been. It'd be good to think Mr Smith felt the same. "Do *you* think I'll be able to have a career?"

"I'm sure you will."

He's been so good to me, I begin to think it would be great to keep in touch. "Mr Smith?"

"Yes?"

But it doesn't feel right. Instead I say thank you, and he says, "Good luck, I'm sure it'll all work out."

He hands me the frisbee, and we part company. Then, while he heads back for Dune Terrace and his car, I start walking on with Toffee. But something makes me turn round: I want to see if he's still in sight. He is, and you'd never guess, from his purposeful stride, how much sadness and disappointment he's suffered recently.

I walk on, with the wind lifting my hair. I've gone about another half-mile when it hits me all over again. *I am going to see Robbie grow up!*

Suddenly I don't feel like walking any more. I want to run, turn cartwheels, do mad things – I want to shake off the past few days.

I shout stuff to Toffee. Stuff about my new life. Understanding every word, he leaps about like we're having the best game ever. I run, like for once I'm winning the race – but he still outruns me. I flop onto the sand and call him back. He thinks this is getting even better and charges over to lick my face. I scream in mock horror – but he wants more kisses.

I have to stop this silly business when a couple look as if they're coming over to see if I'm all right. Standing up,

300

I dust the sand off my jeans, tell Toffee to behave and give them a cheery wave. They look relieved and walk away.

And I smile all the way home.

Chapter Thirty-eight

Even before the end of the holidays I begin helping Mrs Kelly with Robbie: feeding and changing him, taking him out in his buggy. He *loves* this and is starting to notice where we're going. I think he must be able to smell the sea because his wrists twist with excitement whenever we head for the beach. Something else he loves is being with Mum. His eyes widen when she talks to him, and he doesn't care if the finger he grabs is a bit crooked. It's *her* finger and he wants to hang onto it.

It's Mum's birthday today. I've given her slippers with easy fastenings, and a jade green floral scarf. Kirsty, Shaun and Mr Kelly are coming over for tea. Mrs Kelly, though, is staying behind to look after the little ones. They *could* all have come, but it would have been a bit of a squash. Mrs Kelly made me promise not to make a cake, which is probably a good thing – my cakes sink in the middle.

This morning I dusted the front room while Mrs Dundas gave the side table a good polish. Lisa arranged our three cushions and keeps going in there to make sure no one's disturbed the brilliant job she's done. Mum's birthday cards on the mantelpiece make it look bright and welcoming. It also looks like we care about the room for once. Poor little room – it's usually only used for stiff conversations, like the time when Nana Kathleen died and a man from the funeral directors' came to find out what sort of coffin Mum wanted for her. Lisa went out because she thought it was gross. I had to stay because there wasn't anyone else.

I've already filled the kettle. When I've put out the cups – and glasses, in case anyone wants juice – we'll go through with the sandwiches Mrs Dundas helped me make. Plus there's Mum's favourite Bourbon biscuits. Later there should be cake.

And here's my surprise. I've planned for Mum to help Robbie with his bottle: a kind of extra birthday present, one that doesn't need wrapping.

My heart lifts when Toffee goes to sit by the front door. It's like he senses the others are on their way. He gives a sudden loud bark, and Mum, sat on the settee in the front room, laughs. "Sounds like he's heard the car!"

I hurry to the front door. We all talk at once: "Hi! Hello there! Hi!"

Mr Kelly spots Lisa standing behind me. "Lisa," he says quietly, "pop this in the kitchen, would you?" and carefully hands her a shopping bag – pushed out of shape by something large and round. Definitely a tin with a cake in it.

Shaun, in a navy T-shirt I've not seen before, takes up half the hallway. He holds the front door open for Kirsty, who's bearing Robbie, like a gift, in his baby carrier. I say, "Hello, sweetie-pie!" and take the carrier by the handle. I drop a kiss on his head, then watch Mum's face light up as I carry him in to sit beside her in his little seat. Kirsty and her dad follow, saying, "Happy birthday!"

Mum smiles a totally happy smile, and Shaun comes in and sits on the other side of her. Mum touches Robbie on the head. "Hello, sweetheart," she says, "you're looking very smart." She glances at Lisa in the doorway. "Doesn't he look gorgeous, Lisa?"

Lisa nods, and Kirsty says, "Mum's instructions! We're to take as many photos as possible."

Which we do. Or Kirsty and her dad do, on their phones. Mum wants to look at each one as it's taken. I make the tea, then another pot. The pile of egg and cress sandwiches goes down fast, and I put Robbie's bottle to warm in a pan of hot water. I think how happy Mum looks.

After I've handed round the last of the sandwiches, Kirsty gives her dad a nudge, then he gives Lisa a nudge and they both go into the kitchen – where I guess they'll be sorting out the candles on the cake. Kirsty and I stay in the front room, chatting with Mum and Shaun – mostly about the progress Robbie's making and how cute he looks with more hair. When Mum looks soulful and says, "He'll be breaking a few hearts," I remember how I'd thought it was my heart he'd break.

Kirsty says, "Isn't that blue perfect on him?" Then, as if the colour makes her think of Jordan, she says to Mum, "Jordan says happy birthday."

Mum says, "Oh, do thank him for his card. Wherever did he find it? It really made me chuckle!"

Shaun says, "Did you like mine?"

Mum smiles. "I love it, Shaun. Thank you *very* much."

I go into the kitchen. Lisa's gazing at the pink and white cake, its four candles in place: one for every ten years. She says, "When are we cutting it?"

"I thought Mum could feed Robbie first."

She doesn't look particularly surprised. "Aren't *you* going to feed him?"

"It would be great if Mum had a go… D'you want to light the candles?"

She takes matches from the drawer. "Okay."

"Not yet."

"Duh. I wasn't going to."

I test Robbie's bottle in the pan. It's warm enough so I take it, together with a clean tea towel, into the front room. At the sight of it, Robbie gives a little squeak and Mum says, "Listen to him, he doesn't miss a thing!"

Shaun grins at Mum. "He's got Amy's brains, Mrs Preston."

I hover over Shaun. "Can I sit there, please?"

He stands up hurriedly. "Sorry, Amy."

"It's all right, I just need to put this tea towel on Mum's lap." She looks up in surprise, and I say, "Would you like to give Robbie his bottle?"

Her cheeks flush. "Do you trust me?"

Tears prick my eyes, but I blink them back and lift Robbie into her lap. Keeping my arm round him, I ease the bottle into Mum's right hand. She has difficulty, but I help support the bottle and before we know it, Robbie's mouth has clamped round the teat.

He sucks greedily and I lessen my hold on the bottle. Apart from Toffee having a good scratch, the room is quiet as we watch the level of milk go down. When it reaches the bottom, and before Robbie sucks air, I gently take the bottle from Mum. I whisper in her ear, "You haven't lost your touch."

As if from a signal, Shaun crosses to the window and pulls the curtains together. Mum says, "Oh! Don't shut out the daylight, Shaun, it's—" but she breaks off as the room lights up with the flicker of candles on the cake Lisa carries in.

I don't know whose eyes shine more brightly – Mum's or Robbie's. I only know my voice cracks when I take Robbie from Mum's arms and Kirsty gives us a note for "Happy Birthday".

After we've sung – Shaun sounding more like he's

chanting – I hold Robbie, and Lisa lowers the cake in front of Mum. "Blow out the candles," she says, "and make a wish."

Shaun looks earnest. "You mustn't tell us what it is."

Mum blows out three at once. With the last one still to go, she takes another breath, leans closer and blows it out. We clap hard and she sits back, beaming at us.

Mr Kelly takes the cake from Lisa and puts it on the side table. Mum says, "That's a wonderful cake, Frank." She hesitates. "Did Susie make it herself? It looks very professional."

He says, "Actually, *I* made it." Which turns out to be true, though he admits Kirsty's mum iced *Happy Birthday, Lindy* on the top.

When Kirsty hands round slices of feather-light sponge with buttercream in the middle, I notice the plates aren't ours. I recognize the pattern of violets, and realize Mrs Kelly must have slipped them in with the cake. (I won't be pleading with Lisa to help with the washing-up.)

We're all exclaiming over the delicious cake, when Shaun – straight to the point – says, "What's that pong?"

Mum laughs. "Shaun, *really*!" but I'm already on my feet, Robbie in my arms.

"You're right, Shaun," I say. "I'll take him upstairs."

I lay him on my bed, where Kirsty's been thoughtful enough to spread out his changing mat and leave spare nappy sacks and wipes. I lean over him and at first he's perfectly happy, rolling his eyes at the ceiling – as if examining it for cracks. I tug at his little blue shorts and he starts kicking. When I say, "There's a good boy, lie still," he turns his head to look at me. And kicks harder.

I'm used to his little tricks and hook my fingers round his ankles. I hoist his legs above his head and pull open the nappy. Shaun's right about the pong. This is a seriously impressive turnout.

I clean him up and put on a fresh nappy. I'm in no hurry to break the spell of it being just the two of us, and gently stroke his head. He's beginning to look drowsy: the nice warm milk must be working its way down. He's beautiful. Sweet-smelling, relaxed, eyelids quivering. I kneel beside the bed, pull him gently towards me and nuzzle his vest up with my nose. I drink in the scent of his skin. Kiss him all the way up to the soft little dent at the base of his throat, and all the way down again. I ease his nappy and tickle his tummy button. He's very nearly asleep, and doesn't react. I press a kiss where I feel his heartbeat, and whisper, "I love you so, so much. Thank you for being my darling little boy."

Chapter Thirty-nine

At the start of the autumn term it looked like the rain would never let up. Now though, we're having what Mum calls an Indian summer. Which makes such a difference to how she feels – especially on the warmest days, when Shaun rushes home from school to take her down to the sea. Being able to relax about the future is doing her so much good. Plus Mrs Dundas is lovely. She and Mum are still getting on like a house on fire.

Lisa's having to toe the line: get her bed made before Mrs D arrives in the morning. I miss not having a room to myself but, like Nana Kathleen would have said, it's a small price to pay.

Mum's made it clear to Lisa that with my new responsibilities, and even with Mrs Dundas here each morning, she's expecting to rely on her elder daughter for more help around the house. We both realize Lisa will have to look for a job – again. But we'd be able to manage. In some ways there's less work when she's out of the house.

Mr and Mrs Smith have moved on. He's teaching at a school way up towards the Scottish border, and Orchard Cottage is for sale.

My fame – or, more accurately, my *notoriety* (a good word for a bad thing) – spread like wildfire. For the first few days of term Kirsty acted as my bodyguard, ready to give an earful to anyone trying to slag me off. She's showing another side to her character: tough and unafraid. So much for anyone who thinks she looks like butter wouldn't melt.

Our new form tutor, Miss Hill – dry sense of humour – is taking us for English Lit in Mr Smith's place. She's promised she'll rent the DVD of *To Kill a Mockingbird* to show over an afternoon. She's told us we're to "relax and enjoy" before starting to think about AS and A Level set books. Mum's dead jealous of me having an afternoon of Gregory Peck!

Did I say I got an A in GCSE English Lit? I got two other As, the rest Bs. Nine passes in all; plus I can take Maths in November. Kirsty and I were both happy with our results – ecstatic really. Can't believe we're about to start all over again…

It's Sunday morning and Toffee's getting an extra run on the beach. We're on our way back from Kirsty's, where I've given Robbie a feed and helped Mrs Kelly make children's meals for the freezer.

Whiter-than-white surf, whipping up on the incoming tide, rolls towards us. The sun's high in the sky and it's warm for October. I pull my trainers off and race after Toffee. He's at the water's edge, bottom in the air, barking like every slap of water hitting the sand is a personal threat. He jumps back and shakes himself. All over me! Running away laughing, I let him chase me until I realize it's time to think about getting lunch.

Before we go home I breathe in the salty air and stand still for a moment, looking out across the North Sea. Toffee has found a stick. He brings it to me.

I take it and write in the damp sand.

ROBBIE.

Discussion Questions

◆ *Writing in the Sand* is told entirely from Amy's point of view. Why do you think the author chose a first person narrative for this book?

◆ Liam is a significant character in the book, although we never actually meet him. What do you think Amy loved about him and their relationship?

◆ Amy tells a lot of lies in the book, whether it's to her mum's social worker, to the police, or to her friends and family. Is she justified in doing so? Do you consider Amy to be a dishonest person as a result?

◆ Discuss the significance of Toffee's arrival and the book's entwined themes of belonging, responsibility and love. How does Amy's relationship with Toffee offer us insight into other relationships, both actual and potential, in the story?

- Consider Shaun's role in the book. Why do you think he behaves the way he does? What impact does his friendship with Amy have, both on them as characters, and on events in the book?

- Think back to the scene where Gina Smith invites Amy to her home. Why do you think Gina does this? How did this scene make you feel?

- *You've got to stop spending your life worrying about other folk. Start thinking about Number One for a change.* – Lisa
  Think about Lisa's advice to Amy. To what extent do you agree with her, firstly in Amy's case, and also more generally?

- *Writing in the Sand* is set in a small town on the Northumberland coast. How does the sense of place and community contribute to the book's plot and atmosphere? Imagine setting the book in an alternative place, and consider the effect it might have on the story.

A Note from the Author

Like Amy, I loved English at school; though unlike Amy I didn't actually long to be a writer. But I loved the theatre, and – at Saturday morning classes at the Arts Educational School in London – I wrote my own material.

After moving to Yorkshire I began writing seriously, and joined a group called Yorkshire Playwrights, now Script Yorkshire. It was here that Vicky Featherstone, currently the Artistic Director of the Royal Court, said I ought to write for young adults.

I didn't immediately take her advice. Instead I wrote afternoon plays for BBC Radio 4, a serial for *Woman's Hour* and scripts for Granada, Carlton TV and the BBC, as well as audio cassettes for *Coronation Street*.

It was at the finals of a talent contest at Harrogate Theatre that I remembered the advice I'd been given about writing for young adults. On that night there was one particular performer I could not forget – a talented young singer, who I later discovered was a carer for *both* parents.

Suddenly my eyes were opened to the thousands upon thousands of young people acting as carers, and I began to wonder what life must be like for them. How did they juggle caring for their parents with school? What fun things – like sport, or drama or just being with friends – were they missing out on? Or was their love for their parents so strong that they just got on with it?

And what if they ever got sick? Or something utterly unexpected happened? Something that could make their role as a carer difficult...or impossible?

This is where my writer's "what if" came in... Amy became real, and before long, I had finished my debut novel.

I very much hope you have enjoyed reading *Writing in the Sand*, and exploring those "what if"s with me.

Acknowledgements

Most of the time, *Writing in the Sand* has been a labour of love – but, like love, it decided now and then to change direction. This is probably because it heard this rule: that the main protagonist has to go on a journey. Once it understood this, you couldn't see it for dust – and I had a job keeping up.

Luckily, for me and the book, there have been great people to meet along the way. In the early days, Susan Davis at Writer's Workshop helped reinforce my belief in the story. Buoyed up, I approached agents and more than happily found myself with Becky Bagnell, whom I just can't thank enough… Where would I be without your advice and faith in me?

My heartfelt thanks go to my editor, Stephanie King, and to everyone at Usborne. You turn each new stage into an adventure!

I am indebted to the British Association for Adoption

and Fostering. Their advice, and solving of a crucial problem, was invaluable.

My thanks, of course, go to my friends and family – particularly John who has to make allowances for the odd hours I keep – and to my sister, Clare Druce, who first suggested I should write. And thank you to those who have been unstintingly interested to hear what's going on. Okay, Jacky, I mean you.

If you enjoyed *Writing in the Sand*, you'll love...

how to
save
a life

Sara Zarr

"moving, funny, and emotionally honest"
Publishers Weekly

ISBN: 9781409546757
EPUB: 9781409554875   KINDLE: 9781409554882

how to save a life

Jill's life lost all meaning when her dad died. Friends, boyfriend, college – nothing matters any more. Then her mother drops a bombshell. She's going to adopt a baby.

Mandy is desperate for her life to change. Seventeen, pregnant and leaving home, she is sure of only one thing – her baby must never have a life like hers, whatever it takes.

Heart-achingly beautiful, How to Save a Life *is about finding love, truth and your place in the world... all where you least expect it.*

"An achingly poignant read."
The Daily Mail

"An extremely readable and thought-provoking novel."
The Bookseller

"Impossible not to be moved."
We Love This Book

For more compelling, inspiring reads,
visit www.usborne.com/fiction